THE TREMOR OF FORGERY

When Howard Ingham arrived in
Tunisia to collect material for a film he
expected John Castlewood, the film's
producer, to follow within a few days.
But Castlewood does not appear, and
Ingham starts work on a novel rather
than the film.

Using the theme of his book as a
counterpoint to the story of her own,
Patricia Highsmith creates a brilliant
Chinese-box inversion of knowing and
not-knowing, good and evil, truth and
falsity.

There are one, possibly two, fatalities,
but the superb tension comes not from
the proliferation of death and disaster
but from the many facets of Howard
Ingham's uncertainty.

*'Miss Highsmith is a crime novelist whose
books one can re-read many times.'*
– Graham Greene

Also by Patricia Highsmith
in Hamlyn Paperbacks

THE BLUNDERER

THE TWO FACES OF JANUARY

A GAME FOR THE LIVING

THOSE WHO WALK AWAY

THE TREMOR OF FORGERY

Patricia Highsmith

Hamlyn Paperbacks

THE TREMOR OF FORGERY
ISBN 0 600 38780 1

First published in Great Britain 1969
by William Heinemann Ltd
First paperback publication 1970 by Panther Books
Hamlyn Paperbacks edition 1978
Third printing 1982
Copyright © 1969 by Patricia Highsmith

Hamlyn Paperbacks are published by
The Hamlyn Publishing Group Ltd,
Astronaut House,
Feltham,
Middlesex, England

Printed and bound in Great Britain by
Cox & Wyman Ltd, Reading

THE TREMOR
OF FORGERY

For Rosalind Constable
as a small souvenir
of a rather long
friendship

CHAPTER ONE

'You're sure there's no letter for me?' Ingham asked.
'Howard Ingham. I-n-g-h-a-m.' He spelt it, a little uncer-
tainly, in French, though he had spoken in English.

The plump Arab clerk in the bright red uniform glanced
through the letters in the cubbyhole marked I–J, and shook
his head. 'Non, m'sieur.'

'Merci,' Ingham said with a polite smile. It was the second
time he had asked, but it was a different clerk. He had asked
ten minutes ago when he arrived at the Hotel Tunisia
Palace. Ingham had hoped for a letter from John Castlewood. Or from Ina. He had been away from New York five
days now, having flown first to Paris to see his agent there,
and just to take another look at Paris.

Ingham lit a cigarette and glanced around the lobby. It
was carpeted with oriental rugs, and air-conditioned. The
clientele looked mostly French and American, but there
were a few rather dark-faced Arabs in Western business
suits. The Tunisia Palace had been recommended by John.
It was probably the best in town, Ingham thought.

He went out through the glass doors on to the pavement.
It was early June, nearly 6 p.m., and the air was warm, the
slanting sunlight still bright. John had suggested the Café
de Paris for a pre-lunch or -dinner drink, and there it was,
across the street and at the second corner, on the Boulevard
Bourguiba. Ingham walked on to the boulevard, and bought
a Paris *Herald-Tribune*. The rather broad avenue had a
tree-bordered, cement-paved division down its middle on
which people could walk. Here were the newspaper and
tobacco kiosks, the shoeshine boys. To Ingham, it looked
something between a Mexico City street and a Paris street,

but the French had had a hand in both Mexico City and Tunis. Snatches of shouted conversation around him gave him no clue as to meaning. He had a phrase book called *Easy Arabic* in one of his suitcases at the hotel. Arabic would obviously have to be memorised, because it bore no relation to anything he knew.

Ingham walked across the street to the Café de Paris. It had pavement tables, all occupied. People stared at him, perhaps because he was a new face. There were many Americans and English, and they had the expressions of people who had been here some time and were a little bored. Ingham had to stand at the bar. He ordered a Pernod, and looked at his newspaper. The place was noisy. He spotted a table and took it.

People idled along the pavement, staring at the equally blank faces in the café. Ingham watched especially the younger people because he was on an assignment to write a film script about two young people in love, or rather three, since there was a second young man who didn't get the girl. Ingham saw no boy and girl walking along, only single young men or pairs of boys holding hands and talking earnestly. John had told Ingham about the closeness of the boys. Homosexual relationships had no stigma here, but that had nothing to do with the script. Young people of opposite sex were often chaperoned or at least spied upon. There was a lot to learn, and Ingham's job in the next week or so until John arrived was to keep his eyes open and absorb the atmosphere. John knew a couple of families here, and Ingham would be able to see inside a middle-class Tunisian home. The story was to have the minimum of written dialogue, but still something had to be written. Ingham had done some television writing, but he considered himself a novelist. He had some trepidations about this job. But John was confident, and the arrangements were informal. Ingham had signed nothing. Castlewood had advanced him a thousand dollars, and Ingham was scrupulously using the money only for business expenses. Quite a bit of it would go on the car he was supposed to hire for a month. He must get the car tomorrow morning, he thought, so he could begin looking around.

'Merci, non,' Ingham said to a pedlar who approached him with a long-stemmed, tightly bound flower. The over-sweet scent lingered in the air. The pedlar had a handful and was pushing about among the tables yelling, 'Yes-*meen?*' He wore a red fez and a limp, lavender jubbah so thin one could see a pair of whitish underpants.

At one table, a fat man twiddled his jasmine, holding the blossom under his nose. He seemed in a trance, his eyes almost crossed with his daydream. Was he awaiting a girl or only thinking of one? Ten minutes later, Ingham decided he was awaiting no one. The man had finished what looked like a colourless soda pop. He wore a light grey business suit. Ingham supposed he was middle-class, even a bit upper. Perhaps he made thirty or more dinars per week, sixty-three dollars or more. Ingham had been boning up on such things for a month. Bourguiba was tactfully trying to extricate his people from the reactionary bonds of their religion. He had abolished polygamy officially, and disapproved of the veil for women. As African countries went, Tunisia was the most advanced. They were trying to persuade all French business-men to leave, but still depended to a great extent on French monetary aid.

Ingham was thirty-four, slightly over six feet tall, with light brown hair and blue eyes, and he moved rather slowly. Although he never bothered about exercise, he had a good physique with broad shoulders, long legs and strong hands. He had been born in Florida, but considered himself a New Yorker, because he had lived in New York since the age of eight. After college – the University of Pennsylvania – he had worked for a newspaper in Philadelphia and written fiction on the side, without much luck until his first book, *The Power of Negative Thinking*, a rather flippant and juv-enile spoof of positive thinking, in which his pair of nega-tive-thinking heroes emerged covered in glory, money and success. On the strength of this, Ingham had quit journal-ism, and had had two or three rocky years. His second book, *The Gathering Swine*, had not been so well received as the first book. Then he had married a wealthy girl, Charlotte Fleet, with whom he had been very much in love, but he had not availed himself of her money, and her wealth in fact had been a handicap. The marriage had ended after two years. Now and again, Ingham sold a television play or a short story, and he had kept going in a modest apartment in Manhattan. This year, in February, he had had a breakthrough. His book *The Game of 'If'* had been bought for a film for $50,000. Ingham suspected it had been bought more for the crazy love story in it than for its intellectual content or message (the necessity and validity of wishful thinking), but no matter, it had been bought, and for the first time Ingham was enjoying a taste of financial security. He had declined an invitation to write the film script of *The Game of 'If'*. He thought film scripts, even television plays, were not his forte, and *The Game* was a difficult book for him to think of in film terms.

John Castlewood's idea for *Trio* was simpler and more visual. The young man who didn't get the girl married someone else, but wreaked vengeance on his successful rival in a most horrible way, first seducing his wife, then ruining the husband's business, then seeing that the husband was murdered. Such things could scarcely happen in America, Ingham supposed, but this was in Tunisia. John Castlewood had enthusiasm, and he knew Tunisia. And John had known Ingham and had invited him to try the script. They had a producer named Miles Gallust. Ingham thought that if he felt he wasn't getting anywhere, wasn't capable, he would tell John, give back the thousand dollars, and John could find someone else. John had done two good films on small budgets, and the first, *The Grievance*, had had the better success. That had been set in Mexico. The second had been about Texas oil-riggers, and Ingham had forgotten the title. John was twenty-six, full of energy and the kind of faith that went with not knowing much about the world as yet, or so Ingham thought. Ingham felt that John had a future better, more than likely, than his own would be. Ingham was at an age when he knew his potentialities and limitations. John Castlewood did not know his as yet, and perhaps was not the type ever to think about them or recognise them, which might be all to the good.

Ingham paid his bill, and went back to his hotel room for a jacket. He was getting hungry. He glanced again at the two letters in the box marked I–J, and at the empty cubbyhole under his hanging key. 'Vingt-six, s'il vous plaît,' he said, and took the key.

Again taking John's advice, Ingham went to the Restaurant du Paradis in the rue du Paradis, which was between his hotel and the Café de Paris. Later, he wandered around the town, and had a couple of café exprès standing at counters in cafés where there were no tourists. The patrons were all men in these places. The barman understood his French, but Ingham did not hear anyone else speaking French.

He had thought to write a letter to Ina when he got back to his hotel but he felt too tired, or perhaps uninspired. He went to bed and read some of a William Golding novel that he had brought from America. Before he fell asleep, he thought of the girl who had flirted with him – mildly – in the Café de Paris. She had been blonde, a trifle chubby, but very attractive. Ingham had thought she might be German (the man with her could have been anything), and he had felt pleased when he heard her talking French with the man as they went out. Vanity, Ingham thought. He should be thinking about Ina. She was certainly thinking about him. At any rate, Tunisia was going to be a splendid place not to think any more about Lotte. Thank God, he had almost stopped. It had been a year and six months since his divorce, but sometimes to Ingham it seemed like only six months, or even two.

CHAPTER TWO

The next morning, when there was again no letter for him, it occurred to Ingham that John and Ina might have written to him at the Hotel du Golfe in Hammamet, where John had suggested he should stay. Ingham had not yet made a reservation there, and he supposed he should for the 5th or 6th of June. John had said, 'Look around Tunis for a few days. The characters are going to live in Tunis. ... I don't think you'd like to work there. It'll be hot, and you can't swim unless you go to Sidi Bou Said. We'll work in Hammamet. Terrific beach for an afternoon swim, and no city noises. ...'

After a whole day of walking and driving about Tunis, enduring also the long closure of everything except restaurants from noon or twelve-thirty until four, Ingham was ready to go to Hammamet tomorrow. But he thought as soon as he got to Hammamet, he would reproach himself for not having seen enough of Tunis, so he decided to stay on two more days. On one of those days, he drove to Sidi Bou Said, sixteen kilometres away, had a swim and took lunch at a rather chic hotel, as there were no independent restaurants. It was a very clean town of chalk-white houses and bright-blue shutters and doors.

There had been no room free at the Golfe when Ingham had telephoned the day before, but the manager had suggested another hotel in Hammamet. Ingham went to the other hotel, which he found too Hollywood in atmosphere, and at last put himself up at a hotel called La Reine de Hammamet. All the hotels had beaches on the Gulf of Hammamet, but were set back fifty yards or more from the water. The Reine had a large main building, gardens of lime

and lemon and bougainvillaea, and also fifteen or twenty
bungalows of varying sizes, each given privacy by the leaves
of citrus trees. The bungalows had kitchens, but Ingham
was not in the mood to start housekeeping, so he took a room
in the main building with a view on the sea. He immediately
went down for a swim.

There were not many people on the beach at this hour,
though the sun was still above the horizon. Ingham saw a
couple of empty beach chairs. He didn't know if one had to
rent them or not, but he assumed they belonged to the hotel,
so he took one. He put on his sunglasses – another thought
of John Castlewood, who had made him a present of these –
and pulled a paperback out of his robe pocket. After fifteen
minutes, he was asleep, or at least in a doze. *My God*, he
thought, *my God, it's quiet and beautiful and warm.* . . .

'Hello! Good evening! – You an American?'

The loud voice startled Ingham like a gunshot, and he sat
up in his chair. 'Yes.'

'Excuse me interrupting your reading. I'm an American,
too. From Connecticut.' He was a man of fifty or so, greyish-
haired, balding, with a slight bulge at his waistline, and with
an enviable tan. He was not very tall.

'New York here,' Ingham said. 'I hope I haven't taken
your chair.'

'Ha-ha! No! But the boys'll be collecting them in another
half-hour or so. Have to put 'em away, or they wouldn't be
here tomorrow morning!'

Lonely, Ingham thought. Or had he a wife just as
chummy? But one could be lonely with that, too. The man
was looking out at the sea, standing only two yards from
Ingham.

'My name's Adams. Francis J. Adams.' He said it as if he
were proud of it.

'Mine's Howard Ingham.'

'What do you think of Tunisia?' Adams asked with his
friendly smile that bulged his brown cheeks.

'Very attractive. Hammamet, anyway.'

'I think so. Best to have a car to get around in. Sousse and
Djerba, places like that. Got a car?'

'Yes, I have.'

'Good. Well—' He was backing, taking his leave. 'Drop in and see me some time. My bungalow's just up the slope there. Number ten. Any of the boys can tell you which is mine. Just ask for Adams. Come in and have a drink some evening. Bring your wife, if you have one.'

'Thanks very much,' Ingham said. 'No, I'm alone.'

Adams nodded, and waved. 'See you again.'

Ingham sat on another five minutes, then got up. He took a shower in his room, then went downstairs to the bar. It was a large bar with red Persian carpeting that covered the floor. A middle-aged couple were speaking French. Another table of three was British. There were only seven or eight people in the room, a few of them watching television in the corner.

A man came from the television set to the British table and said in a voice without excitement, 'The Israelis have blasted a dozen airports.'

'Where?'

'Egypt. Or maybe Jordan. The Arabs are going to be a pushover.'

'That news came through in French?' asked another of the Englishmen.

Ingham stood at the bar. The war was on apparently. Tunisia was quite a distance from the fighting. Ingham hoped it wouldn't interfere with work plans. But the Tunisians were Arabs, and there was going to be some anti-Western emotion, he knew, if the Arabs lost, and of course they would lose. He must get a Paris paper tomorrow.

Ingham avoided the beach for the next couple of days, and took some drives into the country. The Israelis were mopping up the Arabs, and twenty-five airbases had been destroyed on Monday, the day the war broke out. A Paris paper reported a few cars with Western licence plates overturned in a street in Tunis, and also the windows of the U.S.I.S. library broken on the Boulevard Bourguiba. Ingham did not go to Tunis. He went to the town of Naboul, north-east of Hammamet, and to Bir Bou Rekba inland, and to a few other tiny towns, dusty and poor, whose names he could not remember easily. He ran into a market morning at one, and walked about among camels, pottery, baubles and pins, cotton clothing and straw mats, all spread out on coarse sheets on the ground. People jostled him, which Ingham did not like. The Arabs didn't mind human contact, and on the contrary needed it, Ingham had read. That was everywhere apparent in the souk. The jewellery in the market was shoddy, but inspired Ingham to go to a good shop and buy a silver pin for Ina, a flat triangle which fastened with a circle. They came in all sizes. Since the box was so small for posting, Ingham bought also an embroidered red vest for her – a man's garment, but so fancy, it would look very feminine in America. He posted them the afternoon of the same day, after much time-killing, waiting for the post office in Hammamet to open at 4 p.m. The post office was open only one hour in the afternoon, according to a sign outside.

On the fourth day at the Reine, he wrote to John Castlewood. John lived on West Fifty-third Street in Manhattan.

June 8, 19—

Dear John,

Hammamet is as pretty as you said. A magnificent beach. Are you still arriving the 13th? I am ready to get to work here, chatting with strangers at every opportunity, but the kind of people you want don't always know much French. I visited Les Arcades last night. [This was a coffeehouse a mile or so from the Reine.]

Please tell Ina to write me a line. I've written to her. Sort of lonely here with no word from home. Or maybe as you said the mail is fantastically slow. . . .'

And so he trailed off, and felt a little more lonely after he had written it than before. He was checking with the Golfe every day, sometimes twice a day. No letter or cable had come. Ingham drove to the post office to mail his letter, because he wasn't sure it would get off today, if he left it to the hotel. Various clerks had given him three different times for mail arrival, and he assumed they would be equally vague as to collection.

Ingham went down to the beach around six o'clock. The

beach was approached via a patch of jungle-like palm trees which grew, however, out of the inevitable sand. There was a footworn path which he followed. A few metal poles, perhaps from an abandoned children's playground, stuck up out of the sand and were encrusted near the top with small white snails fastened tightly like barnacles. The metal was so hot, he could barely touch it. He walked on, daydreaming about his novel, and he had brought his notebook and pen. There was really nothing more he could do on *Trio* until John got here.

He went into the water, swam out until he felt slightly tired, then turned back. The water was shallow quite far out. There was smooth sand underfoot, which farther inshore became rocky, then sand again, until he stood upon the beach. He wiped his face on his terry-cloth robe, as he had forgotten to bring a towel. Then he sat down with his notebook. His book was about a man with a double life, a man unaware of the amorality of the way he lived, and therefore he was mentally deranged, or unbalanced, to say the least. Ingham did not like to admit this, but he had to. In his book, he had no intention of justifying his hero Dennison. He was simply a young man (twenty when the book began) who married and led a happy family life, and became a director in a bank at thirty. He expropriated funds from the bank when he could, by forgery mainly, and he was as free with giving and lending as he was in stealing. He invested some of the money with a view to his family's future, but he gave away two-thirds of it (also usually under false names) to people who needed it and to men who were trying to start their own businesses.

As often happened, Ingham's ruminations made him doze within twenty minutes, and after writing only twelve lines of notes, he was half asleep when the voice of the American woke him like a repeated dream:

'Hello, there! Haven't seen you for a couple of days.'

Ingham sat up. 'Good afternoon.' He knew what was coming, and he knew he would go, this evening, to have a drink at Adam's bungalow.

'How long're you here for?' Adams asked.

'I don't quite know.' Ingham had stood up and was putting on his robe. 'Maybe another three weeks. I have a friend coming.'

'Oh. Another American?'

'Yes,' Ingham looked at the spear Adams was carrying, a sort of dart five feet long without apparent means of projection.

'I'm on my way back to my bungalow. Want to come along and have a cooling drink?'

Ingham at once thought of Coca-Cola. 'All right. Thank you. What do you do with that spear?'

'Oh, I aim at fish and never catch them.' A chuckle. 'Actually sometimes I snare up shells I couldn't reach if I were just swimming. You know, in water six or eight feet deep.'

The sand became hot inland, but still bearable. Ingham was carrying his beach shoes. Adams had none.

'Here we are,' said Adams suddenly, and turned on to a paved but gritty walk which led to his blue-and-white bungalow. The bungalow's roof was domed for coolness, in Arabian style.

Ingham glanced over his shoulder at a building he had not noticed before, a service building of some sort where several adolescent boys, waiters and clean-up boys of the hotel, he supposed, leaned against the wall chatting.

'Not much, but it's home just now,' said Adams, opening his door with a key he had fished from somewhere in the top of his swimming trunks.

The inside of the bungalow was cool, the shutters closed, and it seemed dark after the sunlight. Adams evidently had an air-conditioner. He turned on a light.

'Sit ye down. What can I get you? A Scotch? Beer? Coke?'

'A Coke, thanks.'

They had stomped their feet carefully on the bare tiles outside the door. Adams walked briskly and squeakily across the tile floor into a short hall that led to a kitchen.

Ingham looked around. It looked like home, indeed. There were seashells, books, stacks of papers, a writing-table that was obviously much used, with ink bottles, pens, a stamp box, a pencil sharpener, an open dictionary. A *Reader's*

Digest. Also a Bible. Was Adams a writer? The dictionary was English–Russian, neatly covered in brown paper. Was Adams a spy? Ingham smiled at the thought. Above the desk hung a framed photograph of an American country house that looked like New England, a white farmhouse surrounded at a generous distance by a three-railed white fence. There were elm trees, a collie, but no person in the picture.

Ingham turned as Adams entered with a small tray.

Adams had a Scotch and soda. 'You a teetotaller?' he asked, smiling his paunchy little smile.

'No, I just felt like a Coke. How long've you been here?'

'A year,' Adams said, beaming, bouncing on his toes.

Adams had high arches, high insteps and rather small feet. There was something disgusting about Adams's feet, and having looked at them once, Ingham did not look again.

'Your wife isn't here?' Ingham asked. He had seen a woman's photograph on the chest of drawers behind Adams, a woman in her forties, sedately smiling, sedately dressed.

'My wife died five years ago. Cancer.'

'Oh. – What do you do to pass the time here?'

'I don't feel too lonely. I keep busy.' Again the squirrel-like smile. 'Once in a while someone interesting turns up at the hotel, we make acquaintances, they go on somewhere else. I consider myself an unofficial ambassador for America. I spread goodwill – I hope – and the American way of life. Our way of life.'

What the hell did that mean, Ingham wondered, the Vietnam War springing at once to his mind. 'How do you mean?'

'I have my ways. – But tell me about yourself, Mr Ingham. Sit down somewhere. You're here on vacation?'

Ingham sat down in a large scooped leather chair that creaked. Adams sat on the sofa. 'I'm a writer,' Ingham said. 'I'm waiting for an American friend who wants to do a film here. He's going to be cameraman and director. The producer is in New York. It's all rather informal.'

'Interesting! A film on what subject?'

'A story about young people in Tunisia. John Castlewood – the cameraman – knows Tunisia quite well. He lived a few months here with a family in Tunis.'

'So you're a film writer.' Adams was putting on a colourful short-sleeved shirt.

'No, just a writer. Fictions. But my friend John wanted me to do his film with him.' Ingham detested the conversation.

'What books have you written?'

Ingham stood up. He knew more questions were coming, so he said, 'Four. One of them was *The Game of "If"*. You probably haven't heard of it.' Adams hadn't, so Ingham said, 'Another book was called *The Gathering Swine*. Not so successful.'

'*The Gadarene Swine?*' Adams asked, as Ingham had thought he would.

'*Gathering*,' Ingham said. 'I meant it to sound like Gadarene, you see.' His face felt warm with a kind of shame, or boredom.

'You make enough to live on?'

'Yes, with television work now and then in New York.' He thought suddenly of Ina, and the thought caused a throb in his body, making Ina strangely more real than she had been since he got to Europe, or Africa. He could see Ina in her office in New York now. It would be noonish. She would be reaching for a pencil, or a sheet of typewriter paper. If she had a lunch date, she would be a little late for it.

'You're probably famous and I don't realise it,' Adams said, smiling. 'I don't read much fiction. Now and then, something that's condensed. Like in the *Reader's Digest*, you know. If you've got one of your books here, I'd like to read it.'

Ingham smiled. 'Sorry. I don't travel with them.'

'When's your friend due?' Adams stood up. 'Can't I freshen that? How about a Scotch now?'

Ingham agreed to the Scotch. 'He's due Tuesday.' Ingham caught a glimpse of his own face in a mirror on the wall. His face was pink from the sun and starting to tan. His mouth looked severe and a little grumpy. A sudden loud voice, shouting in Arabic just outside the shuttered windows, made him flinch, but he continued staring at himself. This is what Adams saw, he thought, what the Arabs saw, an ordinary American face with blue eyes that looked too sharply at everything, above a mouth not exactly friendly. Three creases undulated across his forehead, and the beginnings of wrinkles showed under his eyes. Maybe not a very friendly face, but it was impossible to change one's expression without being phoney. Lotte had done a little damage. The best he could do, Ingham thought out of nowhere, the proper thing was to be neutral, neither chummy nor standoffish. Play it cool.

He turned as Adams came in with his drink.

'What do you think about the war?' Adams asked, smiling as usual. 'The Israelis have got it won.'

'Can you get the news? By radio?' Ingham was interested. He must buy a transistor, he thought.

'I can get Paris, London, Marseilles, Voice of America, practically anything,' Adams said, gesturing towards a door, which presumably led to a bedroom. 'Just scattered reports now, but the Arabs are finished.'

'Since America is pro-Israel, I suppose there'll be some anti-American demonstrations?'

'A few, no doubt,' said Adams, as cheerfully as if he were talking about flowers pushing up in a garden. 'A pity the Arabs can't see a yard in front of their noses.'

Ingham smiled. 'I thought you might well be pro-Arab.'

'Why?'

'Living here. Liking them, I thought.' On the other hand, he read the *Reader's Digest*, which was always anti-Communist. On the other hand, what was the other hand?

'I like the Arabs. I like all peoples. I think the Arabs ought to do more with their own land. What's done is done, the creation of Israel, right or wrong. The Arabs ought to do more with their own desert and stop complaining. Too many Arabs sit around doing nothing.'

That was true, Ingham thought, but since Adams read the *Reader's Digest*, he suspected anything he said, and thought about it twice. 'Have you a car? Do you think the Arabs will turn it over?'

Adams chuckled comfortably. 'Not here. My car's the black Cadillac convertible under the trees. Tunisia is pro-Arab, of course, but Bourguiba isn't going to allow much trouble. He can't afford it.'

Adams talked about his farm in Connecticut, and about his business in Hartford. He had had a soft drinks bottling plant. Adams obviously enjoyed reminiscing. His had been a happy marriage. He had a daughter who lived in Tulsa. Her husband was a brilliant engineer, Adams said. Ingham thought, *I'm afraid to fall in love with Ina. I'm afraid to fall in love with anyone since Lotte.* It was so obvious, he wondered why he hadn't realised it before, months ago. Why should it come to him now, while talking with this ordinary little man from Connecticut? Or had he said he originally came from Indiana?

Ingham said good-bye with a vague promise to meet Adams in the bar next day around eight o'clock, just before dinner. Adams said he sometimes took dinner at the hotel, rather than cook. As he walked back to the main building of the hotel, Ingham thought about Ina. It wasn't bad, maybe even wise, he thought, the way he felt about her. He was not out of his mind about her. He cared for her and she was important to him. He had taken his film contract for *The Game of 'If'* to show her before he signed it, her approval being just as important to him as his agent's. (In fact, Ina knew all about film contracts, but emotionally as well he had wanted her approval.) She was intelligent, pretty, and physically attractive to him. She was dependable and unneurotic. She had her own work, and she wasn't a bore or a drag – as Lotte had been, out of bed, he had to admit. Ina had some talent for playwriting. She'd have been better than him for this job, in fact, and Ingham wondered why John hadn't suggested her doing the script instead of him? Of maybe he had, and Ina hadn't been able to get away from New York. John and Ina had known each other a little longer than Ingham had known either of them. Ina might not mention it to him, if John had asked her to write 'Trio', Ingham thought.

Suddenly, Ingham felt happier. If there wasn't a letter from John when he got to the hotel, if there was none tomorrow, and if John didn't come on the 13th, Ingham felt he could take it in his stride. Maybe he was acquiring the African tempo. *Don't be anxious. Let the days pass.* He realised that Francis J. Adams had been curiously stimulating. The *Reader's Digest* condensations! The American way of life! Adams was so plainly content with himself, with everything. It was fabulous, in these times. An Arab boy had brought fresh bathtowels while Ingham had been there, and Adams had talked with him in Arabic. The boy seemed to like Adams. Ingham tried to imagine having lived in the hotel for a year. Was Adams some kind of American agent? No, he was much too naïve. Or could that be part of his cover? One never knew these days, did one? Ingham didn't know what to make of Adams.

CHAPTER THREE

June 13th came and went. There was no word from John and, what was even stranger, no word from Ina. On the 14th, inspired by a good lunch at the hotel, Ingham called Ina:

WHAT'S UP? WRITE ME HOTEL REINE HAMMAMET. I LOVE YOU. HOWARD.

He sent it to CBS. At least it would be there the first thing tomorrow morning, Thursday. Ingham had been in Tunisia two weeks now without a word from John or Ina. Even Jimmy Goetz, not one for writing letters, had sent him a postcard of good luck wishes. Jimmy was off to Hollywood to write a film script of someone's novel. His postcard had come to the Hotel du Golfe.

The days began to drag. They dragged for two days, then Ingham picked up mentally, or perhaps slowed down, so that he didn't mind the dragging. He was making some progress in planning his novel, and had the first three chapters clearly in mind.

Ingham was now on demi-pension, so he took lunch or dinner away from the hotel, usually at the restaurant Chez Melik in the town of Hammamet, a kilometre away. He could walk to Hammamet along the beach – more pleasant if it were evening and not so warm – or take his car. Melik's was a terrace restaurant, very cheap and informal, up some steps from the street. The terrace was shaded with grape-vines and one corner of it looked down on a strawy cattle pen, where sheep and goats sometimes stood, waiting to be slaughtered. Sometimes instead of living animals, there was a heap of bleeding sheepskins at which cats pulled, over which flies buzzed. Ingham did not always enjoy looking

23

down there. The good thing about Melik's was the mixed clientele. There were turbaned camel-drivers, Tunisian or French students with flutey instruments or guitars, French tourists, occasionally some British, and ordinary men from the village who lingered over their vin rosé, picking their teeth and nibbling from plates of fruit until midnight. Once Adams came with him to Melik's. Adams had been there before, of course, and was not so fond of the place as Ingham. Adams thought it could be cleaner.

Ingham had met four or five people in his hotel, but he did not care very much for any of them. An American couple had asked him to play bridge, but Ingham had told them he didn't know how to play, which was nearly true. Another was an American named Richard Messerman, a bachelor on the prowl, but having luck, he said, only at the Hotel Fourati, a mile away, where he often spent the night. Ingham did not accept Messerman's invitations to cruise the Fourati. Another was a German homosexual from Hamburg, who had luck only in Hammamet with Arab boys, but plenty of luck, he told Ingham. His name was Heinz something-or-other, and he spoke good English and French, and was usually wearing white tight trousers with colourful belts.

Oddly enough, Ingham found Adams the best company, perhaps because Adams asked nothing of him. Adams had the same affable manner with everyone – with Melik, the pharmacist, the man in the post office, the Arab boys at the hotel. Adams looked happy. Ingham feared that one day he would spring something on him like Christian Science or Rosicrucianism, but after nearly two weeks, Adams hadn't.

It was growing hotter. Ingham found himself eating less and losing a little weight.

He had sent a second cable to Ina, this one to her home in Brooklyn Heights, but still no reply had come. Three days after the second cable, Ingham tried to ring her one afternoon, when it would be morning in New York and she would be at her office. This attempt kept him waiting in the air-conditioned lobby of the hotel for more than two hours, but the hotel could not get through even to Tunis. The lines to

Tunis were too crowded. Ingham had the distinct feeling that a telephone call was hopeless, unless he went to Tunis, which of course he could do; it was only sixty-one kilometres away. But he did not go, and he did not try again to telephone Ina. Instead he wrote a long letter in which he said:

Africa is strangely good for thinking. It's like standing naked in glaring sunlight against a white wall. Somehow nothing is hidden in this bright light . . .'

But his important thought, about being afraid to fall in love, and his consequently even more substantial feeling about Ina, he preferred not to write her. Maybe at some time he would mention it, or maybe it was best left unsaid, because she might misunderstand and think he was not enthusiastic enough about her.

Tell John if he doesn't hurry up and get here, I'm going to start my novel. What's holding him up? It's true it's pleasant here, and it's free (if we sell this thing) but it's turning into a vacation and I don't like vacations. . . . The Arabs are very friendly and informal. They loaf a lot, sitting at tables under trees, drinking coffee and wine. There is a section like the Casbah next to an old fortress which juts out to sea. There the houses are all white, full of plump jolly moms, most of them pregnant again. Never a closed door, so you can see into rooms with mats on the floor, babies crawling, brazier fires with grandma fanning them with the end of her shawl. . . . Car is a Peugeot station wagon, behaving well so far. . . . I wish like mad you were here. Why couldn't John have put us both on this job? . . . Could you send me a snapshot? You know I haven't a single picture of you?

She would probably send him an awful snapshot for a laugh, Ingham thought. He faced the fact that he was terribly lonely. He supposed it would take four or five days for his letter to reach Ina. That meant the 20th or 21st of June. The Israelis had won the war, all right, a blitzkrieg, the papers called it. And as Adams had predicted, there were no serious reverberations in Hammamet, but in Tunis just enough broken glass and street fighting to make Ingham prefer to keep away. If the Arabs in Hammamet cafés were talking about the war, Ingham couldn't tell it, as he could not understand a word. Their conversations had a certain level of intensity and loudness which did not seem to vary.

Ingham had put in a request for a bungalow, and on the 19th of June, one was available. The refrigerator and stove were very new, because the bungalows in this section had been built only in the spring, Adams had said. There was a small but excellently stocked grocery store just inside one driveway of the hotel about a hundred yards from his bungalow, which sold spirits and cold beer, all kinds of canned goods, even kitchen gadgets and toothpaste. If he and John holed up here, Ingham thought, they'd hardly need to leave the bungalow except to take a swim and visit the store for provisions. His bungalow, number three, had only one big room plus kitchen and bath, but it had two single beds. John probably wouldn't want to share it for sleeping, and Ingham didn't much like the idea either, but John could sleep in the main building. The table in the bungalow was a big wooden one, splendid for working. Ingham bought salami, cheese, butter, eggs, fruit, Ritz crackers and Scotch the afternoon he moved in, then he went over about five o'clock to invite Adams for a house-warming drink.

Adams wasn't in, and Ingham supposed he was on the beach. He found Adams lying on a straw mat on his stomach, writing something. Adams, oblivious of Ingham's approach until he was quite close, finished off his sentence or whatever with a satisfied flourish, lifting his pen in the air.

'Hello-o, Howard!' Adams said. 'Got your bungalow?'

'Yes, just now.'

Adams was pleased to be invited, as Ingham had known he would be. He agreed to come to number three at six o'clock.

Ingham went back and did some more unpacking. It was good to have a sort of 'house' instead of a hotel room. He thought of his desk in his apartment on West Fourth Street, near Washington Square. He'd had the apartment only three months. It was air-conditioned and more expensive than any place he'd ever had, and he had taken it only after the film sale of *The Game of 'If'* had become definite. Ina had a set of keys. He hoped she was looking in now and then, but she had taken his few plants to her Brooklyn house, and there weren't any chores for her to do except forward letters that looked important. Ina was brilliant at telling what was important and what wasn't. Ingham had of course told his agent and his publishers that he would be in Tunisia, and by now they knew he was at the Reine.

'Well!' Adams stood at the door with a bottle of wine. 'Looks *very* nice! – Here, I brought you this. For the housewarming. Or for your first meal, you know.'

'Oh, thanks, Francis! That's very nice of you. What'll you have?'

They had their usual Scotch, Adams's with soda.

'Any news from your friend?' Adams asked.

'No, I'm sorry to say.'

'Can't you send a telegram to someone who knows him?'

'I've done that.' Ingham meant Ina.

The boy called Mokta, a waiter at the bungalows' bar-café, knocked on the open door, smiling his wide, friendly smile. 'Good evening, messieurs,' he said in French. 'Is there anything you have need of?'

'I think nothing, thanks,' Ingham said.

'You would like breakfast at what time, sir?'

'Oh, you serve breakfast?'

'It is not *necessary* to take it,' Mokta said with a quick gesture, 'but many of the people in the bungalows take it.'

'All right, at nine o'clock, then,' Ingham said. 'No, eight-thirty.' The breakfast would probably be late.

'Nice boy, Mokta,' Adams said when Mokta had left. 'And they really work them here. Have you seen the kitchen in that place?' He gestured towards the low, square building that was the bungalows' café-with-terrace. 'And the room where they sleep there?'

Ingham smiled. 'Yes.' He had had a glimpse today. The

boys slept in a room that was a field of ten or twelve jammed-together beds. The sink in the kitchen had been full of dirty water and dishes.

'The drains are always stopped up, you know. I make my own breakfast. I imagine it's a little more sanitary. Mokta's nice. But that sour-puss *directrice* works him to death. She's a German, probably only hired because she can speak Arabic and French. If they're out of towels, it's Mokta who has to go to the main building and get them. – How're you doing on your book?'

'I've done twenty pages. Not as fast as my usual rate, but I can't complain.' Ingham was grateful for Adams's interest. He had found out that Adams wasn't a writer or a journalist, but he still didn't know what Adams did, except study Russian in a casual way. Maybe Adams didn't do anything. That was possible, of course.

'It must be hard, writing when you think each day you'll have to drop it,' Adams said.

'That doesn't bother me too much.' Ingham replenished Adam's drink. He served Adams crackers and cheese. The bungalow began to seem more attractive. The waning sunlight shone through half-open, pale-blue shutters on to the white walls. Ingham thought that he and John might spend no more than ten days on the script. John knew someone in Tunis who could help him in finding the small cast. John wanted amateurs.

He and Adams were in good spirits when they went off in Ingham's car to have dinner at Melik's. The terrace was half full, not noisy as yet. Someone was strumming a guitar, someone else tootling a flute hesitantly at a back table.

Adams talked about his daughter Caroline in Tulsa. Her husband, the engineer, was about to be sent off to Vietnam, as he was in some kind of civilian army reserve. Caroline was due to have a baby within five months, and Adams was pleased and hopeful, because her first child had miscarried. Adams was pro-Vietnam War, Ingham had discovered early on. Ingham was sick of it, sick of discussing it with people like Adams, and he was glad Adams did not say anything else about the war that evening. Democracy and God, those were the things Adams believed in. It wasn't Christian Science or Rosicrucianism with Adams – at least not so far – but a sort of Billy Graham, all-round God with an old-fashioned moral code thrown in. What the Vietnamese needed, Adams said in appallingly plain words, was the American kind of democracy. Besides the American kind of democracy, Ingham thought, the Americans were introducing the Vietnamese to the capitalist system in the form of a brothel industry, and to the American class system by making the Negroes pay higher for their lays. Ingham listened, nodding, bored, mildly irritated.

'You've never been married?' Adams asked.

'Yes. Once. Divorced. – No children.'

They were having a smoke after the *couscous*. Not much edible meat tonight, but the *couscous* and the spicy sauce had been delicious. *Couscous* was the name of the African millet flour, Adams had explained, granulated flour that was cooked by steaming it over a broth. It could be made also from wheat. It was tan in colour, bland in flavour, and over it was spooned hot or medium hot red sauce, turnips, and pieces of stewed lamb. It was a speciality at Melik's.

'Was your wife a writer, too?' Adams asked.

'No, she didn't do anything,' Ingham said, smiling a little. 'A woman of leisure. Well, it's past, and it was a long time ago.' He was ready to tell Adams it was longer than a year and a half ago, in case Adams asked.

'Do you think you'll marry again?'

'I don't know. – Why? Do you think it's the ideal life?'

'Oh, I think that depends. It's not the same for every man'. Adams was smoking a small cigar. When his cheeks flattened out, his face looked longer, more like an ordinary face, and when he removed the cigar, the little pouches came back, like a cartoon of himself. Between the cheeks, the thin, pink mouth smiled good-naturedly. 'I was certainly happy. My wife was the kind who really knew how to run a home. Put up preserves, took care of the garden, a good hostess, remembered people's birthdays, all that. Never annoyed when I got delayed at the plant. – I thought of marrying again. There was even one woman – a lot like my wife – I might've married. But it's not the same when you're not young any more.'

Ingham had nothing to say. He thought of Ina and wished she were here, sitting with them now, wished he could take a walk with her on the beach tonight, after they had said good night to Adams, wished they could go back to his bungalow and go to bed together.

'Any girl in your life now?' Adams asked.

Ingham woke up. 'In a way, yes.'

Adams smiled. 'So you're in love?'

Ingham didn't like to talk to anyone about Ina, but did it matter if he talked to someone like Adams? 'Yes, I suppose so. I've known her about a year. She works for CBS-TV in New York. She's written some television plays and also some short stories. Several published,' he added.

The flautist was gaining strength. An Arab song began shakily, reinforced by a wailing male voice.

'How old is she?'

'Twenty-eight.'

'Old enough to know her own mind.'

'Um-m. She had a marriage that went wrong – when she was twenty-one or -two. So I'm sure she's in no hurry to make a mistake again. Neither am I.'

'But you expect to marry?'

The music grew ever louder.

'Vaguely. – I can't see that it matters very much, unless people want children.'

'Is she going to join you here in Tunisia?'

'No. I wish she were. She knows John Castlewood very well. In fact she introduced us. But she has her job in New York.'

'And she hasn't written you either? About John?'

'No.' Ingham warmed a little to Adams. 'It's funny, isn't it? How slow can mail *get* here?'

Their dessert of yoghurt had arrived. There was also a platter of fruit.

'Tell me more about your girl. What's her name?'

'Ina Pallant. – She lives with her family in a big house in

Brooklyn Heights. She has a crippled brother she's very fond of – Joey. He has multiple sclerosis, practically confined to his wheeelchair, but Ina's a great help to him. He paints – rather surrealistically. Ina arranged a show for him last year. But of course he couldn't have got the show unless he was good. He sold – oh, seven or eight out of thirty canvases.' Ingham disliked saying it, but he thought Adams would be interested in figures. 'One picture, for instance, was of a man sitting casually on a rock in a forest, smoking a cigarette. In the foreground, a little girl is running forward, terrified, and a tree is growing out of the top of her head.'

Adams leaned forward with interest. 'What's that supposed to mean?'

'The terror of growing up. The man represents life and evil. He's entirely green. He just sits watching – or not even watching – with an air of having the whole situation in his power.'

Melik's plump son, aged about thirteen, came and leaned on chubby hands on the table, exchanging something in Arabic with Adams. Adams was grinning. Then the boy totted up their bill. Ingham insisted on paying, because it was part of his bungalow-warming.

Downstairs, on the dusty steet, Ingham noticed an old Arab whom he had seen a few times before, loitering around his car. The Arab had a short grey beard and wore a turban and classic baggy red pants held up somehow under the knees. He walked with a stick. Ingham knew he must try the car doors when he – Ingham – wasn't in sight, hoping with indefatigable patience for the day or the hour when Ingham would forget to lock a door. Now as the Arab drifted away from the big Peugeot station wagon, Ingham barely glanced at him. The Arab was becoming a fixture, like the tan fortress or the Café de la Plage near Melik's. Ingham and Adams walked a little way up the main street, but since this became dark, they turned back. The interesting corner, the only alive part of the town at this time of night, was the broad sandy area in front of the Plage, where a few men sat at tables with their coffees or glasses of wine. The yellow light from the Plage's big front windows flowed out on to the first table-legs and a few sandalled feet under them.

As Ingham looked at the front door, a man was rudely pushed out and nearly fell. Ingham and Adams stopped to watch. The man seemed a little drunk. He went directly back into the Plage, and was again shoved out. Another man came out and put an arm around him, talking to him. The drunk had a stubborn air, but let himself be sent off in the direction of the white houses behind the fortress. Ingham continued to watch the unsteady man, fascinated by whatever passion filled him. Just beyond the glow of the café's lights, the man stopped and half turned, staring defiantly at the café door. In the doorway of the Plage now, a tall man and the man who had put his arm around the drunken man were talking together and keeping an eye on the motionless, determined figure two hundred yards away.

Ingham was rapt. He wondered if they were carrying knives. Perhaps, if it was a long-standing grudge.

'Probably a quarrel about a woman,' Adams said.

'Yes.'

'Very jealous when it comes to women, you know.'

'Yes, I'm sure,' Ingham said.

They walked a little on the beach, though Ingham did not like the fine sand getting into his shoes. By the light of the moon, small children were gathering bits off the beach – the second or third wave of scavengers after their parents and elder siblings – and putting their findings away in bags that hung from their necks Ingham had never seen such a clean beach as this one. Nothing was ever left by all the picker-uppers, not even a four-inch-long splinter of wood, because they used the wood for fires, and not even a shell, because they sold all the shells they could to tourists.

Ingham and Adams had a final coffee at the Plage. A smelly, arched doorway to their right revealed a huge 'W.C.' and an arrow, in black paint, on a blue wall three feet beyond. The ceiling was groined, if such a word could be used, by projecting supports ornamented with big yellow knobs that suggested stage footlights. Ingham realised that he had nothing to talk to Adams about. Adams, silent himself must have realised the same thing in regard to

Ingham. Ingham smiled a little as he drank the last of his sweet black coffee. Funny to think of someone like himself and Adams, hanging around together just because they were Americans. But their good night twenty minutes later, on the hotel grounds, was warm. Adams wished him a happy stay, as if he had moved in permanently, or as if, Ingham thought, he were a newcomer to an expedition, doomed to a different and rather lonely life for months to come. But Ingham had no duties at all except those he assigned himself and he was free to go hundreds of miles anywhere in his car.

Before he went to bed that night, Ingham looked through his personal and his business address books, and found two people to whom he might write in regard to John. (He hadn't Miles Gallust's address, or he had left it in New York, and reproached himself for this oversight.) The two people were William McIlhenny, an editor in the New York office of Paramount, and Peter Langland, a free-lance photographer whom John knew pretty well, Ingham remembered. Ingham thought of cabling, but decided a cable would look too dramatic, so he wrote Peter Langland a short, friendly note (they had met at a party with John, and Ingham remembered him more clearly now, a chunky blond fellow with glasses), asking him to prod John and ask John to cable, in case he had not yet written. The probable four or five days until the letter reached New York seemed an aeon to wait, but Ingham tried to make himself be patient. This was Africa, not Paris or London. The letter had to get to Tunis before it could be put on a plane.

Ingham posted the letter the next morning.

CHAPTER FOUR

Two or three days went by. Ingham worked.

In the mornings, Mokta brought his continental breakfast around nine-fifteen or nine-thirty. Mokta always had a question:

'The refrigerator works well?' Or 'Hassim has brought you enough towels?' Always Mokta asked these things with a disarming smile. He was more blond than brunette, and he had grey-blue eyes with long lashes.

Ingham supposed Mokta was popular with both women and men, and though he was only seventeen or so, he had probably had experience with both. At any rate, with his good looks and his manner, he was not going to spend the rest of his life carrying breakfast-trays and stacks of towels across the sand. 'Only one thing I'd like, my friend,' Ingham said. 'If you see a letter for me in that madhouse, would you bring it immediately?'

Mokta laughed. 'Bien sûr, m'sieur! Je regarde tout le temps – tout le temps pour vous!'

Ingham waved a casual good-bye and poured himself some coffee, which was strong enough but not hot. Sometimes it was the other way around. He pulled on his pyjama top. He slept only in the pants. The nights were warm, too. He thought of the desk in the bungalow manager's office. Dare he hope for a letter today by ten-thirty – eleven? Ingham had been told by the hotel's main office that mail came twice a day to the bungalow headquarters and was delivered as soon as it arrived, but this was patently not so, because Ingham had seen people going to the office in the bungalow headquarters and looking through the post there, post that was sometimes sorted and sometimes not. How could he expect Arab boys, or even the harassed, ill-tempered German *directrice* to care very much about people's mail? There was never anyone at the desk. Stacks of towels filled one corner of the office – although when Ingham had asked for a clean towel, having used his for more than a week, the boy had told him he hadn't changed it because it didn't look dirty. Mysterious grey metal files stood against the walls. The absurdity of the contents of this office had given it a Kafka-like futility to Ingham. He felt that he never would, never could receive any letter of significance there. And it was maddening to Ingham to find the door sometimes locked for no apparent reason, no one around to open it, or no one with the key. This would send him forging across the sand to the main building on the off-chance that post had arrived and not yet been brought to the bungalows.

Ingham was working when Mokta came in just before eleven o'clock with a letter. Ingham seized it, automatically fishing in his pocket for some coins for Mokta.

'Hallelujah!' Ingham said. The envelope was a long business airmail, and it was postmarked New York.

'Succès!' said Mokta. 'Merci, m'sieur!' he bowed and left.

The letter was from Peter Langland, strangely enough. Their letters had crossed.

June 19, 19—

Dear Mr Ingham – or Howard,

By now you no doubt know of the sad events of overlast weekend, as Ina said she would write you. John spoke to me just two days before. He was in a crise, as you probably know, or maybe you didn't know. But none of us expected anything like this. He was afraid he couldn't go through with 'Trio' under the circumstances, which made him feel doubly guilty, I think, because you were already in Tunisia. Then he had his personal problems, as you probably know from Ina. But I know he would want me to write a line to you and say he is sorry, so herewith I do it. He simply couldn't stand up to everything that was on his shoulders. I liked John very much and thought very highly of him, as I think everyone did who knew him. We all believed he had a great career coming. It is a shock to all of us, but especially to those who knew him well. I suppose you'll be coming home now, and maybe you've already left, but I trust this can be forwarded to you.

Yours sincerely,
Peter Langland

John Castlewood had killed himself. Ingham walked to the window with the letter in his hand. The blue shutters were closed against the augmenting morning sun, but he stared at the shutters as if he could see through them. This was the end of the Tunisia expedition. How had John done it? A gun? Sleeping pills most likely. *What a hell of a thing,* Ingham thought. And why? Well, he hadn't known John well enough to guess. He remembered John's face – always lively, usually smiling or grinning, pale below the neat, straight black hair. Maybe a trifle weak, that face. Or was that an after-thought? A weak beard, anyway, soft, pale skin. John hadn't looked in the least depressed when Ingham had last seen him, at that last dinner in New York with Ina in a restaurant south of the Square. It had been the evening before the day Ingham caught the plane. 'You know where to go in Tunis for the car rental?' John had asked, making sure of the practical things as usual, and he had asked again if Ingham had packed the street map of Tunis and the *Guide Bleu* for Tunisia, both of which John had lent or given him.

'For Christ's sake,' Ingham muttered. He walked up and down his room, and felt shattered. An anecdote of Adams's drifted into his mind: Adams fishing on a small river (Connecticut? Indiana?) when he was ten years old, and bringing his line up with a human skull on the end of it, a skull so old 'it didn't matter', Adams had said, so he had never told his parents, who he had feared wouldn't believe him, anyway. Adams had buried the skull, out of fear. Suddenly Ingham wanted the comfort of Adams's presence. He thought of going over now to tell Adams the news. He decided against it.

'Good God,' Ingham said, and went to his kitchen to pour

himself a Scotch. The drink did not taste good at that hour, but it was a kind of rite, in Castlewood's honour.

He'd have to think now about starting home. Tell the hotel. See about a plane from Tunis to New York.

Surely he'd hear from Ina today. Ingham looked at the calendar. The weekend Peter meant was the 10th and 11th of June. What the hell was happening over in the great, fast Western world? It was beginning to seem slower than Tunisia.

Ingham went out and walked in the now empty driveway that curved towards the bar-café-mail-office-supply-department of the bungalows. The sand under his tennis shoes was powdery. He walked with his hands in the pockets of his shorts, and when he encountered a huge woman talking in French to her tiny son, who looked like a wisp beside her, Ingham turned aimlessly back. He was trying to think what he should do next. Cable Ina again, perhaps. He might stay on a day or so to get a letter from her – if she had written. Suddenly, everything seemed so doubtful, so vague.

He went back to his bungalow – which he had left unlocked against the advice of Adams who told him to lock it if he were away even one minute – took his billfold and set out, having locked the door this time, for the main building of the hotel. He would cable Ina, and take a look at the newspapers on the tables in the lobby. Sometimes the papers were several days old. There might be something about John in a Paris *Herald-Tribune*. He should look for a Monday June 12th paper, he thought. Or possibly a Tuesday paper, the 13th.

A series of broad, shallow steps led from the beach up to the rear entrance of the hotel. There was an open shower for swimmers at the foot of the steps, and some corpulent Germans, a man and a woman, were yelling and screaming as they de-sanded each other's backs under the water. On going closer to them, Ingham was irked to hear that they were speaking very American American.

At the hotel desk, Ingham sent a cable to Ina:

HEARD ABOUT JOHN FROM LANGLAND. WRITE OR CABLE AT ONCE. BAFFLED. LOVE. HOWARD.

He sent it to Ina's house in Brooklyn, because she would surely get it there, whatever was happening, and she just might not be at work if her brother Joey was having a bad spell and she had to look after him. Neither on the low tables nor on the shelves at the back of the lobby could Ingham find a paper of weekend June 10th–11th, nor a paper in English or French for June 12th or 13th.

'If you please,' Ingham said in careful French to the young Arab clerk at the desk, handing him a five-hundred-millime bill, 'would you see that any letter that comes for me today is delivered at once to my bungalow? Number three. It is very important.' He had printed his name on a piece of paper.

He thought of having a drink at the bar, and decided not to. He did not know what he wanted to do. Oddly enough, he felt he could work on his novel this afternoon. But logically he should make plans about leaving, speak to the hotel now. He didn't.

Ingham went back to his bungalow, put on swimming trunks, and went for a swim. He saw Adams at some distance, bearing his spear, but managed to avoid Adams's seeing him. Adams always went for a swim before lunch, he said.

That afternoon, Ingham found he could write only one paragraph. He was too anxious for a word from Ina, which he felt positive would come in the afternoon post that arrived at any time between four-thirty and six-thirty. But nothing came except something from the U.S. Internal Revenue Department in a windowed envelope, forwarded by Ina. The government wanted three hundred and twenty-eight dollars more. Ingham's accountant had made a slight mistake, apparently. Ingham wrote the cheque and put it in an airmail envelope.

To satisfy himself, Ingham looked first in the bungalow headquarters' office – eight unclaimed letters, but none for him – then walked to the main building. Nothing there for him, either. He walked back barefoot, carrying his sandals, letting the little waves break against his ankles. The declining sun behind him. He stared at the wet sand at his feet.

'Howard! Where've you been?' Adams stood a few yards away, his nose shiny and bown. Now he reminded Ingham of a rabbit. 'Come and have a drink *chez moi*!'

'Thanks very much,' Ingham said, hesitated, then asked, 'When did you mean?'

'Now. I was just on my way home.'

'Did you have a good day?' Ingham asked, making an effort.

They were walking along.

'Very fine, thanks. And you?'

'Not too good, thanks.'

'Oh? What happened?'

Ingham gestured towards Adams's house, a vague forward gesture which he had, in fact, picked up from Adams.

They walked on over the gritty cement path, past the bungalow headquarters, Adams on neat bare feet, Ingham with his heel-less sandals on now, because of the heat of the sand. He felt sloppy in sandals or slippers without heels, but they were certainly the coolest footgear.

Adams hospitably set to work making Scotches with ice. The air-conditioning felt wonderful to Ingham. He stepped outside the door and carefully knocked the sand from his slippers, then came in again.

'Try this.' Adams said, handing Ingham his drink. 'And what's your news?'

Ingham took the drink. 'The man who was supposed to join me killed himself in New York about ten days ago.'

'*What?* – Good heavens! When did you hear?'

'This morning. I had a letter from a friend of his.'

'John, you mean. – Why did he do it? Something wrong with a love affair? Something financial?'

Ingham felt grateful for every predictable question. 'I don't think because of a love affair. But I don't know. Maybe there's no reason at all – except anxiety, something like that.'

'Was he a nervous fellow? Neurotic?'

'In a way. I didn't think *this* neurotic.'

'How did he do it?'

'I dunno. Sleeping pills, I suppose.'

'He was twenty-six, you told me.' Adams's face was full of concern. 'Worried about money?'

Ingham shrugged. 'He wasn't rolling, but he had enough for this project. We had a producer, Miles Gallust. We were advanced a few thousand dollars. – What's the use wondering? There're probably a lot of reasons why he did it, reasons I don't know.'

'Sit down.'

Adams sat down on the sofa with his drink, and Ingham took the squeaky leather chair. The closed shutters made the light in the room a pleasant dusk. A few thin bars of sun came in near the ceiling above Adams's head.

'Well,' Adams said, 'I suppose without John you'll be thinking of leaving here – going back to the States?'

Ingham heard a gloominess in Adam's tone. 'Yes, no doubt. In a few days.'

'Any news from your girl?' Adams asked.

Ingham disliked the term 'your girl'. 'Not yet. I cabled her today.'

Adams nodded thoughtfully. 'When did this happen?'

'The weekend of June tenth and eleventh. I'm sorry I didn't see any papers then. I think the Paris *Herald-Tribune* might have mentioned it.'

'I can understand that it's a blow,' Adams said sympathetically. 'How well did you know John?'

Platitudes.

Adams made them both a second drink. Then Ingham went to his bungalow to put on some trousers for dinner. He had fatuously hoped for a cable from Ina to be lying on the corner of his work-table when he walked into his bungalow. The table was empty of messages as usual.

Melik's was lively that evening. There were two tables with wind instruments, and one guitar somewhere else. A man at another table had a well-behaved German police dog who put his ears back at the noise, but did not bark. It was too noisy to talk comfortably, and that was just as well, Ingham thought. The man with the dog was tall and slender and looked like an American. He wore levis and a blue denim shirt. Adams sat with his pouchy smile, giving an occasional tolerant shake of his head. Ingham felt like a small silent room – maybe an empty room – within a larger room where all this din came from. The American led his dog away.

Adams shouted, for the second time, 'I said, you ought to see more of this country before you take off!'

Ingham nodded his emphatic agreement.

The moon was almost full. They walked a little on the beach, and Ingham looked at the beige, floodlit fortress whose walls sloped gently back, looked at the huddled, domed white Arab houses behind it, heard the still balmy breeze in his ears, and felt far away from New York, from John and his mysterious reasons, even far away from Ina – because he resented her not having written. He hated his resentment and his small-mindedness for having it. Maybe Ina had good reasons for not having written. But if so, what were they? He was not even close to Adams, Ingham thought with a slight start of fear, or loneliness.

Where would he go? Look at the Tunisia map tomorrow, Ingham thought. Or get back to work on the book, until Ina's letter or cable came. That was the wisest thing. His bungalow with breakfast cost about six dollars a day, not that he was worried about money. But much of his Tunisian expenses would obviously have to come out of his own pocket now. Anyway, he ought to wait two or three days for a word from Ina, in case she wrote instead of cabled.

They said good night on the bungalow driveway. 'My thoughts are with you,' Adams said, speaking softly, because people were asleep in the near-by bungalows. 'Get some rest. You've had a shock, Howard.'

CHAPTER FIVE

Ingham meant to sleep late, but he awakened early. He went for a swim, then came back and made some instant coffee. It was still only half past seven. He worked until Mokta brought his breakfast at nine o'clock.

'Ah, you work early this morning!' Mokta said. 'Be careful you do not make the head turn.' He made a circular motion with one finger near his ear.

Ingham smiled. He had noticed that Arabs were always worried about overstraining their brains. One young man he had spoken with in Naboul had told him that he was a university student, but had overstrained his brain, so he was on a vacation of several weeks on doctor's orders. 'Don't forget to see if I have a letter, will you, Mokta? I shall look around eleven, but a letter may come before then.'

'But today is Sunday.'

'So it is.' Ingham was suddenly depressed. 'By the way, I can use a clean towel. Hassim took mine yesterday and forgot to bring a clean one.'

'Ah, that Hassim! I am *sorry*, sir! I hope there are clean towels today. Yesterday, we used them all.'

Ingham nodded. Somebody was getting clean towels, anyway.

'And you know,' Mokta said, leaning gracefully against the door jamb, 'all the boys go to school for *five months* to learn hotel work? You would not believe it, would you?'

'No.' Ingham buttered a piece of toast.

Ingham slept from twelve until one o'clock. He had written nine pages and he was pleased with his work. He took his car and drove to Bir Bou Rekba, a tiny town about seven kilometres away, and had lunch at a simple little restaurant with a couple of tables out on the pavement. The wandering cats were skinnier, ribs showing and all their tails were broken at a painful angle. Breaking cats' or kittens' tails was evidently a minor sport in Tunisia. Most of the cats in Hammamet had broken tails, too. Ingham heard no French. He heard nothing that he could understand. It was appropriate, this environment, he thought, as the main character in his book lived half his time in a world unknown to his family and his business associates, a world known only to himself, really, because he couldn't share with anyone the truth that he was appropriating money and forging cheques with three false signatures several times a month. Ingham sat in the sun dreaming, sipping chilled rosé, wishing – but not desperately at this moment – that time would pass a little faster so that he could have a word from Ina. What would her excuse be? Or maybe a letter from her had got lost, or maybe two had. Ingham had telephoned the Hotel du Golfe the day before yesterday, but not yesterday. He was sick of being told there wasn't anything for him. And anyway, the Golfe was apparently forwarding reliably to the Reine. The sun made his face throb, and he felt as if he were being gently broiled. He had never known the sun so close and big. People farther north didn't know what the sun was like, he thought. This was the true sun, the ancient fire that seemed to reduce one's lifespan to a second and one's personal problems to a minuscule absurdity.

The dramas people invent! Ingham thought. He felt a detached disgust for the whole human race.

A scruffy, emaciated cat looked at him pleadingly, but they had taken away Ingham's plate of fish-with-fried-egg. Ingham tossed the inside of some bread on to the dusty cement. It was all he had. But the cat ate it, chewing patiently with its head turned sideways.

That afternoon, he worked again, and produced five pages.

Monday and Tuesday came and went without a letter from Ina. Ingham worked. He avoided Adams. Ingham felt morose, and knew he would be bad company. In such a mood, he was apt to say something bitter. On Wednesday, when he would have liked to have dinner with Adams, he remembered that Adams had said he always spent Wednesday evenings alone. It seemed to be a law Adams had made for himself. Ingham ate in the hotel dining-room. The cruising American was still here, dining with a man tonight. Ingham nodded a greeting. He realised that he hadn't answered Peter Langland's letter. He wrote a letter that evening.

June 28, 19—

Dear Peter,

I thank you very much for your letter. I had not heard the news, as you know from my first letter, and matter of fact Ina hasn't written me as yet. I was very sorry to hear about John, as I had thought like everyone else that he was doing well. I didn't know him well, as you may know – for the past year, but not well. I had no idea he was in any kind of crisis.

In the next week, I'll probably leave and go back to the States. This is undoubtedly the strangest expedition of my life. Not a word, either, from Miles Gallust, who was to be our producer.

Forgive this inadequate letter. I am frankly still dazed by the news.

Yours,
Howard Ingham

Peter Langland lived on Jane street. Ingham sealed the envelope. He had no stamps left. He would take the letter into Hammamet tomorrow morning.

In the bungalow fifteen feet behind Ingham's, beyond some lemon trees, some French were saying good night. Ingham could hear them distinctly through his open window.

'We'll be in Paris in three days, you know. Give us a telephone call.'

'But of course! Jacques! Come along! – He's falling asleep standing up!'

'Good night, sleep well!'

'Sleep well!'

It seemed very dark beyond his window. There was no moon.

The next day passed like the one before, and Ingham did eight pages. He knocked on Adams's door at 5 p.m. to invite him for a drink, but Adams was not in. Ingham did not bother to look for him on the beach.

On the morning of June 30th, a Friday, a letter from Ina arrived in a CBS envelope. Mokta brought it. Ingham tore it open, in too much of a hurry to tip Mokta.

The letter was dated June 25th, and it said:

Howard dear,

I am sorry I have not written before. Peter Langland said he wrote you, in case you hadn't heard about John, but it was in the Times (London) and the Trib in Paris, so we supposed you'd seen it in Tunisia. I am still so bouleversed, I can't write just now, really. But I will in a day or so, I hope tomorrow. That's a promise. Please forgive me. I hope you are all right.

My love,
Ina

The letter was typewritten. Ingham read it a second time. It wasn't a letter at all. It made him a little angry. What was he supposed to do, sit here another week until she felt in the mood to write? Why was she so bouleversed? 'We thought...' Was she so close to Peter Langland? Had she and Peter been holding John's hand in the hospital before John died? That was, assuming he had taken sleeping pills.

Ingham took a walk along the beach, plodding the same sand he had crossed so many times in quest of a letter from Ina. Maddening, he thought, her letter. She was the kind who could dash off a ten-line letter and give the facts, and perhaps say, 'Details later,' but here there weren't even any facts. It was unexpectedly heartless of her Ingham felt. She might have had the imagination to realise his position, sitting miles away, waiting. And why hadn't she had time to write him in all the days before John did it? And this was the girl he intended to marry? Ingham smiled, and it was a relief. But he felt swimmy and lost, as if he floated in space. Yes, it was understood that they would marry. He had proposed in a casual way, the only way Ina would have liked. She hadn't said, 'Oh, *yes*, darling!' But it was understood. They might not marry for several months. It depended on their jobs and the finding of an apartment, perhaps, because sometimes Ina had to go to California for six weeks or so, but the point was—

His thoughts trailed off, cooked by the sun on his head, discouraged by the sheer effort of imagining New York's unwritten conventions in this torrid Arabic land. Ingham remembered a story Adams had told him: an English girl had smiled, or maybe just stared too long, at an Arab, who had followed her along a dark beach and raped her. That had been the girl's story. An Arab considered a girl's stare a green light. The Tunisian government, to keep in good odour with the West, had made a big to-do, tried the man and given him a long sentence, which had been very soon commuted, however. The story was an absurdity, and Ingham laughed, causing a surprised glance from the two young men – they looked French – who were walking past with skin-diving gear just then.

In the afternoon, Ingham worked, but did only three pages. He was fidgety.

That evening, he had dinner with the man in levis. Ingham had found him in the Café de la Plage, where he went to have a drink at eight o'clock. The man spoke to him first. Again the German police dog was with him. He was a Dane and spoke excellent English with a slight English accent. His name was Anders Jensen. He said he lived in a rented apartment in a street across from Melik's. Ingham tried the *boukhah* which Jensen was drinking. It was a little like *grappa* or *tequila*.

Ingham was in a rather tight-lipped mood, so far as giving information about himself went, but Jensen did not pump him. Ingham replied, to a question from Jensen, that he was a writer and taking a month's vacation. Jensen was a painter. He looked thirty or thirty-two.

'In Copenhagen I had a breakdown,' Jensen said with a

46

tired, dry smile. He was lean and tan with light straight hair and a strangely absent, drifting expression in his blue eyes, as if he were not paying full attention to anything around him. 'My doctor – a psychiatrist – told me to go somewhere in the sun. I've been here for eight months.'

'Are you comfortable where you are?' Jensen had said his place was simple, and he looked capable of roughing it, so Ingham supposed the house was primitive indeed. 'Good conditions for painting, I mean?'

'The light is splendid,' Jensen said. 'Hardly any furniture, but there never is. They rent you a house, you know, and you say, "Where's the bed? Where's a chair? Where's a table, for Christ's sake?" They say that will come tomorrow. Or next week. The truth is, they don't use furniture. They sleep on mats and fold their clothing on the floor. Or drop it. But I have a bed at least. And I made a table out of boxes and a couple of boards I picked up on the street. – They broke my dog's leg. He's just getting over the limp.'

'Really? Why?' Ingham asked, shocked.

'Oh, they just threw a big rock. They dropped it out of a window, I think. Waited their chance when Hasso was lying in the shade by a house across the street. They love to hurt animals, you know. And maybe a thorough-bred dog like Hasso is more tempting than an ordinary dog to them.' He patted the dog who was sitting by his chair. 'Hasso's still nervous from it. He hates Arabs. Crooked Arabs.' Again the distant but amused smile. 'I'm glad he's obedient, or he'd tear the trousers off twelve a day around here.'

Ingham laughed. 'There's one in red pants and a turban I'd like to paste. He haunts my car all the time. Whenever it's parked around here.'

Jensen lifted a finger. 'I know him. Abdullah. A real bastard. Do you know, I saw him robbing a car just two streets from here in the middle of an afternoon?' Jensen laughed with delight, but almost silently. He had handsome white teeth. 'And no one does anything!'

'Was he stealing a suitcase?'

'Clothing of some kind, I think. He can always flog that in the market. – I think I shall not stay here much longer because of Hasso. If they hit him again, they may kill him. Anyway, it's an inferno of heat here in August.'

They got into a second bottle of wine. Melik's was quiet. Only two other tables were occupied, by Arabs, all men.

'You like to take vacations alone?' Jensen asked.

'Yes. I suppose I do.'

'So you are not writing now?'

'Well, yes, I've started a book. I've worked harder in my life, but I'm working.'

By midnight, Ingham was on his way with Jensen to have a look at Jensen's apartment. It was in a small white house with a door on the street which was closed by a padlock. Jensen turned on the feeblest of electric lights, and they climbed a naked white – but grimy – stairs without a banister. There was the smell of a toilet somewhere. Jensen had the next floor, which consisted of one good-sized room, and the floor above, which had two smaller rooms. A confusion of canvases leaned against the walls and lay on tables of the box-and-board variety Jensen had described. In one of the upstairs rooms, there was a little gas stove with two burners. There was one chair which neither of them took. They sat on the floor. Jensen poured red wine.

Jensen had lit two candles which were fixed in wine bottles. He was talking about having to go to Tunis for paint supplies. He said he went by bus. Ingham looked around at the paintings. A fiery orange colour predominated. They were abstract, Ingham supposed, though some of the straight lines and squares in them could have been meant to be houses. In one, a rag, maybe a paint rag, was flattened and painted on to the canvas, crumpled. It was not a light in which to make a judgement, and Ingham didn't.

'Have you got a shower here?' Ingham asked.

'Oh, I use a bucket. Down on the terrace. Or the court. It has a drain.'

There was a sound of two men's voices, arguing, in the street below. Jensen lifted his head to listen. The voices passed on. The tone had been more angry than usual.

'You understand Arabic?' Ingham asked.

'Some. I don't make much of an effort. But languages come easily for me. I get along. I limp, as they say.'

Jensen had put out some dry white cheese and some bread. Ingham did not want anything. The plate of cheese was rather pretty in the candlelight, surrounded by a halo of shadow. The dog, lying on the floor by the door, gave a deep sigh and slept.

Half an hour later, Jensen put his hand on Ingham's shoulder and asked him if he would like to spend the night. Ingham suddenly realised he was queer, or at least was making a queer pass.

'No, I have my car outside,' Ingham said. 'Thank you, anyway.'

Jensen attempted to kiss him, missed and kissed his cheek briefly. He missed because Ingham dodged a little. Jensen was on his knees. Ingham shivered. He was in shirtsleeves.

'You never sleep with men? It's nice. No complications,' Jensen said, rolling back on his heels, sitting down again on the floor only three feet away from Ingham. 'The girls here are awful, whether they're tourists or whether they're – what shall I say – native. Then there's the danger of syphilis. They all have it, you know. They're sort of immune to it, but they pass it on.'

A profound bitterness was audible in Jensen's subdued tone. Ingham was at that moment calling himself an idiot for not having realised that Jensen was homosexual. After all, as a fairly sophisticated New Yorker, he might have been a bit brighter. Ingham felt like smiling, but he was afraid Jensen might think he was smiling at him, instead of at himself, so Ingham kept a neutral expression.

'Lots of boys available here, I've heard,' Ingham said.

'Oh, yes. Little thieving bastards,' Jensen replied with his wistful, absent smile. Now he was reclined on the floor, on one elbow. 'Nice, if you send them straight out of the house.'

Now Ingham laughed.

'You said you weren't married.'

'No,' Ingham said. 'Can I see some of your paintings?'

Jensen put on another light or two. All his lights were naked bulbs. Jensen had a few pictures with huge, distorted faces in the foreground. The red-orange in many of them gave a sense of extreme heat. They were all a trifle sloppy and undisciplined, Ingham thought. But obviously he worked hard and pursued a theme: melancholy, apparently, which he thrust forward in the form of the ravaged faces, backgrounded by chaotic Arabian houses, or falling trees, or windstorms, sandstorms, rainstorms. Ingham did not know, after five minutes, whether he was any good or not. But at least the paintings were interesting.

'You've shown your work in Denmark?' Ingham asked.

'No, only Paris,' Jensen replied.

'Suddenly, Ingham did not believe him. Or was he wrong? And did it really matter? Ingham looked at his watch under a light globe – twelve-thirty-five. He managed to say a few complimentary things, which pleased Jensen.

Jensen was restless and shifting. Ingham sensed that he was as hungry as a wolf, maybe physically hungry, certainly emotionally starving. Ingham sensed also that he was a shadow to Jensen, just a form in the room, solid to the touch, but nothing more. Jensen knew nothing and had really asked nothing about him. Yet they might both be in the bed in the upstairs room this moment.

'I'd better be taking off,' Ingham said.

'Yes. A pity. Just when it's getting nice and cool.'

Ingham asked to use the toilet. Jensen came with him and put on the light. It was a hole in a porcelain floor which sloped downward. Just outside, a tap on the wall dripped slowly into a bucket. Ingham supposed Jensen tossed a bucket of water into the hole now and then.

'Good night, and thanks for letting me visit,' Ingham said, holding out his hand.

Jensen gripped it firmly. 'A pleasure. Come again. I'll see you at Melik's. Or the Plage.'

'Or visit me. I've got a bungalow and a refrigerator. I can even cook.' Ingham smiled. He was perhaps overdoing it, just because he didn't want Jensen to think he had any un-friendly feelings. 'How do I get back to the main road?'

'Go left outside the door. Take the first left, then first right, and you'll come out on the road.'

Ingham went out. The light from Jensen's street-lamp was of no use as soon as he turned the first corner. The street was only six feet wide, not meant for cars. The white walls on either side of him, poked with deep-set black windows, seemed strangely silent – strangely, because there was usually some kind of noise coming from any Arabic house. Ingham had never been in a residential section so late. He tripped on something and pitched forward, catching himself on both hands just in time to avoid hitting the road with his face. It had felt like a rolled-up blanket. He pushed at the thing with his foot, and realised he was slightly tight. It was a man asleep. Ingham had touched a pair of legs.

'Hell of a place to sleep,' Ingham murmured.

No sound from the sleeping form.

Out of curiosity, Ingham struck a match. Coverless, the may lay with one arm crumpled under him. A black scarf was around his neck. Black trousers, soiled white shirt. Then Ingham saw that the black scarf was red, that it was blood. The match burnt his fingers, and Ingham struck another and bent closer. There was blood all over the ground under the man's head. Under his jaw was a long glistening cut.

'Hey!' Ingham said. He touched the man's shoulder, gripped it convulsively, and just as suddenly pulled his hand back. The body was cool. Ingham looked around him and saw nothing but blackness and the vague white forms of houses. His match had gone out.

He thought of going back to get Jensen. At the same time, he drifted away from the corpse, drifted on away from Jensen, towards the road. It wasn't his business.

The end of the alley showed a pale light from the street-lights of the road. His car was a hundred yards to the left, down by Melik's. When Ingham was some thirty yards away from his car, he saw the old humpbacked Arab in the baggy trousers standing by the right rear window. Ingham ran towards him.

'Get the hell away!' he yelled.

The Arab scurried with a surprising agility, hunched over, and disappeared into a black street on the right.

'Son of a bitch!' Ingham muttered.

There was no one about, except two men standing under a tree in the light that came from the Plage's front windows.

Ingham unlocked his car, and glanced into the back seat when the light came on. Hadn't his beach towel (his own, not the hotel's) and his canvas jacket been on the seat? Of course. One rear window was open three inches. The Arab had fished the things out. He cursed the Arab with a new fury. He slammed the door and went to the dark street into which the Arab had vanished.

'Son of a bitch, I hope it *kills* you!' he shouted, so angry now that his face burnt. 'Bastard son of a bitch!'

That the Arab couldn't understand didn't matter at all.

CHAPTER SIX

The next morning, lying in bed at 9 a.m. with the sun already warm through the shutters, Ingham did not remember getting home. He did not remember anything after cursing the humped Arab with the yellow-tan, filthy turban. Then he remembered the corpse. My God, yes, a corpse. Ingham imagined it a hell of a cut, maybe the kind that nearly severed the neck, so that if he had lifted the man, the head might have fallen off. No, he wouldn't tell Ina *that* part of the evening. He wouldn't tell anyone about the corpse, he thought. People might say, 'Why didn't you report it?' Ingham realised he was ashamed of himself. Regardless of the red tape that might have followed, he should have reported the thing. He still could report it. The time he saw the body might be of some significance. But he wasn't going to.

He sprang out of bed and took a shower.

When he came out of the bathroom, Mokta had set his breakfast-tray on the windowsill near his bed. That was good service. Ingham ate in shorts and shirt, sitting on the edge of his chair. He was thinking of a letter he would write to Ina, and before he finished his coffee, he pushed the tray aside and began it on his typewriter.

July 1, 19—
Sat. A.M.

Darling,

A strange day yesterday. In fact all these days are strange. I was furious not to have more news from you. I'll hold this till I hear from you. Would you mind telling me *why* he killed himself and secondly why were you so thrown by it?

It seems fantastic, but I have 47 pages done on my book and I think it is going along pretty well. But I am horribly lonely. Such a new sensation for me, it's almost interesting. I thought I had been lonely many times before and I have been, but never anything like this. I've set myself a mild schedule about working, because if I hadn't that, I think I'd go to pieces. On the other hand, that's just in the last week, since hearing about John. Before that, the days were sort of empty here, thanks to no news at all from John (or from you for that matter) but since his death, the bottom has fallen out – of what? Tunisia, maybe. Not me. Of course I'll leave soon, after cruising around the country a bit, since I'm here.

Last night I had dinner with a Danish painter who turned out to be a faggot and made a mild pass. He is lonely too, poor guy, but I am sure he can find a lot of bed-companions among the boys here. Homosexuality is not against their religion, but alcohol is, and some towns are dry. Stealing is apparently okay, too. One old bastard swiped my canvas jacket and a towel last night from the back seat of my car while I was visiting the Dane – to look at his paintings, ha! I detest this particular Arab, and I know I shouldn't. Why detest anyone? One doesn't, one just focuses a lot of emotions of a nasty kind on one person, and there you are, hating something or somebody. Darling Ina, I have focused the opposite kind of emotions on you, you are everything tangible that I like and love, so why do you make me suffer now with this ghastly long silence? The days may flit by for you, but they drag here. I can see I'm going to post this off today express, even if I don't hear from you. . . .

Since he did not hear from Ina in the morning post, he sent the letter express from the post office at 4 p.m. There was nothing from Ina in the afternoon post, either.

He had dinner with Adams in a fishing town called La Goulette, near Tunis. The town bore a funny similarity to Coney Island, not that it had amusements or hot-dog stands, but it was the elongated shape of the town, the lowness of its houses, the atmosphere of the sea. It also looked rather crummy and cheap and unspoilt. Ingham's first thought was to inquire about hotels here, but the barman at the bar they visited told him there were none. The waiter and the proprietor of the restaurant where they had dinner assured Ingham of the same thing. The waiter knew of a place where they let rooms, but this sounded too sketchy to bother investigating, at least at that hour.

That evening, Adams bored Ingham to a degree. Adams was launched again on the virtues of democracy for everyone, Christian morals for everyone. ('*Everyone?*' Ingham interrupted once, so loudly that the next table turned to look at him.) He thought of the happy pagans, Christless, maybe syphilis-less, too, blissful. But in fact, where were they these days? Christianity and atom-bomb testing had spread themselves just about everywhere. *I swear if he gets on to Vietnam, I'll burst a vein*, Ingham said to himself. But realising the absurdity of his emotions against this absurd little man, Ingham controlled himself, remembered that he had enjoyed Adams's company many times, and reminded himself that he would feel like a fool to make an enemy of Adams, whom he encountered once or twice a day on the hotel grounds or on the beach. His anger was only frustration, Ingham realised, frustration in every aspect of his life just now – except perhaps in his novel-in-progress.

'You can see it in their faces, the men who have turned their back on God,' Adams droned on.

Where was God, that one could turn one's back on him?

Adams's pouches became pouchier. He was smiling and chewing contentedly at once.

'Drug addicts, alcoholics, homosexuals, criminals – and even the ordinary man in the street, *if* he's forgotten the Right Way – they're all wretched. But they can be *shown* the Right Way. . . .'

My God, Ingham thought, was Adams cracked? And why throw in the homosexuals?'

'Oh, I come to the garden alone,
   When the dew is still on the roses.

And the voice I hear,
Falling on my ear,
Is my Saviour's, my Saviour's alone.'

Falling on your *ear*? Can't you come to the garden *sober*?
The remembered schoolboy joke brought irrepressible
laughter, which Ingham gulped down, though tears stood in
his eyes. Fortunately Adams didn't take his smile amiss, because Ingham could not possibly have explained it. Adams
was still smiling complaisantly himself.

'I'm sure you're right,' Ingham said forcefully, hoping to
wind it up. One might be friendly, but one did not make
friends with people like Adams, Ingham was thinking. They
were dangerous.

A few minutes later, as Adams was tapering off, though
still on the subject of Our Way of Life, Ingham asked,
'What about some of the things normal people do in bed?
Heterosexuals. Do you disapprove of those things?'

'What things do you mean?' Adams asked attentively, and
Ingham thought very likely Adams really didn't know about
them.

'Well – various things. Matter of fact, the same things
homosexuals do. The very same things.'

'Oh. Well, they're still male and female. Man and wife,'
Adams said cheerfully, tolerantly.

Yes, if they happened to be married, Ingham thought.
'That's true,' Ingham said. If OWL preached tolerance.
Ingham would not be outdone. But Ingham sensed his mind
beginning to boggle, as it so often did with Adams, his own
unassailable arguments seeming to turn to sand. That was
what happened in brainwashing, Ingham thought. It was odd.

'Have you ever written anything,' Ingham asked, 'on these
subjects?'

Adams's smile became a little sly.

Ingham could see that he had, or wanted to, or was writing
something now.

'You're a man of letters who I think I can trust,' Adams
said. 'I do write, in a way, yes. Come to my bungalow when
we get home and I'll show you.'

Ingham paid for their inexpensive dinner, because he felt he had been a little rude to Adams, and because Adams had driven him here in his Cadillac. Ingham was glad Adams had driven, because half an hour after his dinner, he began to have waves of gripes in his lower abdomen, in fact all over his abdomen, up to the ribs. In Hammamet, back at the bungalows, Ingham excused himself under pretext of getting another pack of cigarettes, and went to the toilet. Diarrhoea, and pretty bad. He swallowed a couple of Entero-Vioform tablets, then went over to Adams's.

Adams showed Ingham into his bedroom. Ingham had never been in the room before. It had a double bed with a very pretty red, white and blue counterpane, which Adams must have bought. There were a few shelves of books, more pictures – all photographs – a cosy, lighted nook within reach of the head of the bed, which contained a few books, a notebook, pen, ashtray, matches.

Adams opened a tall closet with a key, and pulled out a handsome black leather suitcase, which he unlocked with a small key on his keyring. Adams opened the suitcase on the bed. There was a radio of some sort, a tape machine, and two thick stacks of manuscript, all neatly arranged in the suitcase.

'This is what *I* write,' Adams said, gesturing towards the typewritten stacks of papers at one side of the suitcase. 'In fact, I broadcast it, as you see. Every Wednesday night.' Adams chuckled.

'Really?' So that was what Adams did on Wednesdays. 'That's very interesting,' Ingham said. 'You broadcast in English?'

'In American. It goes behind the Iron Curtain. In fact, exclusively behind the Iron Curtain.'

'You're employed then. By the Government. The Voice of America?'

Adams shook his head quickly. 'If you'll swear not to tell anyone—'

'I swear,' Ingham said.

Adams relaxed slightly and spoke more softly. 'I'm employed by a small group of anti-Communists behind the

Iron Curtain. Matter of fact, they're not a small group by any means. They don't pay me much, because they haven't got it. The money comes via Switzerland, and that's complicated enough, I understand. I know only one man in the group. I broadcast pro-American, pro-Western – what shall I call it? Philosophy. Pep talks.' Adams chuckled.

'Very interesting,' Ingham said. 'How long've you been doing this?'

'Almost a year now.'

'How did they contact you?'

'I met a man on a ship. About a year ago. We were on the same ship going from Venice to Yugoslavia. He was a great card-player on the ship.' Adams smiled reminiscently. 'Not dishonest, just a brilliant bridge-player. Poker, too. He's a journalist, lives in Moscow. But of course he's not allowed to write what he thinks. He sticks strictly to the party line when he writes for the Moscow papers. But he's an important man in the underground organisation. He got this equipment for me in Dubrovnik and gave it to me.' Adams gestured with a proud flourish at his tape recorder and sender.

Ingham looked down with, he felt, a dazed respect at the suitcase. He wondered just how much they paid Adams. And why, when Radio Free Europe and the Voice of America were booming the same kind of thing into Russia free? 'Have you a special wavelength or something that the Russians can't jam?'

'Yes, so I was told. I can shift the wavelength, depending on the orders I have. The orders come in code to me here from Switzerland – Italy sometimes. Would you like to hear a tape?'

'I would indeed,' Ingham said.

Adams lifted the tape recorder from the suitcase. From a metal box in the suitcase he took a roll of tape. 'March–April inclusive. We'll try this.' He fixed it in the machine and pushed a button. 'I won't play it loud.'

Ingham sat down on the other side of the bed.

The machine hissed, then Adams's voice came on.

'Good evening, ladies and gentlemen, Russians and non-Russians, brothers everywhere, friends of democracy and of

America. This is Robin Goodfellow, an ordinary American citizen, just as many of you, listening, are ordinary citizens of your own . . .'

Adams had winked at Ingham at the name 'Robin Goodfellow'. He advanced the tape a bit.

'. . . what many of you thought of the news that came from Vietnam today. Five American planes shot down by the Vietcong, say the Americans. Seventeen American planes shot down, say the Vietcong. The Vietcong say they lost one plane. The Americans say the Vietcong lost nine. Someone is lying. Who? Who do you think? What country discloses her failures as well as her successes when it comes to rocket take-offs? When it comes even to the *poverty* in its land – which the Americans are fighting just as hard to erase as they are fighting lies, tyranny, poverty, illiteracy and Communism in Vietnam? The answer is America. All of you . . .'

Adams pushed a button which advanced the tape in jerks. 'Sort of a dull section.' The muted tape screamed, hiccuped, and Adams spoke again. Ingham was aware of Adams's tense, self-satisfied smile as he sat perched on the other side of the bed, though Ingham could not look at him, but kept his eyes on the tape machine. His abdomen was contracting, getting ready for another wave of pain.

'. . . comfort to us all. The *new* American soldier is a crusader, bringing not only peace – eventually – but a happier, healthier, more *profitable* way of life to whatever country he sets foot in. And unfortunately, so often that setting foot' (Adams's voice had dropped dramatically to a hushed tone and stopped) – 'that setting foot means the death of that soldier, the telegram of bad news to his family back home, *tragedy* to his young wife or sweetheart, bereavement to his children . . .'

'Again not too exciting,' Adams said, though he looked very excited himself. More squeaks and gulps from the tape machine, a couple of samples which did not please Adams, then:

'. . . the voice of God will prevail at last. The men who put *people* before all else will triumph. The men who put "the *State*" first, in defiance of human values, will perish. America fights to preserve *human* values. America fights not only to preserve herself but all others who would follow in her path – in our blessed way of life. Good night, my friends.'

Click. Adams turned the machine off.

Our Blessed Way of Life. OBWL. Not pronounceable. Ingham hesitated, then said, 'That's very impressive.'

'You like it. Good.' Adams began briskly putting his equipment away, back into the closet which he again locked.

If it was all true, Ingham was thinking, *if* Adams was paid by the Russians, he was paid because it was so absurd, it was really rather good anti-American propaganda. 'I wonder how many people it reaches? How many listen?'

'Upwards of six million,' Adams replied. 'So my friends say. I call them my friends, although I don't even know their names, except the one man I told you about. A price is on their heads, if they're found out. And they're gaining recruits all the time, of course.'

Ingham nodded. 'What's their final plan? I mean about – changing their government's policy and all that?'

'It's not so much a final plan as a war of attrition,' Adams said with his confident, pouchy smile, and from the happy sparkle in his eyes, Ingham knew that this was where his heart lay, his *raison d'être*, in these weekly broadcasts that carried the American Way of Life behind the Iron Curtain. 'The results may not even be seen in my lifetime. But if people listen, and they do, I make my effect.'

Ingham felt blank for a moment. 'How long are your talks?'

'Fifteen minutes. – You mustn't tell anyone here. Not even another American. Matter of fact, you're the first American I've told about it. I don't even tell my daughter, just in case it might leak out. You understand?'

'Of course,' Ingham said. It was late, after midnight. He wanted to leave. It was an uncomfortable feeling, like claustrophobia.

'I'm not paid much, but to tell you the truth, I'd do it for nothing,' Adams said. 'Let's go in the other room.'

Ingham declined Adams's offer of a coffee or a nightcap, and managed to leave in five minutes, and gracefully. But as he walked in the dark back towards his own bungalow, he felt somehow shaky. Ingham went to bed, but after a moment, his insides began churning, and he was up and in the bathroom. This time he vomited, as well. That was good, Ingham thought, in case the trouble had been the *poisson-complet* – the fried fish with fried egg – at the restaurant in La Goulette. He took more Entero-Vioform.

It became 3 a.m. Ingham tried to rest between seizures. He sweated. A cold towel on his forehead made him too cold, a sensation he had not had in a long time. He vomited again. He wondered if he should try to get a doctor – it didn't seem reasonable to endure this much discomfort for another six hours – but there was no telephone in the bungalow, and Ingham could not face, even though he had a flashlight now, trudging across the sand to the main building, where in fact he might find no one to open the door at this hour. Call Mokta? Wake him at the bungalow headquarters? Ingham could not bring himself to do that. He sweated it out until daylight. He had thrown up and brushed his teeth three or four times.

At six-thirty or seven o'clock, people were up at the bungalow headquarters. Ingham thought vaguely of trying for a doctor, of asking for some kind of medicine more effective than Entero-Vioform. Ingham put on his robe over his pyjamas, and walked in sandals to the bungalow head-quarters. He was chilly and exhausted. Before he quite reached the building, he saw Adams prancing on his little arched feet out of his bungalow, briskly locking his door, briskly turning.

Adams hailed him. 'Hello! What's up?'

Somewhat feebly, Ingham explained the situation.

'Oh, my goodness! You should have knocked me up – as the English say, ha-ha! Throwing up, eh? First of all, take some Pepto-Bismol. Come in, Howard!'

Ingham went into Adams's bungalow. He wanted to sit down, or collapse, but made himself keep standing. He took the Pepto-Bismol, at the bathroom basin. 'Ridiculous to feel so demolished.' He managed a laugh.

'You think it was the fish last night? I don't know how *clean* that place is, after all.'

Adams's words recalled the plate of fish soup with which they had begun their dinner, and Ingham tried to forget he had ever seen the soup.

'Some tea, maybe?' Adams asked.

'Nothing, thanks.' Another trip to the toilet was imminent, but there was some consolation in the thought there could not be much of anything left in him. Ingham's head began to ring. 'Look, Francis, I'm sorry to be a nuisance. I – I don't know if I should have a doctor or not. But I think I'd better get back to my house.'

Adams walked over with him, not quite holding his arm, but hovering just by his side. Ingham had not locked his door. Ingham excused himself and went at once to the toilet. When he came out, Adams was gone. Ingham sat down gently on the bed, still in his bathrobe. The gripes had now become a steady ache, just severe enough to preclude sleep, Ingham knew.

Adams came in again, barefoot, light and quick as a girl. 'Brought some tea. Just one hot cup with some sugar in, it'll do you good. Tea *balls*.' He went to Ingham's kitchen, and Ingham heard water running, a pan clatter, a match being struck. 'I spoke to Mokta and told him not to bring breakfast,' Adams said. 'Coffee's bad.'

'Thank you.'

The tea did help. Ingham could not drink the whole cup.

Adams gave him a cheery good-bye and said he would look in again after his swim, and if Ingham was asleep, he would not wake him. 'Don't lose heart! You're among friends!' Adams said.

Ingham did lose heart. He had to bring a cooking pot from the kitchen to keep by his bed, because every ten minutes or so, he threw up a little liquid, and it was not worth going to the bathroom to do. As for pride, if Adams came in and saw the pot, Ingham had no pride left.

When Adams came back, Ingham was barely aware of it. It was nearly 10 a.m. Adams said something about not coming in earlier, because he thought Ingham might have dropped off to sleep.

Mokta knocked and came in, too, but there was nothing Ingham had in mind to ask him to do.

It was between ten and twelve o'clock, when he was alone, that Ingham experienced a sort of crisis. His abdominal pain continued. In New York, he would certainly have sent for a doctor and asked for morphine, or had a friend go to a pharmacist's to get something to relieve him. Here, Ingham was holding to Adam's advice (but did Adams know how awful he felt?) not to bother about a doctor, that he'd soon feel better. But he didn't know Adams very well, and didn't even trust him. Ingham realised during those two hours that he was very much alone, without his friends, without Ina (and he meant emotionally, too, because if she was really *with* him, she would have written several times by now, would have assured him of her love), realised that he had no real purpose in being in Tunisia – he could be writing his book anywhere – and that the country wasn't to his taste at all, that he simply didn't belong here. All these thoughts came rushing in when Ingham was at his lowest physically, emptied of strength, emptied of everything. He had been attacked, ludicrous as it might be, in the vitals, where it hurt and where it counted, and where it could kill. Now he was exhausted and unable to sleep. The tea had not stayed down. Adams was not back at twelve o'clock, as he had said he would be. Adams might have forgotten. And an hour one way or the other, what would it matter to Adams? And what could Adams do, anyway?

Somehow Ingham fell asleep.

He awoke at the sound of his slightly squeaky doorknob being turned, and raised himself feebly, alert.

Adams was tiptoeing in, smiling, carrying something. 'Hello! Feeling better? I've brought something nice. I looked in just after twelve, you were asleep, and I thought you needed it.' He went on to the kitchen, almost soundless, barefoot.

Ingham realised he was covered in sweat. His ribs were slippery with sweat under his pyjama top, and his sheet was damp. He fell back on his pillow and shivered.

In a very short time, Adams came forth from the kitchen with a bowl of something steaming. 'Try this! Just a few spoonfuls. Very plain, won't hurt you.'

It was hot beef consommé. Ingham tried it. It tasted

wonderful. It was like life, like meat without the fat. It was as if he sipped back his own life and strength that had for so many hours been mysteriously separated from him.

'Good?' Adams asked, pleased.

'It is *very* good.' Ingham drank almost all of it, and sank back again on his bed. Ingham felt grateful to Adams, Adams whom he had so despised in his thoughts. Who else had bothered about him? He cautioned himself that his abject gratitude might not last, once he was on his feet again. And yet, Ingham knew, he would never forget this particular kindness of Adams, never forget his words of cheer.

'There's more there in a pot,' Adams said, smiling, gesturing quickly towards the kitchen. 'Heat it up when you wake up again. Since you missed a night's sleep, I think you ought to sleep the rest of the afternoon. Got the Entero-Vioforms handy?'

Ingham had. Adams brought him a fresh glass of water, then left. Ingham slept again.

That evening, Adams brought eggs and bread, and made a supper of scrambled eggs and toast and tea. Ingham was feeling much better. Adams took his leave before nine o'clock, so Ingham could sleep.

'Thank you *very* much, Francis,' Ingham said. He could smile now. 'I really feel you saved my life.'

'Nonsense! A little Christian charity? It's a pleasure! Good night, Howard, my boy. See you tomorrow!'

CHAPTER SEVEN

A couple of days later, on the 4th of July, a Tuesday, Ingham received a long airmail envelope from a clerk at the Reine's main desk. It was from Ina, and Ingham could tell there were at least two sheets of airmail paper in it. He started to go back to his bungalow for privacy, then realised he couldn't wait, turned back to find an empty sofa to sit on, then changed his mind again and headed for the bar. No one was in the bar, not even a waiter. He sat by a window for light, but out of the sun.

June 28, 19—

Dear Howard,

At last a moment to write. In fact I am staying home from the office today, though I have homework as usual.

The events of the last month are rather chaotic. I don't know where or how to begin, so I will just plunge in. John – first of all – killed himself in your apartment. I had given him the keys once before but only to take your letters from the mailbox (mailbox key being on your ring) and he must have taken the opportunity to have some others made. Anyway, he took an overdose, and because no one thought of looking in your apartment for four days – and anyway when I went there I had no idea I'd find John – we all simply thought he had left town, maybe gone to Long Island. He was of course in a bad state. He had not lost his nerve about the Tunisia work – but he announced that he was in love with me. I was completely surprised. It had never crossed my mind. I was sympathetic. He meant it. He felt guilty because of you. Maybe I was too sympathetic. But I told him I loved *you*. John told me this in

65

the last days of May, just after you left. He must have taken the pills the night of June 10th, a Saturday. He had told everyone he was going away for the weekend. One could say he did it to spite both of us – destroy himself in your apartment, on your bed (but not in it). I did not lead him on, but I admit I was sympathetic and concerned. I made no promises to him . . .

A waiter came and asked what he wanted. Ingham murmured, 'Rien, merci,' and stood up. He went out on the terrace and read the rest of the letter standing up in the sun.

. . . but I hope you can see why I was upset. I don't think he told anyone else of his feelings for me, at least no one that I know. I am sure a psychiatrist would say his suicide was due to other things too (I don't even know what, honestly) and that his sudden emotion for me (itself odd) tipped things the wrong way. He said he felt guilty and could not work with you because of his feelings for me. I asked him to write to you and tell you. I thought it was not for me to do. . . .

The rest of her letter was about her brother Joey, about a serial she had to edit which she thought would be a winner for CBS, about packing up John's things from his apartment, assisted by a couple of friends of John's whom she had not met before. She thanked him for the Tunisian vest, and assured him there was nothing like it in New York.

Why had she had anything to do with packing up John's things, Ingham wondered. Surely John had had a lot of friends closer to him than Ina. *I did not lead him on, but I admit I was sympathetic and concerned.* What did that mean, exactly?

Ingham walked back to his bungalow. He walked steadily, and he looked down at the sand.

'Hello-o! Good morning!' It was Adams hailing him, Adams carrying his silly Neptune spear, wearing his flippers.

'Good morning,' Ingham called back, forcing a smile.

'Got some news?' Adams asked, glancing at the letter in Ingham's hand.

'Not much, I'm afraid.' Ingham waved the letter casually, and walked on, not stopping, not even slowing.

He felt he did not breathe until he closed the door of his little house. That glaring sun, that brightness! It was eleven o'clock. Ingham had closed the shutters. The room was rather dark for a minute. He left the shutters closed.

Killed himself in his apartment. Of all the filthy, sloppy things to do, Ingham thought. Of all vulgar dramatics! Knowing, no doubt, that he'd be found by Ina Pallant, since she was the only person with the key.

Ingham became aware that he was walking round and round his work-table, and he flung himself on the bed. The bed was not yet made up. The boy was late this morning. Ingham held the letter over his head and started reading it again, but couldn't bear to finish it. It sounded as if Ina might have given John some encouragement. If she hadn't, why mention it, or say that she hadn't? *Sympathetic*. Wouldn't most girls have said – more or less – it's no soap, old pal, you'd better forget it? Ina wasn't the mushy, comforting type. Had she really *liked* him? John, in the last fifteen minutes, had become a loathsome weakling to Ingham. Ingham tried and failed to see what about him could have appealed to Ina. His naïveté? His rather juvenile enthusiasm, his self-confidence? But it didn't show much self-confidence to have committed suicide.

Well, what now? No reason to wait for another letter. No reason not to leave Tunisia.

It was funny, he thought, that Ina hadn't said in her letter that she loved him. She hadn't said anything reassuring in that direction. *I told him that I loved* you. That wasn't very forceful. He felt a rush of resentment against Ina, a nasty feeling quite new to him in regard to her. He would answer Ina's letter, but not now. Wait at least until this afternoon, maybe even tomorrow. He wished he had someone to talk to about it, but there was no one. What could Adams say, for instance?

That afternoon, though Ingham had gone for a swim and

67

had a short nap, he found that he could not work. His last few pages were pretty smooth, he knew how he wanted to go on (his hero Dennison had just appropriated $100,000, and was about to tinker with the company books), but the words would not come to him. His mind was shattered, at least that part of it which had to do with writing fiction.

Ingham got into his car, taking a towel and swimming trunks just in case, and drove to Sousse. He arrived at five o'clock. It was a city, compared to Hammamet. An American warship was at anchor beside the long, entry-forbidden pier, and there were several white-uniformed sailors and officers drifting about the town, their faces sun-tanned, their expressions fixed at a certain stony neutrality, Ingham felt. Ingham avoided staring at them, though he wanted to. An Arab boy approached him, offering a carton of Camels at not a bad price, but Ingham shook his head.

He stared into shop-windows. Inferior blue jeans, and lots of white trousers. Ingham laughed suddenly. A pair of blue jeans had the rectangular Levi-Strauss label counterfeited pretty well, glossy white, stapled to the pants, but the printed letters said, 'This Is A Genuine Pair of Louise'. The bottom part of the phoney label trailed off shamelessly in printer's dots. The forgers had given up.

For a while, he daydreamed about his novel. That was a situation he knew and understood. He knew the way Dennison looked, just how big his waistline was, and what made him tick. His theme was an old one, via Raskolnikov, through Nietzsche's superman: had one the right to seize power under certain circumstances? That was all very interesting from a moral point of view. Ingham was somewhat more interested in the state of Dennison's mind, in his existence during the period in which he led two lives. He was interested in the fact that the double life at least fooled Dennison: that was what made Dennison a nearly perfect embezzler. Dennison was morally unaware that he was committing a felony, but he was aware that society and the law, for reasons that he did not even attempt to comprehend, did not approve of what he was doing. For this reason only, he took some precautions. Ingham knew the relationship of the people around Dennison, the girl Dennison had discarded when he was twenty-six and intended to pick up again (but he would not be able to). His novel was more real and definite than Ina, John or anything else. But that was to be expected, Ingham thought. Or was it?

The sight of an old Arab in baggy red pants, with turban, leaning on a stick, made Ingham draw in his breath. He had thought he was Abdullah of Hammamet, but of course he wasn't. Just a dead ringer. It was uncanny how alike some of them could look. Ingham supposed they thought the same thing about tourists.

He shuffled through a narrow, crowded passage into a souk, bumped constantly on arms and back. He felt fingers at his left hip pocket, and glanced around in time to see a boy darting to the left between shopping nets and the billowing, tan burnouses of several women. But his billfold wasn't in that pocket, it was in a left front pocket.

Ingham had a cold lemonade on the strip of pavement down the main street. He sat at a table under a big umbrella against the sun. Then he got back into his car and headed for Hammamet. The dry countryside, empty of people, was a relief. The land was a deep yellow tan. River-beds were wide, cracked and quite dry. Ingham had to pause two or three times to let flocks of sheep clatter across the road. They had mud-caked behinds, and were guided by very small boys or old barefoot women with sticks.

The Reine de Hammamet's bungalows struck him as chi-chi that evening. He did not like his bungalow now, despite its cleanliness and comfort and the little stack of manuscript on the back corner of his work-table. He ought to leave. The room reminded him of his plans to work here with John. The room reminded him of happy letters he had written to Ina. Ingham took a shower. He supposed he would go to Melik's for dinner. He'd had no lunch.

When he opened his closet to get his blue blazer, he didn't see it. He glanced around the room to see if he'd left it on a chair. Ingham sighed, realising he'd been robbed. But he had locked his door today. He hadn't, however, fastened all the shutters from the inside, a fact which he verified now by a glance. Two out of four were not fastened. Ingham looked at his stack of shirts on the shelf above his clothes. The new blue linen shirt was missing. Stud box? Ingham slid a drawer open. It was gone, and an empty circle remained in a jumble of clean socks.

Oddly enough, they hadn't taken his typewriter. Ingham looked around, at his suitcase above his closet, at his shoes in the bottom of the closet. Yes, they'd taken his new pair of black shoes. What would an Arab do with English shoes, Ingham wondered. But the stud box. There'd been the nice old gold links Ina had given him before he left America, and a pair of silver ones that had belonged to Ingham's grandfather. And the tiepin from Lotte, platinum.

'For Christ's sake,' Ingham murmured. 'Maybe they'll even get thirty bucks for it all, if they're sharp.' And of course they were sharp. Ingham wondered if it was the old bastard in the red pants? Surely not. He wouldn't wander a kilometre from Hammamet just to rob him.

Travellers cheques? Ingham had those in the pocket of his suitcase lid. He pulled the suitcase down, and found they were still there.

Ingham went over to the bungalow headquarters to find Mokta.

Mokta was sorting towels and talking in Arabic in an explanatory way to the directrice. Mokta saw Ingham, and flashed a smile. Ingham indicated that he would wait outside on the terrace.

Mokta came out sooner than Ingham had expected. He swept a hand across his forehead to illustrate the ordeal he had just been through, and glanced behind him. 'You want to see me, sir?'

'Yes. Someone was in my house today. A few things were stolen. Do you know who could have done it?' Ingham spoke softly, though there was no one on the terrace.

Mokta's grey eyes were wide, shocked. 'But no, sir. I knew you were away this afternoon. Your car was gone. I remarked it. I was here all afternoon. I didn't see anyone around your bungalow.'

Ingham told him what they had taken. 'If you hear of

anything – if you see any of it – tell me, will you? I'll give you five dinars if you can get anything back.'

'Yes, sir. – I don't think it is any of these boys. Honestly, sir. They are honest boys.'

'One of the gardeners, do you think?' He offered Mokta a cigarette, which Mokta accepted.

Mokta shrugged, but it was not an indifferent shrug. His thin body was tense with the situation. 'I don't know all the gardeners. Some of them are new. – Let me look around. If you tell the directrice' – a flash of hands in a negative gesture – 'she will attack all of us, *all* the boys.'

'No, I shall not tell the directrice or the management. I'll leave it to you.' He slapped Mokta's shoulder.

Ingham went to his car and drove to Melik's. It was late, there was not much left on the menu, but Ingham had lost what appetite he had, and sat merely for the company around him, whose conversation he could not understand. There were no English or French tonight. The Arabic talk – all male voices – sounded guttural, threatening, angry, but Ingham knew this meant nothing. They were having a perfectly ordinary evening. Melik, short, plump and smiling, came over and asked where his friend M. Ah*dam* was tonight? Melik spoke quite a good French.

'I haven't seen him today. I went to Sousse.' It was of no importance, yet it was nice to say to somebody, and Arabs, Ingham knew from the sheer quantity of their speech, must say even less important things in a more verbose manner. 'How's business?'

'Ah – it goes. People get afraid of the heat. But of course lots of French still come in August, the hottest time of the year.'

They chatted for a few minutes. Melik's two sons, the thin one who slunk like Groucho Marx, the fat one who rolled, ministered to the two or three tables that were occupied. From below, Ingham caught a pleasant whiff of baking bread. There was a bakery just next door which functioned during the night. Ingham drank two cups of sweet coffee, not bothering to ask them to make it without sugar. During his second cup, the Dane arrived with his dog on a leash, and stood looking around from the threshold of the terrace, as if to see if a certain friend was here. He saw Ingham, and came towards him slowly, smiling.

'Good evening,' Jensen said. 'All by yourself tonight?'

'Evening. Yes. Have a seat.' There were three empty chairs at Ingham's table.

Jensen sat down opposite, made a sound to his dog, and the dog lay down.

'How is life?' Ingham asked.

'Ah, well, excellent for working. A little boring.'

Ingham thought that that was exactly the way it was. Jensen wore a fresh denim shirt. Above it, his lean face was brown, darker than his hair. His white teeth gleamed when he spoke. Jensen slumped, one elbow on the back of his chair, like a man discouraged.

'Have some wine.' Ingham yelled, '*Asma!*' to empty space. Sometimes someone heard, sometimes not.

Jensen said he had a bottle of wine here, but Ingham insisted on their drinking his. The boy brought another glass.

'Are you working?' Jensen asked.

'Not today. I was in a bad mood.'

'Bad news?'

'Oh, no, just a bad day,' Ingham said.

'The trouble with this country is that the weather is all the same. Predictable. One has to get used to it, accept it, or it can bore one to extinction.' Jensen pronounced 'extinction' with clarity, like an Englishman. 'Today I painted an imaginary bird in flight. He flies downward. Tomorrow I shall paint two birds in one picture, one flying up, one down. They will look like opposite tulips. – There are few basic shapes, you know, the egg which is a variation of the circle, the bird which resembles the fish, the tree and its branches which resembles its own roots and also the bronchi in the lungs. All the more complex forms, the key, the automobile, the typewriter, the tin-opener, are all man-made. But are they beautiful? No, they're as ugly as man's soul. I admit some keys are beautiful. To be beautiful, something must be stylised, that is to say streamlined, which can only be achieved through being alive for centuries of time.'

Ingham found Jensen's monologue soothing. 'What colour are your birds?'

'Pink at present. And they'll be pink tomorrow, I suppose, because I have a lot of pink paint made up and I may as well use it.' Jensen yawned, discreetly. He gave his dog an offhand slap, because the dog had growled as an Arab walked by the table. Jensen turned to look at the Arab briefly. 'Would you like to come to my house for coffee?' Jensen asked.

Ingham begged off, saying that he was rather tired because he had driven to Sousse and back. What really deterred him, he thought, was the idea of walking by that particular spot in the alley where he had seen the corpse. Ingham wanted to ask Jensen if anything had happened that night, after the quarrelling they had heard down in his street, but Ingham repressed it. He didn't want to hear about a corpse and try to feign surprise.

Jensen ordered coffee.

Ingham stood up and took his leave when the coffee arrived.

Back in the bungalow, Ingham thought of adding to his letter in progress to Ina. Perhaps just a paragraph – sympathetic, even commiserating, positively noble. Ingham had composed the lines in his head at Melik's. Now he read over his carefree paragraph about Our Way of Life, OWL, and his broadcasts. He couldn't send that off to Ina, even dating the remainder of his letter with the present date, because the rest of his letter would be so different. He crumpled up the page. Ina was probably not in a mood to appreciate that kind of story now, and as a matter of fact he had promised Adams not to tell anyone. What was the matter with OWL's silly illusions, anyway, if they kept him going, if they made him happy? The harm OWL did (and he might, by his absurdity, and by making nonsense of the Vietnam War, be doing some good) was infinitesimal compared to the harm done by America's foreign policy makers who actually sent people off to kill people. Perhaps it took some illusions to make people happy. Dennison was happy in his idea (not really an illusion) of doing good to the underdog, furthering his friends' businesses, bringing happiness and prosperity to several people. OWL voiced the same objectives. It was rather odd.

And here he was, Ingham thought, with both feet on the ground – presumably – and where did it get him? It got him to melancholy.

John Castlewood had been under his own illusion, because what else was a state of being 'in love'? Blissful if reciprocated, tragic if it wasn't. Anyway, John had had his illusion, and then unfortunately – zip – dead. Despite her sympathy, Ina must have given him a flat no, finally.

CHAPTER EIGHT

The next morning, Ingham made a determined effort, and wrote two pages of his book. He satisfied himself that he was on the rails again. He then stopped and wrote a letter to Ina.

July 5, 19—

Dearest Ina,

Thanks for your letter which came yesterday at last, a small bang for the otherwise quiet Fourth here. I agree, there does seem to be quite a lot that needs to be explained, though maybe I should give up on suicides, at least John's, as I didn't know him at all well and feel now that I didn't know him at all. What else was he upset about besides you? I admit I am annoyed that he chose my apartment to do it in. May I say, without seeming too coarse and unfeeling, that I hope he didn't mess things up too much? I liked that apartment, until now.

It would be nice if you explained your own feelings a bit more. Just how were you sympathetic? Whatever you were, it seems to have been the wrong thing for John. Did you like or love him at all? Or do you now? Of course I can see, unless I'm wildly off the beam, that you never made him any promises (as you said) or else he would not have wanted to do away with himself. What I really can't understand, darling, is why you took so damned long to write to me. If you knew what it's like here, no old chums to talk to, too hot to work comfortably except early morning and evening, no letter for a whole month from the girl I love. – It wasn't a nice month for me. What you haven't explained is why you were so upset, you couldn't write me for twenty-seven days or so, then only a note, until your letter a few days after that. I love you, I want you, I need you. Now more than ever.

I'll try it here for another week, I think. I have to think periods of time like that, otherwise I'd feel lost – as if I don't already. But work is going reasonably well (my book) and I'd like to drive around and see some more of Tunisia, even though the days will be getting hotter, reaching a crescendo or an inferno, I am told, in August. I'll send this express. Please write me at once. I hope you'll be calmer by now, darling. I wish you were here, in this rather pretty room with me, and we could talk and – other things.

All my love, darling.

Howard

In the next days, Mokta brought no news of his missing jacket, shoes or jewellery, and Ingham gave it up. The country was vast. His minuscule possessions had been sucked up and lost for ever. But as the days went on, the loss of Lotte's tiepin, which he almost never wore, and of his grand-father's cuff-links, began to rankle. Compared to what the things meant to him, the pittance the robber would get for them was irritating to think about. Ingham had delayed re-actions, heightened bitternesses (heightened joys, some-times, too), but his realisation of this did little to help. Whenever he saw the old Arab who had stolen from his car definitely, and who might have stolen from his bungalow, Ingham felt like kicking him in whatever lay in the seat of those sordid pants. As a matter of fact, the Arab now scur-ried away at the sight of Ingham in Hammamet, sidling like an old crab into any alley or street that was nearest. It would be even excusable to kick him, Ingham thought, because if a policeman arrived – there was an occasional policeman in tan shirt and trousers on the street in Hammamet – he could say with truth that he had seen Abdullah in flagrante the night of June 30th–July 1st. Ingham remembered the date, because it was the night he had seen the corpse also, and he had thought of speaking to the police about it. He hadn't spoken to the police, not only because he didn't relish becoming involved with them, but because he foresaw that no one would really care.

Ingham had dinner one evening with OWL at Melik's, and mentioned his robbery of a few nights before.

'One of the boys, I'm sure of it. And I'll bet I know which one,' said OWL.

'Which one?'

'The short dark one.'

They were all short and dark, except Mokta and Hassim.

'The one called Hammed. Has his mouth sort of open all the time.' OWL demonstrated, and looked somewhat like a hare-lip, or rabbit. 'Of course, I'm not sure, but I don't like his manner. He's brought my towels a couple of times. I saw him drifting around my bungalow one day, not doing anything, just drifting around looking at the windows. Did you lock your shutters tonight?'

'I did.' Since the robbery, Ingham had locked them from the inside whenever he was out.

'You'll lose your lighter next, then your typewriter. A miracle they didn't take that. Obviously the robber had to get away with something he could conceal – your shoes and stud box wrapped up in the jacket, probably.'

'What do you think of these people, by the way? *Their* way of life?'

'Ah-h! I don't know where to begin!' Adams chuckled. 'They have their Allah, and very tolerant he must be. They're reconciled to fate. Make no great effort, that's their motto. Everything by rote in school, you know, no thinking involved. How does one change a way of life like this? Petty dishonesty is their way of life. Make a handful honest – and they'll be cheated by the majority, and go back to dishonesty as a means of self-preservation. Can you blame them?'

'No,' Ingham agreed. He really did see OWL's point.

'Our country was lucky. We started out so well, with men like Tom Paine, Jefferson. What ideas they had, and they wrote them down for us! Benjamin Franklin. We may have departed now and then from them – but my goodness, they're still there, in our Constitution. . . .'

Was Adams going to say it was all spoilt by Sicilians,

Puerto Ricans, Polish Jews? Ingham didn't care to ask Adams what had spoilt America's idealism. He let Adams ramble on.

'... Yes! That might be the subject of my next tape. The corruption of American idealism. You never get so far, you never make so many *friends*, you know, as when you tell the *truth*. There's always some new failure to talk about. And let's face it, our potential friends' – here Adams beamed, the happy squirrel again – 'are more interested in our failures than in our successes. Failures make people human. They're jealous of us, because they think we're super-men, invincible empire-builders . . .' On and on it went.

And the curious thing, Ingham thought, was that it didn't sound so bad tonight. It sounded true, and almost liberal. No, the chief thing in which Adams was wrong, rotten even, was in saying that communism or atheism was wrong for other people, any and all other people. Well, one rotten apple could spoil the whole barrel, Ingham thought, to use an adage which would surely please OWL. What it always came down to was the dreary fact that men were not as equal as Adams thought, that free enterprise sent certain ones to the top and certain others to the bottom, into the poverty that Adams so detested. But wasn't it possible to have a socialist system with some capacity for competition, some room for personal reward? Of course. Ingham dreamed, while Adams spun.

'Birth control! Now that's vital. A subject also that I have no fear in bringing up on my tapes. Who's more aware of it than China? And who's more aware of China than the Soviet Union? Breeders, the curse of humanity! And I don't omit the United States. Poughkeepsie is a hotbed, the biggest unemployment relief record in the States, the last I heard, mostly due to Puerto Ricans and Negroes. The biggest families, fatherless technically . . .'

Hotbed. On it went. And Ingham couldn't find a thing to deny in what Adams was saying. Of course one could cite – if one had the statistics in hand – Anglo-Saxon families guilty also of ten children, father with no job, maybe also non-existent. But Ingham merely listened.

Jensen came in, without his dog.

'You know each other?' Ingham asked. 'Mr Jensen, Mr Adams.'

'Won't you join us?' Adams asked pleasantly.

'Have you had dinner?' Ingham asked.

'I don't care to eat,' Jensen said, sitting down.

'A good day's work?' Ingham asked, feeling something was the matter with Jensen.

'No, not since noon.' Jensen put his lean forearm on the table. 'I think they've stolen my dog. He's missing since eleven o'clock this morning. I let him out for a pee.'

'Oh, I'm sorry,' Ingham said. 'You looked around?'

'All over the' – Jensen might have repressed a tired curse – 'neighbourhood. Went around calling everywhere.'

'My goodness,' said Adams. 'I remember your dog. I saw him many times.'

'He may be still alive,' Jensen said, somewhat defiantly.

'Of course. I didn't mean to imply he wasn't,' Adams said. 'Is he apt to go off with strangers?'

'He's apt to tear them apart,' Jensen said. 'He hates crooked Arabs, and he can smell them a mile off. That's why I'm afraid they have killed him already. I walked all the streets calling him – until people were yelling at me to shut up.'

'Any idea who did it?' Ingham asked. Jensen took so long to answer – he looked as if he were in a daze – that Ingham asked, 'You think they might be holding him for a reward?'

'I hope so. But so far nobody's told me.'

'Would he be likely to eat any poisoned meat?' Adams asked.

'I don't think so. He's not a dog to gobble up putrid fish on the beach.' Jensen's English was as usual eloquent and distinct.

Ingham felt very sorry for Jensen. He felt the dog was gone, dead. Ingham glanced at Adams. Adams was trying to be practical, Ingham saw, trying to suggest something Jensen might do.

'They'll toss his head in the door tomorrow morning,' Jensen said. 'Or maybe his tail.' He laughed, grimaced, and

Ingham saw his lower front teeth. 'A coffee,' Jensen said to the fat boy who had appeared at the table. 'We shall see,' Jensen said. 'I am sorry to be so melancholic tonight.'

They drank their coffee.

Adams said he had to be getting home. Ingham asked Jensen if he would like to go somewhere for another coffee or a drink. Adams did not care to join them.

'How about the Fourati?' Ingham asked. 'It's cheerful, at least.' It wasn't particularly, it was just an idea.

They got into Ingham's car. Ingham dropped Adams at the bungalows, then he and Jensen went on to the Fourati. Jensen was in levis, but his clothes were always clean, and he looked rather handsome in them. The Fourati had bright lights in its bar. Beyond the bar, people danced on a terrace to a strenuous three-piece band which was augmented unmercifully by amplifiers. Ingham and Jensen stood at the bar, looking over the dozen or so tables. Ingham felt empty, purposeless, yet not lonely. He was staring, looking at faces, simply because he had not seen them before, because they were not Arab, and because he could tell a little bit about the faces, since they were French, American, or English, and some of them German. Ingham's eyes met the eyes of a dark-haired girl in a white, sleeveless dress. After a second or two, Ingham looked down at his drink – a rum on the rocks.

'A little stuffy,' Ingham said, raising his voice over the music. 'The people, I mean.'

'Lots of Germans, usually,' Jensen said, and sipped his beer. 'I saw the most beautiful boy here once. In March. He must have been having a birthday party. He looked sixteen. French. He looked at me. I never spoke to him, never saw him again.'

Ingham nodded. His eyes moved again to the woman in the white dress. She had smooth brown arms. Now she smiled at him. She was with a blond, greying man in a white jacket, who might have been English, a plumpish woman in her forties, and a younger man with dark hair. Her husband? Ingham resolved not to look again at the table. He felt very attracted to the woman in the white dress. How silly could you get in a hot climate?

'Another drink?' Ingham asked.

'Coffee.'

The one boy behind the counter was having a hard time keeping up with orders, so it was a while before their coffee arrived.

Beyond the bar, through the open window on their left, clashing music came now from an Arabic band that was entertaining the people in the dimly lighted hotel gardens. Christ, what a hell of a noise, Ingham thought. He only hoped that the few minutes had cheered Jensen a little, and taken him away from thoughts of his dog. Ingham felt sure he would not see Hasso again. He imagined Jensen going back to Copenhagen alone, a little bitter. How could Jensen help it?

Ingham invited Jensen to the bungalow. Of course, Jensen accepted. But tonight it was out of loneliness, Ingham realised, nothing to do with sex.

'Have you a big family in Denmark?' Ingham asked. They were walking along the sand road towards the bungalow with the aid of Jensen's flashlight, which he always carried in his back pocket.

'Just a mother and father and a sister. My older brother committed suicide when I was fifteen. You know, the gloomy Danes. No, you say melancholy Danes.'

'Do you write them often?' Ingham opened his door. He went tense in the darkness, before he put on a light and saw that there was no one in the room.

'Oh, often enough.'

Ingham saw that his question about Jensen's family hadn't lifted Jensen's spirits in the least.

'A very nice room,' Jensen said. 'Simple. I like that.'

Ingham brought out his Scotch and glasses and ice. They both sat on Ingham's bed, beside which was a table they could use. Ingham was conscious of their respective gloominess, a gloominess for different reasons. He wasn't going to mention Ina to Jensen, and he wasn't going to mention the robbery he had had, as it seemed trivial. And perhaps Jensen's gloom was not entirely due to his dog, but to things he had no intention of telling to Ingham. What did one do in such circumstances to make life a little more bearable, Ingham wondered? Just sit, a yard or more apart, in the same room, silent? Able to speak each other's language, but still silent?

Within fifteen minutes, Ingham was uneasy and bored, though Jensen had begun to talk about a trip he had made to an inland desert town with an American friend a few months ago. They had run into sandstorms that had almost flayed the clothes off them, and they had been very cold at night, sleeping outdoors. His dog had been with them. Ingham's mind drifted. He believed, suddenly, that Ina had been in love with Castlewood, that she had slept with him. My God, maybe even in his own apartment! No, that was a bit too much. John had his own place, and he lived alone. He had thought Ina was so *solid* – solid physically in a very pleasant and attractive way, solid in her attitude towards him, in her love for him. Ingham admitted to himself that he had even been under the illusion that Ina cared more for him than he did for her. What an ass he had been! He must read her letter, her damned ambiguous letter, again tonight, after Jensen had left. He realised he had had quite enough to drink, and his glass was still half full, but he'd ponder the letter anyway and maybe a flash of intuition would enable him to understand it better, to know what had really happened. Why was Ina so coy and devious, if she and John had slept together, She wasn't the kind of girl to call a spade a – a what? Anyway, she called a lay a roll in the hay, or just called it going to bed with someone. She'd been quite frank with him about a couple of her affairs since her marriage.

Jensen left just before one o'clock, and Ingham dropped him off at his street near Melik's, though Jensen had offered, even begged politely, to walk home. As he got back into his car, Ingham heard Jensen's retreating voice in his alley, calling, 'Hasso! Hasso!' A whistle. A rising tone of a curse, something in Danish, a defiant yelp. Ingham remembered the corpse in that same street. A tiny street, but a street full of passion.

Ingham studied Ina's letter once more. He got no further. He went to bed vaguely angry, and decidedly unhappy.

CHAPTER NINE

It was two or three days later, in the morning, that Ingham saw the brunette girl of the Fourati on the beach. She was in a beach chair, and a chair beside her was empty. A small boy was trying to sell her something out of a basket.

'Mais non, merci. Pas d'argent aujourd'hui!' she was saying, smiling but a bit annoyed.

Ingham had just had his noon swim, and was smoking a cigarette, walking along the edge of the water, carrying his robe. From the girl's accent, he supposed her English or American.

'Are you having trouble?' Ingham asked.

'Not really. I just can't get rid of him.' She was American.

'I have no money either, but a cigarette's just as good.' Ingham took two cigarettes from his pack. He thought the boy was selling seashells. The boy seized the cigarettes and ran away on bare feet.

'I thought of cigarettes, too, but I don't smoke and I haven't any.' She had very dark brown eyes. Her face was smooth and tanned, her hair also smooth and pulled straight back from her forehead. *Almond* was the word that came to Ingham when he looked at her.

'I thought you were at the Fourati,' Ingham said.

'I am. But a friend invited me for lunch here.'

Ingham glanced up the beach towards the hotel for the friend – he assumed a man – who must be coming back at any minute. There was a yellow and white towel and a pair of sunglasses on the empty chair beside her. Suddenly Ingham knew, or at least believed, that he would see her this evening, that they would have dinner, and that they would go to bed together, somewhere. 'Have you been in Hammamet long?' The usual questions, the protocol.

She had been here two weeks, and she was going on to Paris. She was from Pennsylvania. She wore no wedding ring. She was perhaps twenty-five. Ingham said he was from New York. At last – and not a moment too soon, because a man in swimming trunks and sportshirt, followed by a waiter with a tray, was walking towards them from the hotel – Ingham asked:

'Shall we have a drink some time before you leave? Are you free this evening?'

'Yes. For a drink, fine.'

'I'll pick you up at the Fourati. About seven-thirty?'

'All right. Oh, my name is Kathryn Darby. D-a-r-b-y.'

'Mine is Howard Ingham. A pleasure. I'll see you at seven-thirty.' He waved a hand and went away, towards his bungalow.

The approaching man and waiter were still thirty feet away. Ingham had not glanced at the man after his first long view of him, and did not know if he was thirty years old or sixty.

Ingham worked well that afternoon. He had done four pages in the morning. He did five or six in the afternoon.

A little after five o'clock, OWL came round and asked him to his bungalow for a drink.

'I can't tonight, thanks,' Ingham said. 'A date with a young lady at the Fourati. How about tomorrow here?'

'A young lady. Well! That's nice!' OWL turned into a beaming squirrel at once. 'Have a good time. Yes, tomorrow would be fine. Six-thirty?'

At seven-thirty, in a white jacket which he had had Mokta take to be washed and returned that afternoon, Ingham rang up Miss Darby from the desk at the Fourati. They sat at one of the tables in the garden and drank Tom Collinses.

She worked for her uncle in a law firm. She was a secretary, and learning a great deal about law, which she would never use, she said, because she had no intention of taking a degree. There was a warmth, a kindness – or maybe it was merely openness – about her for which Ingham was athirst. There was a naïveté, too, and a certain decorum. He was sure she didn't have affairs with just anybody, or very often, but he assumed she did sometimes, and if she happened to like him, that was his good luck, because she was very pretty.

They had dinner at the Fourati.

Ingham said, 'It's a pleasure to be with you. I've been lonely here in the last month. I don't try to meet people, because I have to work. It doesn't keep me from being lonely now and then.'

She asked some questions about his work. Within a few minutes, Ingham told her that the man with whom he had intended to make a film had not come. Ingham also told her he had committed suicide, though he avoided mentioning John's name. He said he had decided to stay on a few weeks and to work on his own novel.

Kathryn (she had told him how to spell it) was certainly sympathetic, and it touched Ingham in a way that Adams's equally genuine sympathy had not. 'What a shock it must have been. Even if you *didn't* know him well!'

Ingham changed the subject by asking her if she had seen other towns in Tunisia. She had, and she enjoyed talking about them and about the things she had bought to send and to take back home. She was on vacation alone, but had flown to Tunisia with some English friends who had been in America, and who yesterday had flown back to London.

Vague thoughts of accompanying her back to Paris, of spending a few days with her, danced in Ingham's mind. He realised they were absurd. He asked if she would like to come to his bungalow for a nightcap and a coffee. She accepted. She did not accept the nightcap, but Ingham made small, strong cups of coffee. She was pleased also at his proposal of a swim – she wearing one of his shirts. The beach was deserted. There was a half-moon.

Back in his bungalow, as she sat wrapped in a large white towel, he said, 'I'd like it very much if you stayed with me. Would you?'

'I would like it, too,' she replied.

It had been simple after all.

Ingham gave her his terry-cloth robe. She disappeared into the bathroom.

Then she got into bed, naked, and Ingham slipped in

beside her. There were lovely, toothpaste-flavoured kisses. Ingham was more interested in her breasts. He lay gently on top of her. But after five minutes, he realised that he was not becoming excited enough to make love to her. He put this out of his mind for a moment or so, as he continued to kiss her neck, but then the realisation came back. And perhaps thinking about it was fatal. She even touched him briefly, perhaps by accident. There were things he might have asked her to do, but he couldn't. Emphatically, not this girl. At last, he lay on his side, and she facing him, both locked in a tight embrace. But nothing happened. Nothing was going to, Ingham realised. It was embarrassing. It was funny. It had never happened to him before, not if he actually wished and intended to make love, as he had. Ina – she had even called him exhausting, and Ingham had been rather proud of that. He said little to Kathryn, a few compliments, which, however, he meant. He felt lost, too lost perhaps to suffer the sense of inadequacy that he should. What was the matter? The bungalow itself? He thought not.

'You're a nice lover,' she said.

He almost laughed. 'You're very attractive.'

Her hand on the back of his neck was pleasant, reassuring, but only vaguely exciting, and he wondered how much she minded, how much he had let her down.

Suddenly she sneezed.

'You're cold!'

'It's that swim.'

He got out of bed and poured a Scotch in the kitchen, came in and struggled into his robe, still holding the glass. 'Do you want it neat?'

She did.

Twenty minutes later, he was driving her towards the Fourati. He had asked if she would like to stay the night, but she had said no. There was no change in her attitude towards him – alas, not as much as there might have been if he had made love to her.

'Shall we have dinner tomorrow night?' Ingham asked. 'If you felt like it, we could cook something at my place. Just for a change.'

'Tomorrow night I promised someone here. – Lunch tomorrow?'

'I don't make lunch dates when I'm working.'

They agreed on the evening after tomorrow, again at seven-thirty.

Ingham went home and got at once into pyjama pants. He sat on the edge of his bed. He felt utterly depressed. He could not see the bottom of his depression without actually going down there, he thought. He realised he had changed a great deal in the past month. And just how? He would know in the next few days, he thought. It was not the kind of question Ingham could answer by thinking about it.

Kathryn Darby was brighter than Lotte, Ingham thought out of nowhere. Which was not to say that anyone had to have an intellect to be brighter than Lotte. Lotte had been a mistake, a strong and powerful, long-lasting mistake. Lotte had left him for another man, because she had been bored with him. The man was one who had come to their parties many times in New York, an advertising executive, witty, extrovert, the kind women always liked, Ingham had supposed, and never took seriously. Then the next thing he knew, Thomas Jeffrey had been asking for her hand, or whatever, and moreover Lotte had wanted to give it to him. Never had anything in Ingham's life, of equal importance, happened so quickly. He'd not had time even to fight, he felt. 'The only time you pay attention to me is in bed,' Lotte had said, more than once. It was true. She hadn't been interested in his writing, or in anyone else's books, and she had a way, which at times had been funny, of demolishing an interesting remark by him or someone else, with a platitudinous remark of her own quite off the subject, yet well meant. Yes, he had often smiled. Though not unkindly. He had worshipped Lotte, and never had any woman had such a physical hold over him. But that was obviously not enough to keep a woman happy. No, he couldn't blame her. She had come of a wealthy family, was badly educated, spoilt, and had really no interests at all, except tennis, which she had slowly given up, perhaps out of laziness.

Or could he somehow do better, if he had another chance

with Lotte? But Lotte was married now. And did he want another chance with her? Of course not. Why had he thought of it?

Ingham went to bed, still depressed, but unbothered, unconcerned even, by Kathryn Darby's scent which still lingered on his pillow.

CHAPTER TEN

'Hasso,' Jensen said, 'is probably four feet under the sand somewhere. Maybe two feet will do.' Jensen looked whipped, broken, slouched over the bar of the Café de le Plage. He was drinking *boukhah*, and looked as if he had had several.

It was noon. Ingham had driven into Hammamet to buy a typewriter ribbon, and, having tried at three likely looking stores that seemed to sell everything, had failed.

'I don't suppose,' Ingham said, 'you could spread the word around that you'd give a reward if somebody found him?'

'I did that the first thing. I told a couple of the kids. They'll spread it. The point is, the dog's *dead*. Or he'd come back.' Jensen's voice cracked. He hunched lower over his bare forearms, and Ingham realised to his embarrassment that Jensen was on the brink of tears.

A pain of sympathy went through Ingham, and his own eyes stung. 'I'm sorry. Really I am. – Bastards!'

Jensen gave a snort of a laugh and finished his little drink. 'What they usually do is toss the head into one of your windows. At least they've spared me that so far.'

'There isn't something, maybe, that they're holding against you? Your neighbours, I mean?'

Jensen shrugged. 'I don't *know* of anything. I never had any quarrels with them. I don't make any noise. I pay my landlord – in advance, too.'

Ingham hesitated, then asked, 'Are you thinking of leaving Hammamet?'

'I'll wait a few more days. Then – sure, for Christ's sake, I'll leave. But I'll tell you one thing, I hate the thought of Hasso's *bones* being in this goddam sand! Am I glad the Jews beat the shit out of them!'

Ingham glanced around uneasily, but as usual there was a din in the place, and probably no one near them understood any English. A couple of men, including the barman, glanced at Jensen because he was upset, but there was no hostility in their faces. 'I'm with you there.'

'It isn't good to hate as I do,' Jensen went on, one fist clenched, the other hand clutching the tiny, empty glass, and Ingham was afraid he was going to throw it. 'It isn't good.'

'You'd better eat something. I'd suggest we have dinner tonight, but I've got a date. How about tomorrow night?'

Jensen agreed. They would meet at the Café de la Plage.

Ingham drove back to his bungalow, feeling wretched, as if he hadn't done enough to help Jensen. He realised he did not want to see Kathryn Darby tonight, and that he would have been less bored, even happier, with Jensen.

That afternoon, along with a letter from Ingham's mother in Florida (his parents had retired and gone there to live), came an express letter from Ina. Ina's letter said:

July 10, 19—

Dear Howard,

It's true I owe you some explanations, so I will try. First of all, why I was upset. I thought for a while that I loved John – and to continue further with the truth, I went to bed with him, twice. You may well ask 'Why?' For one thing, I never thought you were madly in love with me – that is, deeply and completely. It's possible to be slightly in love, you know. Not every love is the grande passion and not every love is the kind on which to found a marriage. I was attracted to John. He was absolutely gone on me – strange as it may seem, developing suddenly, after we'd known each other for a year or so. I made him no promises. He knew about you, as you well know, and I told him you had asked me to marry you and that I had more or less agreed – in our casual way, it was on, I know. I thought John and I – if I tried to play it a bit cool with him (he was fantastically emotional) might find out if we really did or could care for each other. He was a different world to me, full of pictures in his head, which he could visualise so clearly and put into words.

Ingham thought, couldn't *he* do that, too? Or did Ina think him a lousier writer than John had been a cameraman?

Then I began to sense a certain weakness, a shakiness in John. Nothing to do with his feeling for me. That didn't seem shaky at all. It was something in his character which I did not care for, which actually frightened me. It was a weakness he should not have been *blamed* for, and I never thought of blaming him, but having seen or sensed this weakness, I knew it was no go with John and me. I tried to break it off as gently as possible – but things can never be done that way. There is always the moment when the Awful Speech must be made, because the other person won't accept the truth without it. And when I say break it off – this whole 'affair' went on just about ten days. My pulling out, unfortunately, was fatal for poor John. He had five days of decline, during which I tried to help him as much as I could. The last two days, he said he didn't want to see me. I assumed he was in his own apartment. He was dead when I found him. I won't try to describe the horror of seeing him there. I don't know the right words. They don't exist.

So, dear Howard, what do you think of all this? I suspect you want to drop me. I would not blame you – and even if I did? I could have withheld this. No one knows about it but me, unless John told Peter, I mean told him everything. I still like you, even love you. I don't know how you feel now. When you come back, and I assume that will be very soon, we can see each other again, if you like. It is up to you.

I carry on with work, but am dead-tired. (If your employer ask for your lifeblood, give him your corpse also.) The usual amount of take-home work still. It looks like a lull in August and that's when I'll take my two weeks' vacation.

Would you write me soon, even if it's a rather grim letter?

With love,
Ina

Ingham's first reaction was one of slight contempt. What a mistake for Ina to have made! He had thought Ina was so bright. And in the letter, she was more or less begging his forgiveness, in fact pleading, or hoping, that he would take her back. It was all so goddamned silly.

It wasn't even as important as Jensen's dog, Ingham thought.

Ina was right. He wasn't 'madly in love' with her, but he counted on her, he depended on her in a very important and profound way. He knew that, now that he had learned she had betrayed him. The word 'betrayed' came to his mind, and he hated it. It wasn't, he thought, that he was stuffy enough to object to any affair that Ina might have had while he was gone, but the fact that she apparently had sunk so much emotion into this one. She was looking for something 'real and lasting', as practically every woman in the world was, and she'd looked for it in that weak fish John Castlewood.

How he wished that Ina had written that she'd had a silly roll in the hay with Castlewood, which hadn't meant anything, and that Castlewood had taken it seriously! But Ina's letter made her sound like every feather-brained run-of-the-mill—

He wanted a drink, a drink of Scotch on this. The bottle was down to the last inch. He drank this with a splash of water, not bothering with ice, then shoved his billfold in the pocket of his shorts and walked to the bungalows' grocery store. It was a quarter to six. He'd have a couple of drinks before picking Kathryn up. Was Kathryn Darby a bore or not?

As he walked towards the store, Ingham watched a couple of camels on the edge of the main road. One of the camels was ridden by a sun-blackened wraith in a burnouse. The camels were tied together. A donkey-drawn cart, piled high with kindling and topped by a barefoot Arab, paused at the edge of the road, and someone got down. To Ingham's surprise, it was old Abdullah of the red pants. What was he doing here? Ingham watched him look in both directions, then hump across the road to the hotel side and turn in the direction of Hammamet. The cart had come from the Hammamet direction, and it went on. The Arab was lost to view by the hotel's bushes and trees. Ingham went into the grocery shop and bought eggs, Scotch, and beer. The old Arab, Ingham thought, might be going to see the man who ran the curio shop a few yards down the road. And there were fruit and vegetable shops between here and Hammamet, too, run by Arabs. But his presence so near the hotel irked Ingham. Ingham realised he was living through one of the worst, therefore one of the crabbiest, days of his life.

Ingham took Kathryn straight to the Café de la Plage at Hammamet for a pre-dinner drink. She had been in the Plage a couple of times with her English friends. 'We adored it, but it was a little noisy. At least they said so.' Kathryn was a better sport, it seemed, and obviously enjoyed the noise and the sloppiness.

Ingham looked for Jensen, hoping to see him, but Jensen was not there.

From the Plage, they went across the street to Melik's. The bakers were at work next door. One young Arab baker, lounging in shorts and a paper hat in the doorway, looked Kathryn over with interest. There was again the delicious, reassuring smell of baking bread. Melik's was loud. There were two if not three tables with flutes and stringed instruments. The canary, in a cage that hung from a horizontal ceiling pole, was accompanying the music merrily. Ingham remembered one evening when Adams had been droning away, and the canary had been asleep with its head under its wing, and Ingham had wished he might do the same. There was only one other woman besides Kathryn on the terrace. As Ingham had foreseen, the evening was a trifle boring, and yet they were not at a loss for conversation. Kathryn talked to him about Pennsylvania, which she loved, especially in autumn when the pumpkin season was on and the leaves came down. Surely, Ingham thought, she would marry a nice solid Pennsylvanian, maybe a lawyer, and settle down in a town house with a garden. But Kathryn didn't mention a man, gave no hint of one. There was something attractively independent about her. And there was no doubt at all she was very pretty. But the last thing he could have done that night was go to bed with her, the last thing in the world he wished. A nightcap at the Fourati, and the evening was over.

Ingham was pleasantly mellow on food and drink. His anger and irritability had gone, at least superficially, and for this he was grateful to Miss Kathryn Darby of Pennsylvania. What did they say there? 'Shoo fly pie and apple pan dowdy.'

Back in his bungalow, he read Ina's letter again, hoping now to read it without caring a damn, without a twinge of resentment. He did not quite succeed. He dropped the letter on his table, put his head back, and said:

'God, bring Jensen's dog back. *Please!*'

Then he went to bed. It was not yet midnight.

Ingham did not know what awakened him, but he pushed himself up suddenly on one elbow and listened. The room was quite dark. His doorknob gave a squeak. Ingham sprang out of bed and instinctively moved behind his work-table, which was in the centre of his room. He faced the door. Yes, it was opening. Ingham crouched. My God, he'd forgotten to lock it, he realised. He saw silhouetted a somewhat stooped figure: a light, the street-light on the bungalow lane, gave a milky luminosity beyond. The figure was coming in.

Ingham seized his typewriter from the table and hurled it with all his force, shoving it with his right arm in the manner of a basket-ball-player throwing for the basket – but the target in this case was lower. Ingham scored a direct hit against the turbaned head. The typewriter fell with a painful clatter, and there was a yell from the figure which staggered back and fell on the terrace. Ingham sprang to his door, pushed the typewriter aside with one foot, and slammed the door. The key was on the windowsill to the right. He found it, groped with fingertips for the keyhole, and locked the door.

Then he stood still, listening. He was afraid there might be others.

Still in the dark, Ingham went to his kitchen, found the Scotch bottle on the draining-board, nearly knocked it over but grabbed it in time, and had a swig. If he had ever needed a drink, it was now. A second small swallow, and he slammed his palm down on the squeaking cork, replaced the bottle on the draining-board, and looked in the darkness towards his door, listening. Ingham knew the man he had hit was Abdullah. At least, he was ninety per cent sure of it.

There were faint voices, coming closer. The voices were muted, excited, and Ingham could hear that they were speaking in Arabic. A small beam of light swept past his closed shutters and vanished. Ingham braced himself. Were these the man's chums – or the hotel boys investigating?

Then he heard bare feet slapping on the terrace, a grunt, the sweeping sound of something being dragged. The damned Arab, of course. They were dragging him away. Whoever they were.

Ingham heard a whispered 'Mokta'.

The sounds of feet faded, disappeared. Ingham stood in the kitchen at least two minutes more. He could not tell if they had spoken about Mokta, or if Mokta, with them, had been addressed. Ingham started to run out to speak to them. But was he *sure* they were the hotel boys?

Ingham gave a deep, shuddering sigh. Then he heard again soft footfalls in sand, a sound as soft as cotton. There was another faint slap, different. Someone was wiping the tiles with a rag. Wiping away blood, Ingham knew. He felt slightly sickened. The soft tread went away. Ingham waited, made himself count slowly to twenty. Then he set his reading lamp on the floor, so its light would not show much through the shutters, and turned it on. He was interested in his typewriter.

The lower front part of the frame was bent. Ingham winced at the sight of it, more for the surprising appearance of the typewriter than for the impact it must have made against the forehead of the old Arab. Even the spacer had been pushed awry, and one end stuck up. A few keys had been bent and jammed together. Ingham flicked them down automatically, but they could not fall into place. The bend in the frame went in about three inches. That was a job for Tunis, all right, the repairing.

Ingham turned his lamp out and crept between the sheets again, threw the top sheet off because it was hot. He lay for nearly an hour without sleeping, but he heard no more sounds. He put the light on again and carried his typewriter to his closet, and set it on the floor beside his shoes. He did not want Mokta or any of the boys to see it tomorrow morning.

CHAPTER ELEVEN

Ingham was interested in what Mokta's attitude would be when he brought his breakfast. But it was another boy who brought his breakfast at ten past nine, a boy Ingham had seen a couple of times, but whose name he did not know.

'Merci,' Ingham said.

'A votre service, m'sieur.' Calm, inscrutable, the boy went away.

Ingham dressed to go to Tunis. The typewriter went into its case still. It crossed his mind to bring his car outside the bungalow, then put his typewriter into it, because he felt shy about being seen by one of the boys carrying his typewriter up the lane. But that was absurd, Ingham thought. How would anyone know what the old man had been hit with?

At 9.35 a.m., Ingham locked his bungalow and left it. He had put his car far up the lane, almost at Adams's bungalow, because last night he had thought to knock on Adams's door, if he had seen a light, but Adams's lights had been off. Ingham's car was on the extreme left, under a tree, and there were two other cars to the right of him, and parallel. Ingham wondered if the old Arab, not perhaps seeing his car, had assumed he was out? But how would the Arab have known what bungalow was his? Unless one of the boys told him? and that was unlikely, Ingham thought. The Arab had probably gently tried the door of every bungalow where he saw no light.

Mokta was not around.

Ingham flinched a little at the sight of Adams, coming barefoot, spear and flippers in hand, up from the beach towards his bungalow.

'Morning!' Adams called.

'Morning, Francis!' Ingham had put his typewriter in the back of his car on the floor. Now he closed the door.

'Taking off somewhere?' Adams was coming closer.

'I thought I'd go to Tunis to get a couple of typewriter ribbons and some paper.' He hoped Adams wouldn't want to come along.

'Did you hear that scream last night?' Adams asked. 'Around two? Woke me up.'

'Yes. I heard *something*.' Ingham suddenly realised, forcibly, that he might have killed the Arab, and that this was what was making him so uneasy.

'It came from your direction. I heard a couple of the boys go out and see what was up. They didn't come back for an hour. I hear everything they do, being so close.' He gestured towards his bungalow, ten yards away. 'There's a little mystery there. One boy came back to the house here' – a gesture towards the headquarters building – 'then ran out again after a minute.'

Had he come to get the cloth, Ingham wondered. Or a shovel?

'The funny thing is, the boys won't say what it was. Maybe a fight, you know, somebody hurt. But why were they gone for an hour, eh?' Adams's face was lively with curiosity.

'I dunno what to say,' Ingham said, opening his car door. 'I'll ask Mokta.'

'He won't tell you anything. – Are you in the mood for a drink and dinner tonight?'

Ingham was not, but he said, 'Yes, fine. Come to my place for a drink?'

'Come to mine. Got something I'd like to show you.' The squirrel face winked.

'All right. At six-thirty,' Ingham said, and got into his car.

Ingham had to go through Hammamet to get on to the Tunis road. In Hammamet he glanced at the post office corner, at the outdoor tables of the Plage, for the old Arab in the red pants. He did not see him.

It took him forty minutes in Tunis, on foot, to find a repair shop, or the right repair shop. One or two said they could do it, but that it would take at least two weeks, and they did not

98

sound convincing either about the repair or the time. At last, in a busy commerical, street, he found a rather efficient-looking shop, where the manager said it could be done in a week. Ingham believed him, but regretted the length of time.

'How did this happen?' the man asked in French.

'A maid in my hotel knocked it off a windowsill.' Ingham had thought of this beforehand.

'Bad luck! I hope it didn't fall on someone's head!'

'No. On a parapet of stone,' Ingham replied.

Ingham left the shop with a receipt. He felt weightless and lost without the typewriter.

On the Boulevard Bourguiba, he went to a café to have a beer and to look at the *Time* he had bought. The Israelis were standing firm with their territorial gains. It was easy to foresee a growing Arab hatred against the Jews, a worse resentment than had existed before. Things would be seething for quite a time.

He went to have lunch at a ceiling-fan-cooled restaurant on the other side of the Boulevard Bourguiba, one of the two restaurants that John Castlewood had mentioned. His scallopine milanese was well-cooked, he should have welcomed it after Hammamet fare, but he had no appetite. He was wondering if the Arab were possibly dead, if the boys had reported it to the hotel, the hotel to the police – but if so, why hadn't the police or someone from the hotel arrived early this morning? He was wondering if the boys had become frightened at finding the Arab dead, and had buried him in the sand somewhere? There were quite dense clumps of pine trees on the beach, fifty yards or so from the water. No one walked through those groves of trees. People walked around them. There was good burial ground there. Or was he influenced by Jensen's fears about his dog?

It crossed Ingham's mind to tell Jensen about last night's adventure. Jensen, at least, would understand, Ingham thought. Ingham was now regretting that he hadn't opened the door, when he heard the boys. Or when he had heard the one mopping up the tiles.

He was back at the Reine by two-forty-five. The interior of

his bungalow felt actually cool. He took off his clothes and got under a shower. The cold water was chilling, but it was also blissful. And it could not last long. Two minutes, and one became bored, shut the water off, and stepped out once more into the heat. He might ask Adams tonight how to go about getting an air-conditioner. Ingham got naked between his sheets and slept for an hour.

He awakened, and immediately thought of where he was in the chapter he was writing, a scene that was unfinished, and sat up and looked towards his typewriter. The table was empty. He had been very soundly asleep. A week with no typewriter. To Ingham, it was like a hand cut off. He disliked even personal letters with a pen. He took another shower, as he was again sweaty.

Then he dressed in shorts, a cool shirt, sandals, and went out to find Mokta. One of the boys at the headquarters, languidly sweeping sand from the cement before the door-way, said that Mokta had gone on an errand to the main building. Ingham ordered a beer, sat on the terrace in the shade, and waited. Mokta came in about ten minutes, a huge stack of tied-together towels balanced on one shoulder. Mokta saw him from a distance and smiled. He was in shirt-sleeves and long dark trousers. A pity, Ingham thought, that the boys weren't allowed to wear shorts in this heat.

'Mokta! – Bonjour! Can I speak with you a moment, when you have time?'

'Bien sûr, m'sieur!' There was only a brief flash of alarm in Mokta's smiling face, but Ingham had seen it. Mokta went into the office with his stack of towels. He was back at once.

'Would you like a beer?' Ingham asked.

'With pleasure, thank you, m'sieur. But I can't sit down.' Mokta ran around the corner of the building to get his beer from the service door. He was back quickly with a bottle.

'I was wondering, how do I hire an air-conditioner?'

'Oh, very simple, m'sieur. I shall speak to the directrice, she will speak to the manager. It may take a couple of days.' Mokta's smile was as broad as usual.

Ingham studied his grey eyes casually. Mokta's eyes

shifted, not in a dishonest way, but simply because Mokta, Ingham thought, was alert to everything around him, even to things that weren't always there, like a shout from a superior. 'Well, perhaps you can speak to her. I would like one.' Ingham hesitated. He did not want to ask outright what they had done with the unconscious or dead Arab. But why wasn't Mokta bringing it up? Even if Mokta hadn't come to the bungalow with the others last night, he would have heard all about it.

Ingham offered Mokta a cigarette, which he accepted.

Was it too public here for Mokta to talk, Ingham wondered. Mokta's eyes flickered to Ingham's and away. Ingham was careful not to stare at him, not wanting to embarrass the boy. And no doubt, Mokta was waiting for him to begin. Ingham couldn't. Why didn't Mokta say something like, 'Oh, m'sieur, what a *catastrophe* last night! An old beggar who tried to get into your bungalow!' Ingham could hear Mokta saying it, and yet Mokta wasn't saying it. After a minute or two, Ingham felt very uncomfortable. 'It's warm today. I was in Tunis this morning,' Ingham said.

'Ah, oui? It is always warmer in Tunis! Mon Dieu! I am glad I work here!'

After accepting another cigarette for the road, Mokta departed with their two beer bottles, and Ingham went back to his bungalow. He went over his notes for his chapter-in-progress, and made a few notes for the next chapter. He could have been writing an answer to Ina's last and more explanatory letter, but he did not want to think about Ina just now. It would be a letter that required some thought, unless he dashed off something that he might later regret. Ingham paper-clipped his notes and put them on a corner of his desk.

He wrote a short letter to his mother, explaining that his typewriter was undergoing a repair in Tunis. He told her that John Castlewood, whom he had not known very well, had killed himself in New York. He said he was working on a novel, and that he was going to try, despite his disappointment at the job's falling through, to gain what he could from Tunisia. Ingham was an only child. His mother liked to know what he was doing, but she was not a meddler, and did not become upset easily. His father was equally concerned, but a worse correspondent than his mother. His father almost never wrote.

Ingham still had half an hour before his appointment with OWL. He wanted very much to take a walk on the beach, past Adam's bungalow and towards Hammamet, in order to look at the sand among the trees there. He longed to find a torn-up patch that resembled a grave, he longed to be sure. But he realised that gentle rakings of sand with feet, with hand, could make a grave in the morning (or even at once) look like all the sand around it. No soil was more traceless than sand after a few minutes, even a slight breeze would smooth things out, and the sun would dry any moisture that the digging might have turned up. And he didn't care to be seen peering around at the sand. And what was the Arab worth? Next to nothing, probably. That was the un-Christian thought that came to his mind, unfortunately. He locked his bungalow, and walked over to OWL's.

Adams's greeting was, as usual, hearty. 'Come in! Sit ye down!'

Ingham appreciated the coolness of the room. It was like a glass of cold water when one was hot and thirsty. One drank this through the skin. What would August be like, Ingham wondered, and reminded himself that he ought to leave soon.

Adams brought an iced Scotch and water.

'I got stung by a jelly-fish this afternoon,' Adams said. '*Habuki*, they call them. July's the season. You can't see them in the water, you know, at least not until it's too late. Ha-ha! Got me on the shoulder. One of the boys got some salve from the office, but it didn't do any good. I went home and got some baking soda. It's still the best remedy.'

'Any particular time they come out? Time of day?'

'No. It's just the season now. By the way—' Adams sat down on his sofa in his crisp khaki shorts. 'I found out something more today about that yell last night. It was just outside your door. Of your bungalow.'

'Oh?'

'That tallish boy – Hassim. He told me. He said Mokta was with them when they went to investigate. – You know the boy I mean?'

'Yes. He cleaned my bungalow at first.' They had, for some reason, put a new boy on in the last few days.

'Hassim said it was an old Arab prowling around, and he bumped his head on something and knocked himself out. They dragged him off your terrace.' Adams again chuckled, with the delight of someone who lives in a place where nothing usually ever happened, Ingham thought. 'What interests me is that Mokta claims they didn't find *anyone*, though he said they looked around for an hour. Someone's lying. Maybe the old Arab did bump himself, but it could be that the boys beat him up and even killed him, and won't admit it.'

'Good Lord,' said Ingham, with genuine feeling, because he was imagining the boys doing just that. 'By accident, you mean, beating him up too much?'

'Possibly. Because if it was a prowler they found and threw out, why should they be so cagey about it? There's a mystery there, as I said this morning. – You didn't hear anything?'

'I heard the yell. I didn't know it was so near me.' He was lying like the boys, Ingham realised, and suppose it all came out, through one of the boys, that the bump was a pretty bad fracture, a crush of the bone, and that the man was dead when they found him?

'Another thing,' Adams said, 'the hotels always hush up anything about thieves. Bad for business. The boys would hush anything up, because it's part of their job to keep an eye on the place and not let any prowlers in. Of course there's the watchman, as you know, but he's usually asleep and he never walks around patrolling the place.'

Ingham knew. The watchman was usually asleep in this straight chair, propped against the wall, any time after ten-thirty. 'How often does this kind of thing happen?'

'Oh – only one other time in the year I've been here. They got two Arab boys who were prowling around last November. A lot of the bungalows were empty then, and the staff was smaller. Those boys were after furniture, and they broke a couple of door locks. I didn't see them, but I heard they were beaten up by the hotel boys and thrown out on the road. The Arabs are merciless with each other in a fight, you know.' Adams took both their glasses, though Ingham was not quite finished. 'And what do you hear from your girl?' Adams asked from the kitchen. 'Ina, isn't it?'

Ingham stood up. 'She wrote me. – It was she who found John Castlewood's body. He'd taken sleeping pills.'

'Really! Is that so? – In his apartment, you mean?'

'Yes.' Ingham hadn't told Adams that it had happened in his own apartment. Just as well.

'She's not coming over?'

'Oh, no. It's a long way. I should be getting back in a week or so. Back to New York.'

'Why so soon?'

'I can't stand the heat very well. – Didn't you say you had something to show me?'

'Ah, yes. Something for you to listen to. It's short!' Adams said, holding up a finger. 'But I think it's interesting. Come in the bedroom.'

Another blasted tape, Ingham thought. He had hoped that Adams might have found an ancient amphora on the sea bottom, or speared a rare fish. No such luck.

Once more the suitcase on the bed, the reverently handled recording machine. 'My latest,' Adams said softly. 'Scheduled for Wednesday next.'

The tape hissed, and began:

'Good evening, friends, everywhere. This is Robin Goodfellow, bringing you a message from America, land of the ...' Adams raced the tape, explained that it was his usual introduction. The tape chattered and squeaked, then slowed down to '... what we might call democracy. It is true the Israelis have achieved a crushing victory. They are to be congratulated from a military point of view for having won over superior numbers. Two million seven hundred thousand Jews against an *Arab* population of one hundred and ten million. But who in fact struck the first blow? – I leave this, friends, to your governments to tell you. If they are honest governments, they will say that Israel did.' (Long pause. The tape floated expectantly.) 'This is an historic fact. It is not damning, not fatal to Israel's prestige, it is not going to' – apparently groping for a word, though Ingham was sure he had the whole thing written and rewritten before he began – '*blacken* Israel, at least not in the eyes of pro-Israel countries. But! Not content with mere triumph and the displacement of thousands of Arabs, the seizure of Arab territory, the Israelis now show signs of the arrogant nationalism which was the hallmark of Nazi Germany, and for which Nazi Germany at last went to her doom. I say, much as Israel was provoked by threats to her homeland, her womenfolk, and by border incidents – and there were and are incidents to the discredit of Israel that might be cited – it would be well for Israel to be magnanimous in her hour of victory, and above *all* – to guard against that overweening pride and chauvinism which has been the downfall of greater countries than she . . .'

'Or should I have said "her"?' Adams whispered.

Ingham suppressed a crazy mirth. 'I think both are okay.'

'. . . should not be forgotten that half the population of Israel speaks Arabic as a native tongue. This is not to say that they are always Arabs *per se*. The Israelis boast of having broadcast wrong directions in Arabic to Jordanian planes and tanks, implying some mental achievement. They boast of having become great farmers, now that there is no law saying they have no profession but money-lending. There is no law against their becoming farmers in the United States, but very few are. The Israeli Jews are mainly of different origin from the American Jews, who are considerably less eastern, less Arabic. The rankling Arab–Israeli antipathy shows signs of becoming one long, merciless struggle of Arab against near-Arab, fierceness against fierceness. Sanity must prevail. *Magnanimity* must prevail . . .' (Adams skipped again.) '. . . must sit down as brothers and discuss . . .'

'Oh, well,' Adams said, clicking it off. 'The rest is wind-up, recapitulation. What do you think?'

Ingham finally said, 'I suppose the Russians will approve, since they're anti-Israel.'

'The Russian *Government* is anti-*American*,' Adams said, as if he were informing Ingham of something he did not know.

'Yes, but—' Ingham's mind boggling again. *Were* the Russians so anti-American, except for the Vietnam thing? 'The Israeli arrogance may be only temporary, you know. After all, they've got a right to a little crowing, after what they did.'

Adams gesticulated, more vigorously than Ingham had yet seen. 'Temporary or not, it's dangerous while it's there, it's dangerous at any time. It's a dangerous sign.'

Ingham hesitated, but could not refrain from saying, 'Don't you think America's just a bit arrogant in supposing that *her* way of life is the only one in the world, the very best for everybody? Furthermore, killing people daily to foist it on them, whether they like it or not? Is that arrogance, or isn't it?' Ingham put out a half-finished cigarette, and swore to himself not to say another word on the subject. It was ludicrous, maddening, stupid.

Adams said, 'America attempts to sweep away dictatorships in order to give people the freedom to vote.'

Ingham did not reply. He continued to stab his cigarette gently into the ashtray. Adams was upset. This could be the end of their friendship, Ingham thought, or the end of any real liking between them. Ingham didn't care. He did not feel like saying anything mitigating. The awful thing was, there was just a grain of truth in what Adams said about Israeli nationalism. The very countries on whom Israel was dependent had suggested she give back some of the territory she had just taken, and Israel was refusing. Both people were irritating, the Israelis and the Arabs. The only thing for any non-Jew or non-Arab to do was keep his mouth shut. If one said anything pro-Israel or pro-Arab, one ran the risk of being pounced on. It wasn't worth it. The problem was not his. He had no influence.

'I don't know what to do with the damned Arabs,' Ingham said. 'Why the hell don't they work more? Pardon my language. – But if a poor country's ever going to pull itself up – it shouldn't have all these hundreds of young men sitting in cafés from early morning until midnight, doing bloody nothing.'

'Ah, you've got something there,' Adams said, warming, smiling now.

'So between the two countries, I'm bound to say the Westerner admires the Jews more, because they're not *always* on their asses. Maybe not ever, from what I hear.'

'It's the climate here, it's the religion,' Adams chanted, eyes to the ceiling.

'The religion, maybe. Norman Douglas concludes his book on Tunisia with a wonderful statement. He says people think the desert made the Arab what he is. Douglas says the Arab made the desert. He let the land go to hell. When the Romans were in Tunisia, there were wells, aqueducts, forests, there was the beginning of agriculture.' Ingham could have gone on. His own passion surprised him. 'Another thing,' he said as Adams was putting away his equipment. 'Oh, thank you for letting me hear the tape. I know it's possible to find the Arabs interesting, to study their fatalistic religion, admire their mosques and all that, but it all seems such whimsy, even tourist whimsy, compared to the important fact they're holding themselves back with all this nonsense. What's the use of swooning over an embroidered – house-shoe or whatever, or admiring their resignation to fate, if lots of them are begging or stealing, and from us?'

'I agree completely,' Adams said, locking his closet. 'And, as you say, if they depend on fate, why beg from Western tourists who don't believe in fate, but simply in working, in trying? Ah, some religions—' Adams abandoned his sentence in disgust. 'Let me freshen your drink. Yes, and the French and American money pouring in!'

'A half, please,' Ingham said. He followed Adams into the pleasant living-room, the stainless-steel kitchen. 'As to funny religions, don't you think our charming West is guilty, too? Look at all the kids who come into the world entirely because the Catholic church doesn't permit sufficient birth control. The Catholic church ought to be *entirely* responsible for the welfare of these kids, but no, they say, let the State do it.' Ingham laughed. 'The Pope's nose! I wish somebody would rub it in some of the things that are going on in Ireland!'

Adams handed Ingham his drink, scrupulously one-half. 'All true! – There's one thing I didn't put into my tape, because it isn't very pertinent to the people behind the Iron Curtain. Or is it? I had a letter from a Jewish friend in the States just now. Now he's very much a Jew, suddenly. Before he was a Russian, or an American of Russian descent. This is what I mean by chauvinism. Let's go in and sit.'

They sat down in the living-room in their usual places.

'You see what I mean?' Adams said.

Ingham saw, and he hated it. He hated it because he knew it was true. Ingham might have remarked that the Russians had quite a reputation for Anti-Semitism, but that, presumably, was the attitude of the Russian Government, not the Russian or Communist-controlled people whom Adams was concerned with.

'What about the young lady at the Fourati?' Adams asked. 'Is she nice?'

Adams's question sounded studiedly polite and casual, almost like a spy's, Ingham thought. He answered equally carefully, 'Yes, I saw her last evening for dinner. She's from Pennsylvania. She's leaving on Wednesday.'

They had scrambled eggs with fried salami and a green salad, which Adams made in his kitchen. Adams put on his radio, and they had background music of a concert from Marseilles, background music, too, of a yelled conversation from the boys at the bungalow headquarters. Adams said it was nothing unusual. It was a quiet evening. But Ingham was a little on guard with Adams now. He did not like Adams's speculative eyes on him. He did not want Adams to know that his typewriter was being repaired, because Adams might guess that he had thrown it at the Arab. Ingham thought he could manage to be polite and still not invite Adam to his bungalow for the next week. Or if Adams came, he could say that he was taking a few days off from work. And presumably the typewriter would be in the closet.

CHAPTER TWELVE

Ingham awakened early the next morning, Sunday, to the prospect of a day without typewriter, without post, without even the consolation of a good newspaper. The Sunday papers (English, not American) arrived Tuesday or Wednesday at the main building of the hotel, a couple of copies each of the *Sunday Telegraph, Observer,* and the *Sunday Times,* which were maddeningly sometimes appropriated by the guests and taken up to their rooms.

There was, of course, his novel, the comforting stack of nearly a hundred pages on his desk. But he didn't care to think about it any further today, because he knew where he was going when he got his typewriter back.

And there was also Ina's letter to answer. Ingham had decided on a calm, thoughtful reply (basic tone being kindly, without reproach) which would say that he agreed with her, their feelings for each other were perhaps too vague or cool to be called love (whatever that was), and that the fact she had been so taken with John for a time proved the point. He intended to say he did not resent anything, and that he would certainly like to see her again when he returned to the States.

This mentally written letter, however, was simply diplomatic and cautious, face-saving, Ingham realised. He had been nastily stung by Ina's little affair with John. He was simply too proud to let Ina know that. And he reckoned he had nothing to lose by writing a diplomatic letter, and that he could keep his pride by doing so.

But he didn't care to spend an hour of the relatively cool morning writing it in longhand. After his breakfast – served by Mokta – Ingham drove into Hammamet.

Again, having parked his car near Melik's, Ingham looked around for the old Arab, who was always drifting about on a Sunday morning. But not this morning. Ingham stopped for a cold rosé in the Plage. He was alert for any staring at him, but he did not think there was any. The possibility of retaliation had occurred to him, in case a few Arabs learned that he had hit, or killed, the old man. That news could certainly spread via the hotel boys. But Ingham saw and sensed nothing that suggested animosity. The retaliation might take the form of a slashed car tyre, a broken windscreen. He didn't anticipate a personal attack.

He went next door to the wineshop, where he bought a bottle of *boukhah*, then he walked through the alley towards Jensen's house. He looked at the road where he had seen the man with the cut throat. The sun was shining full on it in a bright strip, but Ingham saw no sign of blood. Then just as he was about to look away, he did see a darkish patch in the hard soil, nearly obscured by the drifting dust. That was it. But no one, not knowing, would have taken the spot for blood, he thought. Or was he wrong? Had someone dropped a bottle of wine there a couple of days ago? He went on to Jensen's.

Jensen was in, but it took some time for him to answer Ingham's knock because, he said, he had been asleep. He had wakened early, worked, then gone back to bed. He was glad to see the *boukhah*, but the gloom of the missing Hasso still hung about him. Jensen looked thinner. He had evidently not shaved in a couple of days. They poured the *boukhah*.

Ingham sat on Jensen's tousled bed. There were no sheets on it, only a thin blanket in which Jensen evidently slept.

'Still no news of Hasso?' Ingham asked.

'Nope.' Jensen was stooped, washing his face in a white metal basin on the floor. Then he combed his hair.

There was no sign of his leaving, packing up, Ingham saw. He did not want to ask Jensen about that. 'Can I have a glass of water with this?' Ingham asked. 'Stuff's pretty fiery.'

Jensen smiled his shy, naïve smile, which always came at nothing in particular. 'And to think it is distilled from the sweet fig,' he said sourly. He went out and reappeared with a tumbler of water. The glass was not clean, but the water looked all right. Ingham was in no mood to care.

'My typewriter's being repaired till next Saturday,' Ingham said. 'I was wondering if you'd like to go on a trip with me somewhere. Maybe Gabes. Three hundred and ninety-four kilometres – that is, from Tunis. In my car, I mean.'

Jensen looked blank and surprised.

'I thought we might stay away two nights. More if we feel like it.'

'Yes. – I think that sounds very nice.'

'We might try a camel trip somewhere. Hire a guide, maybe – that's on me – and sleep out on the desert. Gabes is an oasis, you know, even though it's on the sea. I thought a change of scene might pick you up. I know I need it.'

In the next half-hour, on two or three more *boukhahs*, Jensen slowly brightened like a windblown candle given the shelter of a hand. 'I can contribute blankets and a little cooking-stove. Thermos, torch. – What else do we need?'

'We'll be driving through Sfax, which looks pretty big on the map, and we can buy things there. I'd like to go to Tozour, but it looks rather far. Do you know it?' (Jensen didn't know Tozour.) 'It's a famous old oasis inland, past the Chott. My map has an airport marking at Tozour.' Ingham, inspired by the *boukhah*, was about to propose flying there, but restrained himself.

Jensen showed Ingham his latest painting, a canvas four feet high, tacked on to pieces of wood Jensen had probably found. The picture shocked Ingham. Maybe it was shockingly good, Ingham thought. It was of a disembowelled Arab, split like a steer in a butcher's shop. The Arab was screaming, not at all dead, and the red and white bowels hung down to the bottom of the canvas.

'Jesus,' Ingham murmured involuntarily.

'Do you like it?'

'I *do* like it,' Ingham said.

They decided to take off the next morning. Ingham would call for Jensen between a quarter to ten and ten o'clock.

Jensen was happily tight now, but at least happy for the nonce.

'Have you got some toothpaste?' Ingham asked. Jensen had some. Ingham rinsed his mouth with the remainder of his glass of water, and at Jensen's insistence spat it out of the window which gave on the little court below where the toilet was. The *boukhah* left a powerful taste, and Ingham felt it could be smelt six feet away.

Ingham drove to the Fourati. He thought he should invite Miss Kathryn Darby for dinner tonight, and if she was not free, he would at least have been polite. She was leaving on Wednesday, and he expected to be away Wednesday. Miss Darby was not in, but Ingham left a message that he would call for her at seven-thirty to go to dinner, but if she was not free, perhaps she could leave a message for him at the Reine by five o'clock.

Then Ingham went back to his bungalow, took a swim, had a bite of lunch from his refrigerator, and slept.

When he woke up, feeling no ill-effects from the *boukhah*, he took his smaller suitcase from his closet and began in a happy leisurely way to pack for the jaunt to the south. It would be even hotter, that was definite.

Mokta knocked on his door at a quarter to five. Miss Darby was not free tonight. Ingham gave Mokta a tip.

'Oh, merci, m'sieur!' His face broke into his attractive smile that made him look more European than Arab to Ingham.

'I'm going away for three days,' Ingham said. 'I'd like you to keep an eye on the bungalow. I'll lock everything – also the closets.'

'Oui, m'sieur. You are going on an interesting trip? Maybe to Djerba?'

'Maybe. I thought I would drive to Gabes.'

'Ah, Gabes!' he said as if he knew it. 'I have never been there. Big oasis.' Mokta shifted on his feet, he smiled, his willing arms swung, but there was nothing for him to do. 'What time will you leave? I will help you with your suitcases.'

'Thanks, it's not necessary. Only one suitcase. – Have you

heard anything more about the man who was prowling Friday night?'

Mokta's face went blank, and his mouth hung slightly open. 'There was no *man*, m'sieur.'

'Oh – M'sieur Adams told me Hassim said there was. The boys took him away – somewhere. I was told it was near my bungalow.' Ingham was ashamed of his dishonesty, but Mokta was equally dishonest in denying the whole thing.

Mokta's hands fluttered. 'The boys talk, m'sieur. They make up stories.'

Ingham did not think it proper to quiz him any further. 'I see. Well – let's hope there are no prowlers when I'm away.'

'Ah, I *hope*, m'sieur! Merci, au revoir, m'sieur.' The smile again, a bow, and he went.

Ingham would never see Miss Darby again, he supposed, which mattered neither to her nor to him. He was reminded of a passage in the Norman Douglas book which he had liked, and he picked up the book and looked for it. Douglas was talking about an old Italian gardener he had met by accident somewhere in Tunisia. The passage Ingham had marked went:

... He had travelled far in the Old and New Worlds; in him I recognised once again that simple mind of the sailor or wanderer who learns, as he goes along, to talk and think decently; who, instead of gathering fresh encumbrances on Life's journey, wisely discards even those he set out with.*

That appealed very much to Ingham now. Miss Darby was certainly not one of his encumbrances, but Ina might be. A terrible thought, in a way, because he had considered her – for a year at least – a part of his life. He had counted on her. And knowing himself, Ingham knew he had not had the whole reaction he would have, a little later, from her letter. The curious thing, the comforting thing was that Africa would help him to bear it better – if he was going to have

* *Fountains in the Sand* by Norman Douglas. First published 1912; Penguin, 1944.

any bad reaction. It was strange, he couldn't explain it, to be floating like a foreign particle (which he was) in the vastness of Africa, but to be absolutely sure that Africa would enable him to bear things better.

He decided not to think about his letter to Ina, the letter he would write in a few days. Let her wait, say, five or six days, ten including the time the letter would take to get there. She had made him wait a month.

Ingham went over to say goodbye to OWL.

OWL was washing his flippers in the kitchen sink. He shook his flippers neatly, like a woman shaking out a dish-cloth, and stood them upside down on the draining-board. They looked seal-like, but somehow as repellent as Adams's feet.

'I'm going away for a couple of days,' Ingham said.

'Going away where?'

Ingham told him. He did not mention Jensen.

'Are you giving up your bungalow?'

'No. I wasn't sure I could get it back.'

'No, you're right. Would you like a drink?'

'I wouldn't mind a beer, if you have one.'

'Got six, ice cold,' Adams said cheerfully, and got a can from the refrigerator. Adams made himself a Scotch. 'You know, I found out a little something today,' he said as they went into the living-room. 'I think – I'm pretty sure—' Adams looked around at the windows, as if for eaves-droppers, but because of the air-conditioning, his windows were all shut, even all the shutters closed except the one behind Ingham's chair where there was no sun. 'I think I know who the prowler was the other night. Abdullah. The old Arab with the cane. The one you said stole your jacket or something.'

'Oh. One of the boys told you?'

'No, I heard it in town,' Adams said with a faintly satisfied air, as if he were in the secret service and had ferreted out something.

Ingham's heart had tripped. He hoped he did not look pale, because he felt pale.

'At the Plage,' Adams continued, 'they were talking about

"Abdull", a couple of Arabs at the bar. There're lots of Abdullahs, but I saw the barman give the fellows a sign to pipe down, because of me. They know I'm at the Reine. I understood enough of what they said to know he was "gone" or "disappeared". I wanted to ask them about him, because something had just made a connection in my mind. I didn't ask, I didn't want to butt in. But I remembered seeing Abdullah by the curio shop near the hotel here Friday night. It was a night I drove into Hammamet around eight to have dinner. I'd never seen the old fellow around here before, so I remembered it. And I noticed yesterday and today, he wasn't around town. I was in Hammamet three times lately, and he wasn't around, not since Friday. It's *strange*.' Adams looked at Ingham, his head a little cocked.

Silence for a few seconds.

'Well, won't somebody report him missing?' Ingham asked. 'Won't the police do something?'

'Oh – his neighbours might miss him. I presume he's got a room to sleep somewhere, probably with six other people. I doubt if he's got a wife and family. Would a neighbour go to the police?' Adams pondered this. 'I doubt that. They're fatalistic. *Mektoub!* It is the will of Allah that Abdullah should disappear! Voilà! It's a far cry from the American Way, isn't it?'

CHAPTER THIRTEEN

Jensen was punctual the next morning, standing on the road near the narrow alley, with a brown suitcase at his feet. He wore pale green cotton trousers, neatly pressed. Ingham pulled up a bit past Melik's on the other side of the road, and Jensen walked over. Ingham helped him stow the suitcase in the back of the car. They had plenty of room, even with Jensen's knapsack and dangling gear of cooking-stove and pots.

'You know, Anders, you ought to put on shorts,' Ingham said. 'It's going to be a hot drive. You ought to save those good pants.' He spoke gently, always afraid somehow to hurt Jensen's feelings.

'All right,' Jensen said, like a willing, polite little boy. 'I'll change up in Melik's loo.' Jensen opened his suitcase and dragged out a pair of shorts made from old levis. He went up the steps to Melik's.

Ingham stood outside his car and lit a cigarette.

Jensen was back in a moment. He had lean brown legs with golden hairs. He put his trousers away carefully in his suitcase.

Ingham took the road southward, along the sea. The morning was still cool. The emptiness of the clear blue sky seemed to promise a reward, or pleasure, ahead of them. In a quarter of an hour they reached Bou Ficha, a village, and in about the same time something larger called Enfidaville. Jensen held the map. The road was good to Sousse. They did not stop at Sousse even for a coffee, but went on southward on the shorter inland route towards Sfax, where they intended to have a late lunch. Jensen reeled off the names:

'Msaken next ... Bourdjine ... Amphithéatre! Well! No,

that's not a town, it's a fact. They have one. Probably Roman.'

'I find it amazing,' Ingham said, 'there's so little remains of the Romans, Greeks, Turks and so forth. Carthage was a disappointment. I expected it to be so much bigger.'

'No doubt it has been pillaged a thousand times,' Jensen said with resignation.

In Sfax, where they lunched at a very decent restaurant with pavement tables, Jensen was of great interest to a boy of about twelve. At least that was the way Ingham saw it. He hadn't seen Jensen make a single inviting move. The boy hung around, smiling broadly, rolling big dark eyes, leaning against a metal pole some six feet away. At last the boy spoke to Jensen, and Jensen murmured something that sounded bored in Arabic. The boy giggled.

'I asked him,' said Jensen, 'do I look like I have a millime? Scram!'

Ingham laughed. The boy was rather handsome, but dirty.

'They don't bother you?' Jensen asked.

One had approached him in Tunis, but he said, 'No, not yet.'

'Little bores. Little nuisances,' Jensen said, as if he spoke of a minor vice of his own which he could not shake.

Ingham anticipated that Jensen might find a boy or two on this trip. He thought it might pick Jensen up. 'How much money do they want, usually?'

'Oh!' Jensen laughed. 'You can get them for a packet of cigarettes. Half a packet.'

They made it easily to Gabes by 6 p.m., even stopping for half an hour at a town called Cekhira for a swim. It was the hottest time of the afternoon, just after three o'clock. They stepped out of the already ovenlike car, which had been lumbering over sandy soil towards the beach, into something worse, a bigger oven. Ingham changed as fast as possible into swimming trunks, while standing at one side of the car. There was no living thing in sight. What could have stood the heat? They ran down to the sea and jumped in. The water was refreshing to Ingham, though Jensen said the water was not cold enough. Jensen was an excellent swimmer, and could stay under water for so long that Ingham grew alarmed at one point. Jensen swam in his shorts. When they came back to the car, the door handles were too hot to touch. Ingham had to take off his trunks and use them to grip the handle. In the car, Jensen sat in his wet shorts on a towel.

Gabes was Ingham's first view of the desert, stretching inland to the west behind the town, flat and yellow-orange in the light of the setting sun. The town was quite big, but the buildings were not all jammed together as at Sousse or Sfax. There were spaces through which one could see distant palm trees with fronds stirring in the breeze. It was not so warm as Ingham had feared. They found a second-class hotel, which was respectable enough to be listed in Ingham's *Guide Bleu*, however. Jensen was a little proud about paying his way, and Ingham did not want to let him in for much expense. It would be odd, Ingham thought, if Jensen were really quite well off, and had simply decided to rough it for a while. That could go, Ingham supposed, as far as buying a cheap brown suitcase to begin with, and if one roughed it long enough, the suitcase could look like Jensen's at this moment. Ingham didn't care one way or the other. He found Jensen a good travelling companion, uncomplaining, interested in everything, and willing to do anything Ingham proposed.

Only Ingham's room had a toilet and shower. Jensen took a shower in Ingham's room. Then they both went out to walk around the town. The jasmine sellers were here, too. The oversweet scent had become the scent of Tunisia to Ingham – its cosmetic scent, at any rate – as certain scents evoked certain women. Lotte's had been Le Dandy. Ingham could not think of the name of Ina's now, though he had bought some for her once or twice in New York. He certainly could not recollect how it smelt. The olfactory memory might be long and primitive, ante-dating words, but it seemed one couldn't call up a smell in memory as one could call up a word or a line of poetry.

They went into a bar and stood. *Boukhah* again. Then Ingham had a Scotch. The transistor, though tiny on the bar shelf, was blaring, and made talking difficult. The song whined on with no end in sight, and there was off and on singing, by a male or female voice, it was impossible to tell. When the voice stopped for a bit, the twanging, insinuating stringed instruments whammed in, as if to back up the griping vocalist with a *'Yeah! That's what I've been saying all along!'* And what were they complaining *about?* Ingham wanted to laugh.

'Good God,' he said to Jensen, shaking his head.

Jensen smiled slightly, apparently able to shut out the noise.

At their feet was a swill of cigarette butts, sawdust, and spit. 'Let's go somewhere else,' Ingham said.

Jensen was willing.

Eventually they found a restaurant for dinner. Ingham could not eat his squid, or whatever it was, which he had ordered through a mistake of his own in the language, but at least he had the satisfaction of giving it to a grateful cat.

The next morning they paid their bill, and asked the hotel manager about camels.

'Ah, bien sûr, messieurs!' He quoted prices. He knew a camel-driver and where to find him.

They went off with their luggage to find the camel-drivers. The business took some time, because Jensen decided to wait for a driver due at ten or ten-thirty, according to the other camel-drivers. The drivers leaned casually, their pointed sandals crossed, against the round bodies of their camels, which were all lying around on the sand with their feet tucked in like cats. The camels looked more intelligent than their drivers, Ingham thought. It was a disturbing intelligence in their faces, a look of knowledge that could not be acquired by going to any school. All the camels regarded him and Jensen with an amused curiosity, as if to say, 'Well, well, two *more* suckers!' Ingham was vaguely ashamed of his unromantic thoughts.

The awaited driver arrived on one camel, leading three others. Jensen struck the bargain. Six dinars each for overnight.

'They always make a big thing about having to feed the

camels,' Jensen explained to Ingham, 'but the price isn't bad.'

Ingham hadn't been on a camel since a certain trip to the zoo when he was a boy. He rather dreaded the lurching ride, and tried to anticipate falling off – nine feet down to the sand – so that it wouldn't hurt so much if he did. The camel jolted him up, and they were off. After a few hundred yards, it was not as bad as Ingham had feared, but the undulant movement imposed by the camel's gait made him feel silly. He would have preferred to gallop, leaning forward, in the manner of Lawrence of Arabia.

'Hey, Anders!' Ingham yelled. 'What's our destination?'

'We're going towards Chenini. That little town we looked up last night.' Jensen was on the camel ahead.

'Wasn't it ten kilometres away?'

'I think so.' Jensen spoke to the driver, who was on the lead camel, then turned back to Ingham. 'We can't walk in the desert all day, you know. We'll have to have shelter from eleven to four somewhere.'

The desert was widening about them. 'Where?' Ingham asked, unalarmed.

'Oh, trust him. He's no doubt making a bee-line for a shelter.'

This was true, but it was eleven-forty before they reached a tiny town, or cluster of houses, and Ingham was glad to stop. He had covered his head with a handkerchief. Jensen had an old canvas cap. The place had a name, but it slipped from Ingham's mind as soon as he heard it. There was a grocery store-restaurant which sold bottled drinks from a Pepsi-Cola dispenser tank, but there was no ice in the tank, only tepid water. A lunch was produced by the proprietor of the place, chick peas with lumps of inedible sausage, Jensen and Ingham ate at a tiny round table, their metal chairs slanting crazily in the sand. Ingham could not imagine why, or how, people lived here, though there was a road of sorts leading to and from the place, a ghostly trail in the sand which a jeep or a Land-Rover could use, he supposed. They drank some *boukhah* after their lunch. Jensen had picked up a bottle somewhere. Jensen said the only thing to do was sleep for an hour or so.

'Unless you want to read. I might make a sketch.' Jensen got a drawing pad from his suitcase.

There were two more stops in the course of the day. Jensen had quite a conversation with the driver, which he said was on the subject of where they would spend the night. The driver knew of a grove of palms, though it was not an oasis. They arrived there just before seven o'clock. The sun had just set. The horizon was orange, the landscape empty, but there was a cardboard carton, some old tins under the trees, which suggested that this spot might be a favourite for camel-drivers to bring their customers to. Ingham was not fussy. He thought it all quite wonderful. Venus was shining.

Jensen had bought tins of beans and sardines *en route* from the hotel to the camels this morning. Ingham did not care if the food was hot or cold, but Jensen set up his cooking-stove. He invited the driver to partake, but he declined politely, and produced his own food from somewhere. He also declined Jensen's offer of a *boukhah*.

Before he ate, the driver read in the failing light from a little book.

Jensen glanced at the driver and said to Ingham, 'It takes imagination to enjoy a drink. There he is with the Koran, no doubt. You know, they either drink like maniacs or they're stubborn – dries. What do you call them?'

'Teetotallers,' Ingham said. 'He's not very friendly, is he?'

'Maybe he thinks he can't do me, because I know some Arabic. But I have the feeling he has just had a sadness of some kind.'

'Really?' Ingham imagined that Arabs were more or less always the same from one day to the next, that no external event could much affect them.

After dinner out of a mutual pot, eaten with spoons, Jensen and Ingham lay on their blankets and smoked, facing the direction in which the sun had gone down. A palm tree half sheltered them. The *boukhah* bottle was between them, pushed into the sand so it would stand upright. Ingham drank mostly from Jensen's canteen of water. The stars came out more and more, and became powdery with profusion. There was no sound except an occasional swish of breeze in the palm leaves.

Just as he was about to speak, Ingham saw a shooting star. It went on a long way downward in the sky – seven inches, he thought, if the sky had been a canvas and had been of a certain nearness. 'Remember the night,' Ingham said, 'about three weeks ago, when I went to your house the first time? As I was leaving, walking towards the road, I came across a dead man. In that second stretch, after the turn. Lying in the alley.'

'Really?' asked Jensen without too much surprise.

Ingham was speaking softly. 'I stumbled over him. Then I lit a match. The fellow'd had his throat cut. The body was even cold. You didn't hear anything about it?'

'No, I didn't.'

'What do you think happens to the body? Somebody has to remove it.'

Jensen paused for a swig from the bottle. 'Oh, first somebody would cover it up to hide it. Then a couple of Arabs would haul it away on a donkey, bury it in the sand somewhere. That is, if there's some reason to hide it and there usually is if a man's murdered. Excuse me a minute.' Jensen got up and disappeared somewhere in the palm grove.

Ingham put his head down on his forearms. The camel-driver had settled himself under robes next to one of his camels, and might be asleep by now. He was out of hearing, and probably could not understand English, but Ingham disliked his closeness. Ingham stood up as Jensen came back. 'Let's walk a little bit away,' Ingham said.

Jensen took his flashlight. It was very dark when they left the cooking-stove. The flashlight's beam bobbed on the irregular ripples of sand before them. Ingham imagined the ripples mountains, hundreds of feet high, imagined that he and Jensen were giants walking on the moon; or perhaps their actual size, walking on a new planet populated by tiny people to whom these ripples were mountains. They walked slowly, and both glanced behind to see how far they had gone from the palm trees. The trees were not visible, but the stove glowed like a spark.

Ingham plunged in. 'I had an attempted robbery at my bungalow a few nights ago.'

'Oh?' said Jensen, sounding English as he did sometimes, weaving a little in the soft sand. 'What happened?'

'I was asleep and I woke up when the door was being opened. I'd forgotten to lock my door. Someone started to come in. I picked up my typewriter and threw it as hard as I could. I hit the man right in the forehead.' Ingham came to a stop, and so did Jensen. They faced each other without seeing each other. Jensen's torch pointed at their feet. 'The thing is – I think I might've killed the man. I think he was the one they call Abdullah. You know, the old fellow with the turban and the red pants? The one who stole something out of my car?'

'Yes, sure,' Jensen said attentively, as if waiting for the rest.

'Well – I'd got behind my table, you see, as soon as I heard someone coming in. Then I grabbed the first thing to hand, my typewriter. He gave a howl and fell, and I shut the door. After a minute or so, I heard some of the hotel boys come and drag the fellow away.' A longer pause. Jensen wasn't saying anything. 'The next morning I asked one of the boys, Mokta. He said he didn't know anything about it, which I know isn't true. The point is, I think the Arab was dead and they took him somewhere and buried him. I certainly haven't seen Abdullah since.'

Jensen shrugged.

Ingham sensed the shrug without actually seeing it.

'He could be recovering somewhere.' Jensen laughed a little. 'When was this?'

'The night of July fourteenth–fifteenth. A Friday night. That's eleven days ago. – I'd like to know for sure, you see. It was a hell of a blow right in the forehead. It bent my typewriter frame. That's why my typewriter's being repaired.'

'Oh, I see.' Jensen laughed.

'Have you see Abdullah lately?'

'I hadn't thought about it. – You know, he doesn't dare to walk in my little street, they hate him so there.'

'Really?' Ingham said weakly. He realised he did not

appreciate the information. He felt a little faint. 'Let's walk back. Another thing makes me think it was Abdullah. I saw him that evening around six near the hotel. And Adams also said he saw him by the gift shop on the road there. The same night.' Ingham knew these details bored Jensen, but he could not stop himself from saying them.

'Did you tell this story to Adams?' Jensen asked, and Ingham could tell Jensen was smiling.

'No, I lied.'

'Lied?'

'Well – Adams knows it was Abdullah. He knows since a couple of days, because of something he heard in the Plage. About Abdullah being gone, missing or something. Adams heard someone yell that night. Not only that, but one of the boys told Adams the Arab was on my terrace.'

'But where did you lie?'

'I told Adams I'd heard a yell, but I said I didn't know anything about it. I didn't even admit I'd got out of bed.'

'Just as well,' Jensen said, and paused to light a cigarette.

What do you think'll happen if he's dead? Ingham wanted to ask, but he waited for Jensen to speak.

Jensen took so long, Ingham thought he was not going to speak, or was thinking of something else – maybe because the story was so commonplace, it did not much interest him.

'If I were you, I'd forget about it. You can't tell what happened,' Jensen said.

It was vaguely comforting. Ingham realised he needed a great deal of reassurance.

'I hope you got him,' Jensen said in a slow voice. 'That particular Arab was a swine. I like to think you got him, because it makes up a little for my dog – just a little. However, Abdullah wasn't worth my dog.'

Ingham felt suddenly better. 'That's true.'

They lay down again, face down, faces buried in their sweatered arms for warmth. Jensen had blown the fire out.

CHAPTER FOURTEEN

It was Friday, July 28th, before they got back to Hammamet. They had visited the city of Medinine and the island of Djerba. They had roughed it in a small town with no hotel, sleeping in a room above a restaurant where they had eaten. Ingham, like Jensen, had shaved every other day. In Metouia, an ancient town near Gabes where they stopped for coffee one afternoon, Jensen found a boy of about fourteen whom he liked, and went off with him, after asking Ingham if he minded waiting a few minutes. Jensen was back after only ten minutes, smiling, carrying a woollen mat with a black and red pattern. Jensen said the boy had taken him to his house, in no room of which had there been any privacy. Jensen had made him accept five hundred millimes, and the boy had stolen the mat behind his mother's back, in order to give Jensen something. The boy said his mother had woven it, but did not receive five hundred millimes from the shopkeeper to whom she sold her mats. 'He's a nice boy. I'm sure he'll give the money to his mother,' Jensen said. The story lingered in Jensen's mind, pleasantly. What had the mother thought of Jensen's coming home with her son, or did it happen a couple of times a day? And what did it matter if it did?

When Ingham returned to his bungalow, the neat blue and white cleanliness seemed to have a personality of its own, to be on guard, and to hold something unhappy. Absurd, Ingham thought. He simply hadn't seen anything comfortable for five solid days. But the distaste for the bungalow persisted. There were four or five letters, only two of which interested him: a contract by his agent for a Norwegian edition of *The Game of 'If'*, and a letter from Reggie

Muldaven, a friend in New York. Reggie was a free-lance journalist, married, with a small daughter, and he was working on a novel. He asked Ingham how long he was going to be in Tunisia, and what was he doing there since Castlewood's suicide? *How is Ina? I haven't seen her in a month or so, and I only said hello in a restaurant that time. . . .* Reggie knew Ina pretty well, however, well enough to have rung her and talked with her. Ingham was sure Reggie was being diplomatic in saying nothing more about her. Ingham felt sure that people like Reggie would have heard about John's relationship with Ina. People always wanted to know the reasons for a suicide, and kept asking questions until they found out.

Ingham unpacked, showered and shaved. He moved slowly, thinking of other things. He was to pick up Jensen at eight o'clock, and they were going to have dinner in the hotel dining-room. It was now six-thirty.

He remembered the letter he owed to Ina, and when he had dressed, he sat down and began it in longhand, not that he was in the mood, but because he did not want it hanging over his head any longer.

July 28, 19—

Dear Ina,

Yes, your letter was rather a surprise. I had not known things had gone so far, shall we say. But no hard feelings here. Typewriter is being repaired, so I don't write this with my usual ease.

Of course I don't see why we shouldn't see each other again, if we both wish to. And of course I understand that, from your point of view, I perhaps seemed lukewarm. I was cautious, no doubt about that. I have a past, you're familiar with it, and it wasn't and hasn't been easy to get through – I mean this past year and a half until I met you and began to love you. And when was that? Nearly a year ago. The whole time, now a year and eight months (since my divorce) seems a sort of prolonged nightmare without sleep (matter of fact I did not sleep well for nearly a year, as I've told you, and even after meeting *you*) but I hate to think what it would have been if I had not met you at all. You at least lifted me back among the living, you lifted my morale more than I can ever say. You made me realise that someone could care for me again, and that I could care for someone. I'll always be grateful. You might even have saved my life, who knows, because even though I was able to work always, I was going downhill mentally, losing a little weight and so forth. How long could that have lasted?

That was not bad, Ingham thought, and it was certainly sincere. He continued:

I've just got back from a five-day trip south in the car. Gabes (oasis), camel rides, the island of Djerba. Much desert. It changes one's thinking. I think it makes people see things more clearly, or not so close up. More *simply*, perhaps. Let us not take all this so seriously. Don't feel guilty for what happened. If you'll forgive me, I must tell you that I was laughing one night at the thought that: 'John sacrificed his love for Ina on the altar of Howard's bed.' Somehow this had me in stitches.

He was interrupted by a knock. It was OWL.

'Well, hello! Greetings!' Ingham said as heartily as OWL usually greeted him.

'Greetings to you! When did you get back? I saw your car.'

'Around five. Come in and have a drink.'

'No, you're working.'

'I'm only writing a letter.' Ingham persuaded Adams in, then at once became aware of his absent typewriter. 'Sit down somewhere. Anywhere.' Ingham went into the kitchen. He was glad the boys had not cut the refrigerator off, so there was ice.

'Whereabouts did you go?' Adams asked.

Ingham told him, and told about the freezing night on the desert, when he had got up at 5 a.m. and stomped around to get warm.

'By the way, I went with Anders Jensen, the Danish fellow.'

'Oh, did you? Is he a nice fellow?'

Ingham didn't know what Adams meant by 'nice'. Maybe

it included Jensen's politics. 'He's good company,' Ingham said. 'He still can't find his dog. He's sure the Arabs got him, and he's a little bitter about that. I can't blame him.'

It got to be seven-thirty. Ingham replenished Adams's drink, then his own. 'I'm meeting Anders at eight and we're going to have dinner at the hotel. Would you like to join us, Francis?'

OWL brightened. 'Why, yes, thanks.'

Ingham and Jensen found Adams in the hotel bar a little after eight o'clock. They stood at the bar and had a Scotch. Ingham noticed that the cash register showed the alarming figure of 480.00. A bang from a waiter, and the figure jumped to 850.00. Ingham leaned closer and saw that the register had been made in Chicago. It was registering millimes, and the dollar sign had been removed.

Jensen and OWL chatted pleasantly. Ingham had asked Jensen if everything had been all right at his house, and everything had, except that there was no news about his dog. Jensen said he had spoken to the Arab people next door, with whom he was on good terms.

Jensen ate like a starved wolf, though his table manners, in this ambience, were perfect. They had *kebab tunisien*, kidneys on a skewer. Ingham ordered a second bottle of rosé. The blonde Frenchwoman and her small son were still here, Ingham noticed, but otherwise most of the people had changed since he had last been in the dining-room.

'There's still no sign of Abdullah,' Adams said to Ingham in a lull in the conversation.

'And *tant – mieux*,' Jensen said firmly.

'Oh, you know about Abdullah?' Adams asked.

Ingham and Jensen were opposite each other. Adams sat at one end of the table, between them, partly in the path of waiters.

'Howard told me the story,' Jensen said.

Ingham shifted and kicked Jensen deliberately with his right foot under the table, but since Adams looked quickly at Ingham at this moment, Ingham was not sure he had not kicked Adams.

'Yes, you know it happened right outside Howard's bungalow. I think the fellow was killed,' Adams said to Jensen.

Jensen gave Ingham a quick, amused glance. 'And so what? One less thief in this town. Plenty more to go.'

'Well—' Adams tried to smile with good humour. 'He was still a human being. You can't just—'

'That could be debated,' Jensen said. 'What makes a human being? The fact something walks on two legs instead of four?'

'Why, no. Not merely,' Adams said. 'There's the brain.'

Jensen said calmly, buttering yet another bit of bread, 'I think Abdullah used his exclusively for thinking about how to get his hands on other people's property.'

Adams managed a chuckle. 'That doesn't make him any less a human being.'

'Any *less*? Why not? It makes him exactly that,' Jensen replied.

'If we started figuring that way, we'd just kill everybody who annoyed us,' Adams said. 'That wouldn't quite do, as the English say.'

'The nice thing is, half the time they manage to get themselves killed, one way or another. Do you know Abdullah couldn't even walk in the little street where I live? The Arabs chased him out with stones. You call him a loss? That walking bag of rags and—' Jensen couldn't think of a word. '*Merde,*' he said finally.

Ingham glanced at Jensen, trying to convey that he didn't want Jensen to go too far. Jensen knew that, of course, but Ingham could practically feel the heat of Jensen's boiling blood across the table.

'*All* people can be improved, given a chance at a new way of life,' said OWL.

'If you'll forgive me, I won't be alive to see much of it, and while I'm here I prefer to trust to my own experience and my own eyes,' said Jensen. 'When I came here about a year ago, I had quite a wardrobe. I had suitcases, cuff-links, a good easel. I was renting a private house in Sidi Bou Said, that picturesque, immaculate little village of blue and white houses' – Jensen waved a hand airily – 'noted for delicately wrought bird-cages, for its coffee-houses where you can't get an honest drink for love nor money, a town where you can't buy a bottle of wine in a shop. They cleaned me out there, even took a lot of my landlord's furniture. All my canvases. I wonder what they did with them? After that, I decided to live like a beatnik, and maybe I wouldn't get robbed again.'

'Oh, bad luck,' said Adams sympathetically. 'Your dog. – He didn't guard the house?'

'Hasso at that time was at a vet's in Tunis. Somebody had thrown hot water on his back. He was in pain, and I wanted to make sure the hair would grow back. – Oh, no, I don't think these mongrels would come into any house if Hasso was there. They knew he was gone for a few days.'

'Good God,' Ingham said. The story depressed him. No use asking if Jensen ever found out who robbed him, Ingham supposed. No one ever found out.

'You cannot fight or change an enormous tide,' Jensen said with a sigh. 'You must give it up, become reconciled. And yet I am human enough – yes, *human* – to be glad when one of them gets what he gave. I mean Abdullah.'

OWL looked a little squelched. 'Yes. Well, maybe the boys at the hotel did finish him off. But—' Adams glanced at Ingham. 'That night, the boys didn't leave their bunks until they heard someone yell. I think he was killed by that one blow, whatever it was.'

A blow now, not a bump. An insane amusement, perhaps caused by tension, made Ingham set his teeth.

'Maybe one of his own people stabbed him,' Jensen said and gave a titter. 'Maybe two Arabs were after the same house!' Now Jensen sat sideways, threw an arm over the back of his chair, and laughed. He was looking at Adams.

Adams looked surprised. 'What do you know about it?' Adams asked. 'Do you know something?'

'I don't think I would say if I did,' Jensen said. 'And do you know why? Because it just – doesn't – matter.' With the last two words, he tapped a cigarette on the table, then lit it. 'We speculate about Abdullah's death as if he were President Kennedy. I don't think he's quite that important.'

This quietened Adams, but it was a resentful silence, Ingham could tell. Jensen daydreamed and brooded, speaking, when he did speak, in monosyllables. Ingham was sorry

Jensen had made his personal resentments seem resentments against Adams. And Ingham felt that Adams had guessed that he had told Jensen something about that night that he had not told to Adams. Adams knew, too, that Ingham was essentially in accord with Jensen's outlook on life, which was not exactly OWL in nature.

They drove to the Plage in Ingham's car. Ingham had thought Adams would prefer to say good night when they left the Reine's dining-room, but he did not. Jensen now stood the drinks.

'A bitter young man. It's too bad all that happened to him,' Adams said when Jensen was at the bar ordering.

They were sitting at a table. Again, it was hard to talk in the place. Livened by wine and beer, the shouted conversations now and then exploded in startling whoops and roars.

'I'm sure he'll get over it – when he gets back to Denmark.'

Ingham had thought Jensen might ask Adams to come to his house and see his paintings, but Jensen did not. Adams would have come, Ingham was sure. They left after the single round of drinks.

'I'll be seeing you!' Ingham said to Jensen on the road.

'A bientôt. Thank you very much for dinner. Good night, Francis.'

'Good night, good night,' said Adams.

Silence as they drove back to the Reine. Ingham felt Adams's thoughts turning. Ingham put his car up near Adams's bungalow. Adams asked if he would like to come in for a nightcap.

'I think I'm a little tired tonight, thanks.'

'I'd sort of like to speak with you for a minute.'

Ingham came with him. The bungalow headquarters was silent and dark. The side door, where the kitchen was, stood open for air. To the left of the kitchen was the room where ten or twelve boys slept. Ingham declined another drink, but he sat down, on the edge of the sofa this time, elbows on his knees. Adams lit a cigarette and walked slowly up and down.

'I just have the feeling, if you'll forgive me – that you're not telling the truth about that night. You *needn't* forgive me for asking, if you don't want to.' He smiled, not so pouchily, and in fact it was not a real smile. 'I've been frank with you, you know, about my tapes. You're the only person in Tunisia who knows. Because you're a writer and an intellectual and an honest man.' He cocked his head for emphasis.

Ingham disliked being called an intellectual. He was silent, and for too long, he felt.

'First of all,' Adams said, ever so gently, 'It's funny you wouldn't have opened your door or at least listened that night after hearing that yell. And since it was on your terrace – what am I supposed to think?'

Ingham sat back. There was a comfortable pillow to lean back against, but he did not feel comfortable. He felt he was fighting a silly duel. What Adams said was true. He couldn't continue lying without obviously lying. Ingham wished very much he could claim some kind of diplomatic immunity for the moment, put off an answer at least until tomorrow. His real problem was, he did not know the importance of whatever he might say. If he told the truth, for instance, would Adams say anything to the police? What would happen then? 'I forgive you for asking,' Ingham began, a statement whose falseness he realised as soon as he had uttered it. He could have gone on, *Do you mind if I reserve the right. . . . After all, you're not the police.* 'It happened that night as I told you. You can call me a coward for not opening the door, I suppose.'

Now Adams's smile was paunchy, the shiny little squirrel again. 'I simply don't believe you – if you'll forgive me,' he said, even more gently. 'You can trust me. I want to *know.*'

Ingham felt his face grow warm. It was a combination of anger and embarrassment.

'I can see you're not telling the whole story. You'll feel better if you tell me,' Adams said. 'I know.'

Ingham had a brief impulse to jump up and sock him. Was he a Father Confessor? Or just an old snoop? Holier-than-thou, whatever he was. 'If you'll forgive me,' Ingham said, 'I don't see I'm under any obligation to tell you anything. Why are you quizzing me?'

Adams chuckled. 'No, Howard, you're not under an obligation. But you can't throw off your American heritage just because you've spent a few weeks in Africa.'

'American heritage?'

'You can't laugh it off, either. You weren't brought up like these Arabs.'

'I didn't say I was.'

Adams went to the kitchen.

Ingham stood up and followed him. 'I really don't want a drink, thanks. If I may, I'll use your john.'

'Go ahead! Just here to the right,' Adams said, happy to be able to offer something. He put on the light.

Ingham had never been in Adams's bathroom before. He faced a mirror, and rather than look at himself, opened the medicine cabinet and stared into it as he made use of the toilet. Toothpaste, shaving cream, aspirin, Entero-Vioform, a lot of little bottles with yellow pills. Everything neat as an old maid. The tubes of things had American brand names like Colgate's, Squibb's and so forth. Jensen wouldn't take this load of crap, Ingham told himself, and he flushed the toilet and left the bathroom with a self-assured air. By load of crap, he meant his American heritage. Just precisely what did that mean?

Adams was seated in the straight chair at his desk, but turned sideways so that he faced Ingham, who was again on the sofa. 'The reason I sound so positive,' Adams began affably, smiling a little; his bluish eyes terribly alert now, 'is because I talked with the people in the cottage behind you. They're French, a middle-aged couple. They heard the yell that night – and a clatter of some kind like something falling, and then they heard a door slam. Your door. – It must've been you who closed it.'

Ingham shrugged. 'Why not somebody in another bungalow?'

'They're positive where the sound came from.' Adams was using the dogged, argumentative tone that Ingham had heard on his tapes. 'Did you hit him with something that made a clatter?'

Ingham now felt only a faint warmth in his cheeks. He thought he was as deadpan as a corpse. 'Is there any *purpose* in your asking me all this? Why?'

'I like to know the truth about a story. I think Abdullah's dead.'

And he's not Kennedy, Ingham thought. Should he stick to his story and continue to be heckled by Adams (the alternative seemed to be to leave Hammamet), or tell the truth, suffer the shame of having lied, defy Adams to do anything about it, and at least have the satisfaction of having told the truth? Ingham chose the latter course. Or should he wait until tomorrow? He'd had a few drinks, and was he making the right decision? Ingham said, 'I've told you what happened, Francis.' He smiled a little at Adams. But at least it was a real smile. Ingham was amused, and as yet he did not dislike Francis J. Adams. And his smile widened as a funny possibility crossed his mind: could it be that some very rich man – of Communist persuasion – was paying OWL his stipend for his weekly broadcasts just for a joke, a joke that he could afford? Some man who didn't live in Russia? Because certainly OWL's broadcasts helped the Russians. Adams's earnestness made this possibility all the more hilarious to Ingham.

'What's amusing?' Adams asked, but he asked it pleasantly.

'Everything. Africa does turn things upside down. You can't deny that. Or are you – immune to it?' Ingham stood up. He wanted to leave.

'I'm not immune to it. It's a contrast to one's – home-spun morals, shall we say. It doesn't change them or destroy them. Oh, no! If you would only realise it, it makes us hang on all the harder to our proven principles of right and wrong. They're our anchors in the storm. They're our backbone. They *cannot* be shed, even if we wished.'

An anchor for a backbone! Was that one's ass? Ingham had not the faintest idea what to say, though he wanted to be polite as he left. 'You're probably right – I must go, Francis. So I'll say good night.'

'Good night, Howard. And sleep well.' There was no sarcasm in the 'sleep well'.

They shook hands.

CHAPTER FIFTEEN

The next morning was Saturday, the day when Ingham could get his typewriter. Ingham was at the post office at a quarter to ten, and dropped Ina's letter into the box. Then he walked to Jensen's house, this time avoiding a glance at the spot where the dead Arab had lain.

Jensen was not up, but at last he stuck his head out of the window. 'I'll open the door!'

Ingham walked into the little cement court. 'I'm going to Tunis to pick up my typewriter. Can I get anything for you?'

'No, thanks. I can't think of anything.'

Jensen had bought some painting supplies in Sousse, Ingham remembered. 'I was wondering if I could find a place like yours to rent in Hammamet. Do you know of anything?'

Jensen took a few seconds to let this sink in. 'You mean a couple of rooms somewhere? Or a house?'

'A couple of rooms. Something Arab. Something like you've got.'

'I can ask. Sure, Howard. I'll ask this morning.'

Ingham said he would look in when he came back from Tunis. He wanted to tell Jensen about his conversation with Adams last night.

His typewriter was ready. They had kept the old frame, its brown paint worn at the corners down to the steel. Ingham was so pleased, he did not mind the bill, which he thought a bit excessive, seven dinars or slightly more than fourteen dollars. He tried the machine on a piece of paper in the shop. It was his old typewriter, as good as ever. Ingham thanked the man in the shop, and walked out to his car, happily weighted again.

He was back in Hammamet before twelve-thirty. He had bought newspapers, *Time*, *Playboy*, tins of smoked oysters, potted ham, and Crosse & Blackwell soups. Jensen was in the alley, straightening a bent garbage can, presumably his own, with a foot.

'Come in,' Jensen said. 'I've got some cold beer for us.'

Jensen had the beer in a bucket of water. They sat in his bedroom.

'There's a house a quarter of a kilometre this way,' Jensen said, pointing in the Tunis direction, 'but there's nothing in it, and I wouldn't trust the owner to put anything in it, no matter what he says. There's a sink, but no loo. Workmen still creeping around. Forty dinars a month, I'm sure I can get him down to thirty, but I think that's out. Now the couple of rooms below me are free. Thirty dinars a month. There's a little stove there, about like mine, and there's a sink and a sort of bed. Want to see it? I got the key from old Gamal.' Gamal was Jensen's landlord.

Ingham went downstairs with Jensen. The door was just to the right of the hole-in-the-floor toilet, which projected from the wall. The larger room was next to the street, with one rather high arched window on the street. A door opposite the street led into a small square room with two windows, both on the tiny court – which had the virtue of not being overlooked, Ingham had noticed. This room had a good-sized sink and a two-burner stove on a low wooden table. The bed was a flush door, or so it appeared, with a thin mattress resting on three wooden fruit crates. Presumably white, the interior was not really white but grey with dirt, and tan in patches where the paint had been knocked off. A crumpled khaki blanket lay on the door-bed. There was an ashtray full of cigarette butts on the floor.

'Is any one sleeping here now?' Ingham asked.

'Oh, one of Gamal's nephews or something. He'll throw him out quickly enough, because he isn't paying anything. Is this all right or – is it too tatty?' Jensen asked with a facetious swish.

'I suppose it's okay. Is there any place where I could buy a table? and a chair?'

'I'm sure I can get something. I'll put the people next door on to it.'

So the deal was on. Ingham was optimistic. The bedroom door had a padlock that could be switched on a chain from inside to outside. His front door key would be the same as Jensen's. They'd have the same awful john, but as Jensen pointed out, it had at least a door, which Jensen had put on himself. Ingham felt a little safer being so close to Jensen. If something went wrong, if he had an invader, at least he had an ally within shouting distance. Ingham said he would like to move in on Monday, and he gave Jensen fifteen dinars to give Gamal to clinch the thing. Then Ingham drove on to the Reine.

It would be just his luck, Ingham thought, to run into OWL as he was taking his typewriter from the car to the bungalow. He even wanted to look around, from his car, and if he saw OWL to postpone removing the typewriter, but he felt ashamed of his queasiness, and at the bungalows' parking place stopped his car, and without a look around at all, opened the other door and took his typewriter out. He locked his car, then walked to his bungalow. OWL, evidently, was not around at the moment.

Monday would leave time, he thought, to give the hotel decent notice, to find a table and chair, and to write, perhaps another ten pages on his novel. Last night, oddly enough after his disturbing conversation with Adams, Ingham had thought of a title for his book, *The Tremor of Forgery*. It was much better than the two other ideas he had had. He had read somewhere, before he left America, that forgers' hands usually trembled very slightly at the beginning and end of their false signatures, sometimes so slightly the tremor could be seen only under a microscope. The tremor also expressed the ultimate crumbling of Dennison, the dual personality, as his downfall grew imminent. It would be a profound yet unrealised crumbling, like a mountain collapsing from within, undetectable from the outside for a long while – in fact until the complete crash – because Dennison had no pangs of conscience which he recognised as such, and hardly any apprehension of danger.

Ingham went over and spoke to the hotel, and asked them to make up his bill through Sunday. Then he went back to his bungalow and answered, in a rather gay tone, Reggie Muldaven's letter. He said he didn't know what Ina was up to, and that she had shown a strange disinclination to write to him. He said he had started a novel. And of course he expressed regret at Castlewood's suicide. Then Ingham worked and did eight pages between three and six o'clock, when he went for a swim. He felt, for some reason, extremely happy. It was pleasant, first of all, to have a little money, to be able to send a cheque for a rather expensive apartment in New York every month, to be staying at a comfortable hotel here, and to think nothing of the cost. Money wasn't everything, as OWL might say (or would he?), but Ingham had known the mind-pinching torment of being even slightly short of it.

He met Jensen by appointment at the Plage around eight o'clock, and they had a drink before going to Melik's. Jensen said the family next door had promised to find a table by tomorrow. A chair was a little more difficult, and they might have to scout the souk or buy or borrow one from Melik. Jensen had only one.

'Don't sit next to any English.' Ingham said as they climbed the steps to Melik's terrace. 'I'd like to talk to you.'

They shared a table with two shirtsleeved Arabs who talked constantly to each other.

Ingham said, 'What do you think? Adams went on with it last night. He said the people in the bungalow behind me heard the yell, plus a clatter, plus a door being shut. Slammed. Imagine OWL going to the trouble to quiz the neighbours? Like Inspector Maigret?'

Jensen smiled. 'What do you call him?'

'OWL. Our way of life. The American Way. He's always preaching it, or haven't you noticed? Goodness, Godness – and democracy. They'll save the world.'

The *couscous* looked better than usual, with more meat.

'Last night, I denied hearing anything except the yell,' Ingham went on. 'I denied having opened my door.' Jensen so patently took Abdullah's death as no more important than a flea's death. Ingham found that he could speak more lightly of it himself now, even practically lie about it with ease.

Jensen smiled, and shook his head as if in wonderment that anyone could spend so much time on such an unimportant matter.

Ingham tried to amuse Jensen further. 'Adams is trying the soft treatment, à la Porfyrivitch – or the English investigators. "I see that you're not telling the whole truth, Howard. You'll feel better if you do, you know."'

'What do the French people behind you say?'

'They've left. A pair of Germans there now, man and wife, I presume. – And you know, Anders, last night I was on the brink of telling OWL the truth? As you say, so what? What could he do? Gloat? Because he's solved a mystery? I don't think it would bother me.'

'He couldn't do a thing, not a thing. Are you talking about the machinery of justice? Bugger it. The last thing this country wants is to bring the thieves and the tourists face to face – in a court, that is. – Americans are funny.'

The next day, Ingham moved one suitcase into his new quarters, and he and Jensen went to the souk to buy a few things, a couple of bath-towels, a broom, some cooking-pots, a little mirror to hang on the wall, a few glasses, cups and saucers. The family next door had come up with a table, not very big but of the right height and sturdy. The chair was more difficult, but Jensen persuaded Melik to part with one of his for a dinar five hundred millimes.

On Monday morning, Ingham moved in. He had wiped the kitchen shelf down, so it was reasonably clean. He was not at all fussy. It was as if he had shed, suddenly, his ideas about cleanliness, spotless cleanliness, anyway, and of comfort also. A fruit crate was his night-table, the ceiling light his reading light, causing him to move the head of his bed under it, if he wanted to read in bed. His second blanket, the steamer rug, rolled up, served as a pillow. Any dirty clothes, Jensen told him, could be laundered by the 'teen-aged girl of the family next door.

On Monday and Tuesday, Ingham wrote a total of seventeen pages. Jensen lent him three canvases of Ingham's choice. Ingham had not chosen the disembowelled Arab, because Jensen seemed to like to live with it, and Ingham found it disturbing. He borrowed a picture of the Spanish fortress, very roughly painted, pale sand in foreground, blue sea and sky behind. Another picture was of a small boy in a jubbah sitting on a white doorstep, the boy looking round-eyed and abandoned. The third picture was one of Jensen's orange chaoses, and Ingham could not tell what it was, but he liked the composition.

Ingham went daily to the Reine's main desk and to the bungalow headquarters for post, though he had written his agent and Ina his new address – 15 Rue El Hout. Once he saw Mokta and bought him a beer. Mokta was amused and amazed that Ingham had moved where he had. Mokta knew the street.

'All Arabs!' Mokta said.

'It is *interesting*.' Ingham smiled also. 'Very simple.'

'Ah, I believe it!'

The air-conditioner Ingham had applied for had never appeared, Mokta had not mentioned it, so Ingham didn't.

On Wednesday, Ingham invited Adams for a drink. He gave one of Melik's boys a couple of hundred millimes in exchange for a tray of ice cubes. Ingham stood on the street to meet Adams and to guide him to the house. Adams looked around with interest as they walked through the narrow alleys. The Arabs had almost stopped staring at Ingham, but a few of them stared at Adams now.

Ingham had turned his work-table into a cocktail-table. His typewriter and manuscript, papers and dictionary were arranged neatly on the floor in a corner.

'Well! It's certainly simple!' Adams said, laughing. 'Practically bare.'

'Yes. Don't bother with compliments on the décor. I'm not expecting any.' He extricated what was left of the ice from the tray, put some in a couple of glasses, and put the ice back into the metal tray because it was cooler.

'How're you going to get along without a refrigerator?' asked Adams.

'Oh, I buy things in small tins and finish them. I buy a couple of eggs at a time.'

Adams was now contemplating the bed.

'Cheers,' Ingham said, handing Adams his drink.

'Cheers. — Where's your friend?'

Ingham had told him his apartment was below Jensen's. 'He's coming down in a few minutes. He's probably working. Sit down. On the bed, if you like.'

'Is there a bathroom?'

'There's a thing outside in the court. A toilet.' Ingham hoped that Adams wouldn't want to have a look at it. A few minutes ago, he wouldn't have cared, Ingham realised.

Adams sat down. 'Can you work here?' he asked dubiously.

'Yes. Why not? Just as well as at the bungalow.'

'You should be sure you get enough food. And *clean* food. Well—' He lifted his glass again. 'I hope you'll like it here.'

'Thank you, Francis.'

Adams looked at Jensen's orange chaos. It was the only picture of the three that was signed. Adams smiled and jerked his head to one side. 'That picture makes me hot just looking at it. What is it?'

'I don't know. You'll have to ask Anders.'

Jensen came down. Ingham gave him a Scotch

'Any news of your dog?' Adams asked.

'No.'

Their conversation was dull, but friendly.

Adams asked for how long Ingham had rented the rooms, and what they cost. There was no ice for their second drink. Jensen finished his second rather quickly, and excused himself, saying he was still at work upstairs.

'Any news from your girl?' Adams asked.

'No. She's just had time to get a letter of mine. Today probably.'

Adams looked at his watch, and Ingham suddenly remembered that today was Wednesday, that Adams had to be home this evening for his broadcast. Ingham was a little relieved, as he did not want to go out to dinner with Adams.

'I was in Tunis yesterday,' Adams said. 'Saw a nasty word written in Arabic on a tailor's shop – probably a Jewish shop.'

'Oh?'

Adams chuckled. 'I didn't know what the word meant, but I asked an Arab. The Arab laughed. It's a word that doesn't bear repeating!'

'I'm sure the Jews have a hard time just now,' Ingham said, feebly. The picture of 'Arabia Aroused' in the *Observer* one Sunday had been enough to scare the hell out of anyone: a sea of open, yelling mouths, of raised fists, ready to smash anything.

Adams got up. 'I should be getting back. It's Wednesday, you know.' He drifted towards the door. 'Howard, my boy. I don't know how long you're going to stick this out.'

He was near enough to the open door to have seen the toilet, Ingham realised. Jensen had just used the toilet, and he never shut the door when he came out. 'I don't find it bad at all – in this weather.'

'But you can't be very comfortable. Wait till you want an ice-cold lemonade – or just a good night's sleep! You seem to be punishing yourself with this – "going native". You're living like a man who's broke, and you're not.'

So that was it. 'I like a change now and then.'

'There's something on your mind – something bothering you.'

Ingham said nothing. Ina was maybe bothering him, vaguely. But not Abdullah, in case Adams was thinking of that.

'It's no way for a civilised man, a civilised writer to do penance,' Adams said.

'Penance?' Ingham laughed. 'Penance for what?'

'That's within yourself to know,' Adams said more briskly, though he smiled. 'I think you'll find all this primitiveness just a waste of time.'

And who was he to talk about wasting time, Ingham thought, with his hours of fish-spearing, never catching anything? 'I can't say it's that if I'm working, which I am.'

Ingham immediately hated that he'd begun to justify himself with Adams. Why should he?

'It's not your cup of tea. You're going against the grain.'

Ingham shrugged. Wasn't the whole country against his grain, wasn't it a foreign country? And why should everything he did be *with* his grain? Ingham said pleasantly, 'I'll walk down with you. It's easy to lose the way.'

CHAPTER SIXTEEN

In the next week, Ingham's thoughts took a new and better turn in regard to his novel. He was sure his change of scene, uncomfortable as his two rooms actually were – the worst was the lack of a place to hang clothes – was responsible for the jogging of his thoughts. Dennison, being mentally odd, was not to experience a collapse when his embezzlement was discovered. And the people whom he had befriended, nearly all of whom were responsible and successful men themselves now, came to his assistance and repaid whatever money Dennison had given them. Since Dennison had himself been investing embezzled money for twenty years, his appropriations had trebled. His infuriated employers at the bank, therefore, might have lost the earnings of three quarters of a million dollars over twenty years, but they could get the $750,000 back. What would justice do then? Therefore, the title *The Tremor of Forgery* wasn't fitting. It might almost do, but since Dennison never trembled to any extent worth mentioning, Ingham felt it wasn't right. It was Ingham's idea to leave the reader morally doubtful as to Dennison's culpability. In view of the enormous good Dennison had done in the way of holding families together, starting or helping businesses, sending young people through college, not to mention contributions to charities – who could label Dennison a crook?

Ingham was only sorry to part with the title.

Between paragraphs, Ingham often walked up and down his room in his blue terry-cloth robe, which he soaked in cold water and wrung out, over a pair of underpants. It was cooler than anything else. It also seemed less silly, in this neighbourhood, than shorts and a short-sleeved shirt. None of the Arab men wore shorts, and they must know the coolest garb, Ingham thought. Jensen had kidded him: 'Are you going to buy yourself a jubbah next?'

Usually Jensen had dinner with him, or he with Jensen upstairs. It didn't much matter, as they shared dishes and food, and the table situation was the same for both of them. One or the other had to clear away his work. Ingham liked eating with someone every night, it was a little thing to look forward to while he worked, and with Jensen he did not have to make an effort, either in cooking or conversation. There were evenings when Jensen chose to say hardly a word.

Ingham had some odd moments when he would be deep in his book and get up to walk about the room in his detestable but cool heel-less slippers. A transistor would be wailing somewhere, an Arab woman shouting at a child, a pedlar hawking something, and now and again Ingham caught a glimpse of his own stern face in the mirror he had hung on the wall by the kitchen door. His face was darker and thinner, different. He was at these moments conscious (as he had been when suffering the gripes at the bungalow) of being alone, without friends, or a job, or any connection with anybody, unable to understand or to speak the main language of the country. Then, being more than half Dennison at these moments, he experienced something like the unconscious flash of a question: 'Who am I, anyway? Does one exist, or to what extent does one exist as an individual without friends, family, anybody to whom one can relate, to whom one's existence is of the least importance?' It was strangely like a religious experience. It was like becoming nothing and realising that one was nothing anyway, ever. It was a basic truth. Ingham remembered reading somewhere about a man from the Eastern Mediterranean who had been taken away from his village. The man had been nothing but what his family, his friends, and his neighbours had thought he was, a reflection of their opinion of him, and without them he had collapsed and had a breakdown. And whatever was right and wrong, Ingham supposed, was what people around you said it was. That was truer than all OWL's blabble about the American Heritage.

It seemed to be OWL's point that one carried around a set of morals one had been brought up to believe in. But was it true? To what extent did they remain, to what extent could one act on them, if they were not the morals of the people by whom one was surrounded? And since this was not entirely off the subject of Dennison, Ingham would drift back to his typewriter and begin writing again almost at once. He had a bit more than two hundred pages. In his second week in his rooms, he enjoyed a good streak of work.

Then on a Friday, an express letter came from Ina. Ingham had not thought of her, in regard to getting a letter from her, for several days, but now he realised (rather automatically, out of habit) that she might have written him at least five days ago, if she had immediately answered his letter telling her his new address. He read:

Aug 8, 19—

Dearest Howard,

Your change of address was a surprise. You sound as if you'll be there for some time and I suppose that is what is surprising. Anyway you mentioned a month. I'm glad, by the way, the book is going well.

I am mopey and restless and it can't be helped, or I can't help it. Anyway, I thought I would fly over to see you. I have two weeks and I'm pretty sure I can wangle three. I want very much to see you – and if we both fight like cats and dogs, or if we both say it's all off, then I can go on to Paris. But you don't seem inclined to move from that place and I do want badly to see you. I have a reservation for Pan-Am flight 807, arriving Tunis Sun. Aug. 13 at 10.30 a.m., your time. A night flight. If you want me to bring you anything, wire me.

I hope this isn't too much of a surprise. I just couldn't go off to Maine or Mexico and convince myself I'd be enjoying it. I wish I could say something amusing. But here's one New York remark in case you haven't heard it: 'Some of my best friends are Arabs.'

I hope to see you at the airport in Tunis. If you can't make it for some reason, I'll find my way to Hammamet.

My love, darling,

Ina

Ingham was bowled over. He couldn't believe it for a minute. Ina here? In these rooms? Well, for Christ's sake, no, she'd flip. He would find her a hotel room, of course.

Sunday. Day after tomorrow. Ingham wanted to run up and tell Jensen. But Jensen had never heard of Ina.

'Damn it,' Ingham said softly, and walked around the table with the letter in his hand. He thought he should go at once to see about a room. August was a rather crowded month.

Ingham locked the street door lest the *fatma* – their vague cleaning girl who turned up more or less twice a week at any time that suited her – should come in now. He took a bucket shower in the vicinity of the toilet. The bucket was always under the tap, catching a drip. Ingham had tried to turn the tap on once, and found it so impossibly difficult, or perhaps it was already turned on full, that he had given it up.

'What's the hurry?' Jensen called from his upstairs window.

'Oh, was I hurrying?' Ingham slowed up, replaced the bucket under the tap, and walked casually into his room, drying himself.

Ingham got a room with a bath at the Reine de Hammamet for Sunday afternoon. Their last one, said the clerk, but Ingham doubted that. It was a double room, two dinars eight hundred with taxes and breakfast, for one. Ingham felt slightly better with that accomplished. He walked out to his car, not even bothering to ask for any post that they might not have forwarded.

That day he worked, but not with such concentration as usual.

It was Melik's that night. Ingham invited Jensen.

'Another contract?' asked Jensen.

'No. But I think I've got only two more weeks' work till I finish my first draft.'

It was not difficult, after all, to say that he had a friend named Ina Pallant, aged about twenty-eight, coming on Sunday. Jensen was not the kind to ask questions like, 'Is she a girl friend?'

Jensen said simply, 'Oh? What's she like?'

'She works for the Columbia Broadcasting System. Television. She's a script editor, also a writer herself. Very talented. Quite nice looking, blondish.'

'Has she been here before?'

'I don't think so.'

Then they talked of other things. But Ingham knew it was all going to come out when Ina was here. He was too close – also physically where they lived – for Ingham to hope to keep the essentials from him.

Ingham said, 'I think I told you that the man I was supposed to work with here – an American – committed suicide in New York.'

'Yes. You did tell me that.'

'Ina knew him, too. He was in love with her. She broke it off. So he killed himself. But they – From what Ina told me, John had been in love with her just for a couple of weeks. At least, Ina knew about it only a couple of weeks before he killed himself.

'How strange!' Jensen said. 'Is she in love with you?'

'I don't know. I honestly don't.'

'Are you in love with her?'

'I thought I was when I left New York. When she wrote me about John, she told me she'd been very fond of him – for a time. I don't know.' It sounded like a mess, Ingham supposed. 'I don't want to bore you. That's the end of it. I thought I'd tell you.'

Jensen bared his front teeth and slowly extricated a fishbone. 'It doesn't bore me. She must be coming here because she loves you.'

Ingham smiled. 'Yes, maybe. Who knows? I booked a room for her at the Reine.'

'Oh. She wouldn't stay with you?'

He laughed suddenly. 'I doubt it!'

CHAPTER SEVENTEEN

The Tunis air terminal presented a confused picture. Vital direction signs vied with aspirin advertisements, the 'Information' desk had no one at it, and several transistors carried by people walking about, warred with louder music from the restaurant's radio on the balcony, absolutely defeating the occasional voice of a female announcer, presumably giving planes' arrival and departure times. Ingham could not even tell if the announcer was speaking in French, Arabic or English. The first three uniformed (more or less) people he asked about flight 807 from New York referred him to the bulletin board where flights were announced in lights, but ten minutes after Ina's plane was due, nothing had been said about it. It wasn't like Ina to have made a mistake, Ingham thought as he lit his third cigarette, and just then 807 flashed on: from New York, arriving at eleven-ten. A bit late.

Ingham had a café-cognac standing up at the bar counter of the balcony restaurant. There were some thirty white-clothed tables and a buffet-table of cold cuts near the big windows which gave on the airfield. Ingham was amused to see two clusters of waiters, four in each group, chatting in corners of the room, while irate people half rose from their untended tables, clamouring for service. Ina was going to be entertained, no doubt of that!

He saw her through a half-glass fence or wall which he was not allowed to pass. Ingham raised an arm quickly. She saw him. She was in a loose white coat, white shoes, carrying a big colourful pocket-book and a sack which looked like two bottles of something. There was a passport check at booths on the left. She was only ten feet from him.

Then she rushed into his arms, he kissed her on both cheeks, then lightly on her lips. He recognised the perfume that he had forgotten.

'Did you have a good trip?'

'Yes. All right. It's funny to see the sun so high.'

'You haven't seen any sun till you see this one!'

'You look so brown! And thinner.'

'Where's your luggage? Let's get that settled.'

In less than ten minutes, they were in Ingham's car, the two suitcases stowed in the back.

'Since we're in Tunis – practically,' Ingham said, 'I thought we'd have lunch there.'

'Isn't it early? They fed us—'

'Then we'll go and have a drink somewhere. Some air-conditioned place. Do you think it's awfully hot?'

They went to the air-conditioned Hotel Tunisia Palace and had a drink in the plushy red bar-room.

Ina looked well, but Ingham thought there were some new lines under her eyes. She had probably lost sleep in the last days. Ingham knew what it would be like, winding up her office work, plus her tasks in the Brooklyn Heights household, which were formidable. He watched her small, strong hands opening the pack of Pall Malls, lighting one with the strange-looking matchbook from New York, dark red with an Italian restaurant's name printed on it in black.

'So you like it here?' she asked.

'I dunno. It's interesting. I've never seen a country like it. Don't judge by this bar. It might as well be Madison Avenue.'

'I'm eager to see it.'

But her eyes looked eager only for him, only curious about him, and Ingham looked down at the matchbook in his fingers. Then he faced her eyes again. She had blue eyes with flecks of grey in them. Her cheekbones were a trifle broad, her jaw small, her lips well-shaped, determined, humorous, intelligent, all at once. 'I took a hotel room for you in Hammamet,' he said. 'On the beach. Where I was first, the Reine de Hammamet. It's very pretty.'

'Oh.' She smiled. 'Your place isn't big enough? Or are you

living alone, by the way?' she added through a laugh that sounded more like her.

'Ha! Am I alone? What else? My place is small and definitely on the primitive side, as I told you. Well, you'll see.'

They spoke of Joey. Joey was about the same. There was a girl called Louise, whom Ingham had never met, who came to see Joey a couple of times a week. Louise and Joey were in love, in a crazy frightened way, Ingham gathered. It was very sad. Joey would never marry the girl, though Ina said Louise would be willing. Ina had told Ingham about Louise before. She was twenty-four, and this had been going on for two years. Now Ina only touched lightly on it, to Ingham's relief. He could not have embarked now on sympathetic remarks about Joey and Louise.

He took her to the restaurant on the other side of the Avenue Bourguiba, where the ceiling fans, and the patio beyond gave a certain sense of coolness.

'This is one of two restaurants that John recommended,' Ingham said. 'His recommendations were very good, all of them.'

'You must have been flabbergasted at the news,' Ina said.

'Yes, I was.' Ingham looked at her across the table. She had combed her hair in the hotel, and the marks of the comb showed in the dark-blonde, dampened hair at her temples. 'Not so flabbergasted as you, I suppose – finding him. Good God!'

She said it slowly, like a confession, 'The most awful moment of my life. I thought he was asleep. Not that I expected to see him there at all. Then—' She was suddenly unable to speak, but not from tears. Her throat had tightened. She looked into space somewhere beyond Ingham's shoulder.

He had never seen her like this. Surely part of it was the strain of the trip, he thought. 'Don't try to talk about it. I can imagine – Try this Tunisian starter. Turns up on every menu.'

He meant the antipasto of tuna, olives, and tomatoes. Ingham had persuaded her to have scallopine, on the grounds that *couscous* was all too prevalent in Hammamet.

They took long over lunch, and had two coffees and many cigarettes. Ingham told her about Jensen and a little about Adams.

'And that's all the people you've met?'

'I've met others. Most of the people here are just tourists, not too interesting. Besides, I'm working.'

'Did you hear from Miles Gallust, by the way?'

Gallust was the producer, the man who might have been the producer, of *Trio*. Typical of Ina to remember his name, Ingham thought. 'I had a letter in early July. He regretted and all that. I only saw him once, you know. Briefly.'

'So this trip is costing you something. Hiring a car and so forth.'

Ingham shrugged. 'But it's educational. John gave me a thousand dollars, you know, and also paid the plane fare.'

'I know,' said Ina, as if she knew quite well.

'The country isn't wildly expensive. Anyway, I'm not broke.'

Ina smiled. 'That reminds me. You know your story "We Is all"?'

'Of course I do.'

'It's winning a prize. First Prize for the O. Henry Awards. In the yearly prize story thing.'

'Really? You're joking!' The story had appeared in a little quarterly somewhere, after many a rejection.

'I'm not joking. I have a friend on the committee of judges or whatever it is, and he knows I know you, so he told me on condition I wouldn't tell anyone – else, that is.'

'What does that mean? A money prize or what?'

'Money? I don't know. Maybe just distinction. It *is* a good story.'

Yes, it was a good story, based on Ingham's imagining the life, or the periodic crises, of one of his friends in New York who was schizophrenic. 'Thank you,' Ingham said quietly, but his face was warm with pride, with a shyness born of sudden glory.

'Are you sure my luggage is safe in the car?'

Ingham smiled. 'Reasonably. But what a sensible question! Let's take off.'

When they drove off from the restaurant, Ingham stopped and bought some day-old papers and the Saturday-Sunday edition of the Paris *Herald-Tribune*. Then they drove on towards Hammamet.

'Are you tired?' he asked.

'I don't know. I should be. What is it? Nine in the morning to me, and I've been up all night, more or less.'

'Get some sleep this afternoon. What do you think of this view?'

The blue gulf was on their left, in full sunlight. It spread low and wide, and looked as if it covered half the earth.

'Quite terrific! And goodness, it's warm!' She had removed her white coat. Her blouse was flower-patterned and sleeveless.

At last Ingham said, 'Here's Hammamet!' and realised his joyous tone, as if he were saying, 'Here's home!'

They left the wider road – a trio of camels was strolling along the verge, but Ina did not seem to notice them – and rolled on to the dusty asphalt that curved into the village.

'This doesn't look like much,' he said. 'The town's mainly a lot of little Arab houses and fancy hotels, but they're all on the beach, the hotels. Ahead.'

'Where do you live?'

'To the left. Just here.' They were passing his street. Ingham saw Jensen between their alley and the Plage, heading for the Plage, no doubt. Jensen, with his back towards Ingham and his head down, did not see him. 'I'm sure you'd like to go to your hotel room before you see my place.'

'Oh, I don't know.'

But they were rounding the curve now towards the beach hotels.

'What a marvellous castle!' Ina said.

'That's an old fort. Built by the Spanish.'

Then they were at the Reine, going through the broad gates, rolling on to crunchy gravel between tall palms, bougainvillaea, and sturdy little grapefruit and lemon trees. It *was* rather spectacular! Ingham felt a surge of pride, as if he owned the place.

'This looks like an old plantation!' Ina said.

Ingham laughed. 'Massa's a Frenchman. Wait till you see the beach.' Ingham ran directly into Mokta as he was opening the front door. 'Have you got two minutes, Mokta?'

Mokta was for once empty-handed. 'Mais oui, m'sieur!'·

Ingham introduced him to Mlle Pallant, and explained that Mokta worked at the bungalows. Mokta got the key to number eighteen, and helped them with the luggage.

The room was lovely, with a window on the sea, and a door that went on to a good-sized whitewashed terrace with a curving white parapet.

'It's really terribly pretty!' Ina said.

The sun was sinking on their right, into the sea, and looked unnaturally huge.

'I'm dying for a shower,' Ina said.

'Go ahead. Shall I—'

'Can you wait for me?' She was unbuttoning her blouse.

'Sure.' He had brought the newspapers and wanted to look at them.

'So you're picking up Arabic?'

Ingham laughed. 'You mean what I said to Mokta? "Thank you, see you soon"? I don't know *anything*. What's so irritating is, words are spelled differently in different phrase books. "Asma" is sometimes "esma". And "fatma"—' Ingham laughed. 'I thought at first it was our cleaning girl's name, a form of Fatima. Turns out to mean "girl" or "maid". So just yell "fatma" if you want the maid here.'

'I'll remember that.'

A flowery scent of soap drifted out to Ingham, but it was not steamy. No doubt she was taking a cool shower. Ingham stared at the Paris *Herald-Tribune*.

Ina came out wrapped in a large white towel. 'You know what I'd like to do?'

'What?'

'Go to bed.'

Ingham got up. 'How nice. You know that was what I was wanting, too?' He put his arms around the towel and her and kissed her. Then he went and locked the door.

He locked also the tall shutters on to the terrace.

This time it was all right. It was like former times, like all the times with Ina. It erased the silly memory of the girl from Pennsylvania, and made Ingham think that that minor mishap had been due to the fact that he loved only Ina. She adored him. She was a lovely size in bed. Why had he been so insane all these past weeks, Ingham wondered. Why had he thought he didn't love her? They smoked a cigarette, then embraced each other again. And twenty minutes after that, Ingham could have begun all over again.

Ina laughed at him.

Ingham smiled, breathless and happy. 'As you see, I've been saving myself for you.'

'I begin to believe you.'

Ingham reached for the telephone. He ordered champagne on ice, in French.

'Aren't you going to get dressed?'

'Partially. The devil with them.' He got out of bed and put on his trousers. Then his shirt which he did not at once button. He had a malicious desire to ask, 'Was John any good in bed?' He repressed it.

Ina looked beautiful, hands behind her head, face sleepily smiling at him, eyes half-closed, satisfied. Under the sheet she spread her legs and brought them together again.

Ingham drew with contentment on his cigarette. Was this what life was all about, he wondered. Was this the most important thing? Was it even more important than writing a book?

'What are you thinking?'

Ingham fell down beside her on the bed and embraced her through the sheet. 'I am thinking – you are the sexiest woman in the world.'

There was a knock on the door.

Ingham got up. He tipped the waiter, then gave him a couple of dinars and a lot of change, which the waiter said would pay for the champagne.

'To you,' Ingham said, as he lifted his glass.

'To you, darling – and your book. Do you like it?'

'I suppose I like it or I wouldn't be writing it. It's a theme that's been done before, but—'

'But?'

'I hope to say something else, something different. – I'm not so much interested in the story as in people's moral judgements on the hero. Dennison. I mean people in the book. Well, readers, too. And in Dennison's opinion of himself.' Ingham shrugged. He didn't want to talk about it now. 'It's funny, of all the books I've written, you could say this is the least original yet it interests me as much as any of them have.'

Ina set her glass on the night-table, holding the top of the sheet over her breasts with the other hand. 'It's what you put into it. Not how original the theme is.'

That was true. Ingham didn't say anything. 'After another glass of this, I'll leave and let you sleep. We can have dinner as late as nine or so. Do you think you'd like dinner in the hotel or at a crummy – well, Arab place in the town?'

'An Arab place.'

'And – would you like to meet Jensen or would you rather be alone?'

Ina smiled. She was on one elbow. She had just the beginning of a double chin, or a fullness, under her jaw, and Ingham thought it charming. 'I wouldn't mind meeting Jensen.'

Ingham left the Reine in a glow of happiness, on the wings of success. And he had not forgotten the prize, the kudos or whatever it was, coming to him from the O. Henry Award thing.

CHAPTER EIGHTEEN

Jensen was out when Ingham got home at five-thirty. He was either at the Plage or taking a walk along the beach, Ingham thought. Ingham straightened up his rooms a little, gave them a sweep, then went out with the double purpose of finding Jensen and buying some flowers. Flowers in a vase, even if the vase was a glass, would look nice on the table, he thought, and he reproached himself for not having had flowers in Ina's room awaiting her. But how could he have known that the afternoon would turn out as well as it had?

Ingham was about to go into the Plage, when he saw Jensen walking slowly up from the beach, barefoot, carrying something that at first Ingham thought was a child: a long dark object which he held in both arms. Jensen plodded forward, blond and thin, like some starving Viking landed after a shipwreck. Ingham saw that what he carried was a big piece of wood.

'Hey!' Ingham called, approaching him.

Jensen lifted his head a little in acknowledgement. His mouth was open with his effort.

'What's that?'

'A log,' Jensen said. 'Maybe for a statue. I don't know.' He gasped and set it down. It was water-logged.

Ingham had an impulse to help him, but he was in a good shirt, and his mind was on flowers.

'Not very often one finds a nice piece of wood like this. I had to go into the water for it.' The legs of Jensen's levis were damp.

'I'm bringing my friend over at eight. I hope you can join us for dinner. Can you?'

'Okay. Sure. Do I have to get dressed up?'

'No. I thought we'd go to Melik's. – Do you know where I can pick up some flowers? Just a few cut flowers?'

'You can try the souk. Or maybe the jasmine guy's at the Plage.' Jensen smiled.

Ingham pulled his fist back as if to hit him. 'I'll be home in a few minutes,' he said and walked off to the left, in hopes of seeing a flower vendor sitting on the pavement between here and the little Hammamet bank. Ingham couldn't find any flowers, and gave it up after ten minutes. He twisted off a couple of pine twigs from the trunk of a tree by the beach, and at home stuck them in a glass of water. They looked insanely nordic. Once more, he put his typewriter and papers on the floor. Then he took off his shirt and trousers and flung himself on his bed and slept.

He awakened feeling happier than when he had left the Reine, though a little dopey in the head from the heat. He took a bucket shower in the court. He was now expert at saving the right amount of water to get the soap off. He might introduce the revolutionary idea of two buckets, since the one bucket was often overflowing. He had been correct, the tap didn't come on any further, but he could always draw water from the kitchen sink.

Ingham went to Melik's and reserved a table for between quarter to nine and nine o'clock. Then he drove on to pick up Ina. Ina was downstairs in the Reine's lobby, sitting on a big sofa, smoking a cigarette. She was in a pink sleeveless dress with a big, cool-looking green flower printed on the dress above one breast.

'I'm not late, am I?' Ingham asked.

'No. I'm just looking over the people.' She got up.

'Did you have a nap?'

'I had a swim *and* a nap. The beach is divine!'

'I forgot to say, you can get demi-pension here if you prefer. You might like lunch or dinner here, I don't know.'

'I don't want to be pinned down just yet.'

Ingham stopped the car in the usual place near Melik's, and asked Ina to wait a minute. He ran up the steps to the terrace. He had arranged to pick up ice. Then Ingham went back to Ina with the ice-tray, locked his car, and they walked into the first narrow alley.

Ina looked around, fascinated, at everything. And the Arabs, what few there were in the alley, or leaning in doorways, looked back at her, wide-eyed and faintly smiling.

Ingham stopped at his door, a door like many others, except that his was closed and most were open.

'I must say it looks like the real McCoy!' Ina said.

Ingham was glad the toilet door was not open. 'This is where I work. And also sleep,' Ingham said, letting her precede him into his room.

'*Really?*' said Ina, in a tone that sounded amazed.

'A little Robinson Crusoe, maybe, but actually I don't need any more than this.' His mind was on getting her to sit down in the most comfortable place – the bed. He now had a dark red pillow that one could lean against, but only if one slumped, as the bed was rather wide.

Ina wanted to see the kitchen. 'Reasonably neat,' she said, still smiling, and Ingham felt that his tidying had been worthwhile. 'And I suppose it's dirt cheap.'

'Two dollars a day,' Ingham said, coping with the ice now.

'And the john?'

'Well, that's just an outside thing. In the court. I have to wash here.' The ice fell into the sink and at the same time he cut his thumb slightly on the metal grill of the tray. 'Scotch and water? I have soda.'

'Water's fine. Whose paintings are these?'

'Oh, those are Anders's. Do you like them?'

'I like the abstract. I'm not so fond of the little boy.'

'I didn't tell him you liked painting.' Ingham smiled, happy that Ina and Jensen would have something to talk about. 'Here, darling.'

She took her drink and sat down on the door-bed. 'Oof!' she said, bouncing a little, or trying to. 'Not exactly springy.'

'The Arabs aren't much for beds. They sleep on mats on the floor.'

Ina wore pale green earrings. Her hair was shorter. It waved naturally, and she wore it without a parting. 'A strange people. And just a little frightening. By the way, were there any repercussions here after the war? Or during it?'

'Yes, quite a few. Cars overturned in Tunis, windows of the American Information Service library busted right in the middle of town. I didn't—'

Jensen appeared in the doorway, and knocked. He was in his green trousers, a clean white shirt.

'Anders Jensen, Miss Pallant. Ina.'

'How do you do,' Ina said, looking him over, smiling, not extending a hand.

Jensen made an abortive bow. 'How do you do, Miss – Ina.' He could sometimes look like an awkward, well-meaning six-teen-year-old.

'Fix you a stone,' Ingham said, going to the kitchen. Jensen was amused by the adjective 'stoned', and he often called a drink a stone. Ingham heard Ina ask:

'Have you been here a long time?'

Ingham brought Jensen his drink, a good big one.

They talked about Jensen's paintings. Jensen was pleased that she had noticed them, and that she liked the orange abstract. Ina did not mention her brother. Jensen said he was working now on a sand picture, inspired by the trip he and Ingham had made to Gabes.

'We slept out on the sand,' Jensen said. 'There wasn't any storm as in my picture, but one gets a very close view with one's eyes – at sand level.'

The conversation rolled on pleasantly. Ina's quick eyes took in everything, Ingham felt, Jensen's white leather shoes, their uppers perforated, his thin hands (yellow paint under one thumbnail), his profoundly troubled face that could look tragic and merry and tragic again in a matter of seconds. Ina's forehead grew shiny with perspiration. Ingham hoped there was a breeze on Melik's terrace. She fished a gnat out of her second, iceless, drink.

'The insects here are alcoholic,' Jensen said, and Ina laughed.

'At Melik's, it was *couscous*, of course. Ina thought the place charming. The canary was in good voice. There was also a flute, not too loud, and a breeze, faint but still a breeze.

'Are women *allowed* here?' Ina asked softly and Ingham laughed. 'They have such funny laws. Where are the women?'

'Home cooking their own dinner,' Jensen said. 'And these men – they've probably spent the afternoon with their girl friends, and after dinner they will visit other girl friends and finally go home – where their wives are also pregnant.'

This amused Ina. 'You mean, it doesn't cost much to have a lot of girl friends? These fellows don't look exactly affluent.'

'I think Arab women dare not say no. I dunno. Don't ask me,' said Jensen with a languid wave of a hand. He looked into space.

'Not wearing your cuff-links?' Ina said to Ingham.

Ingham was wearing very ordinary cuff-links he had bought in Tunis. 'I thought I wrote you. I had a slight robbery at the Reine. In my bungalow. They took my stud box with everything I had like that – all my cuff-links, a tiepin, a couple of rings.' The robbery had included his gold wedding ring, Ingham suddenly realised.

'No, you didn't mention it,' Ina said.

'Also a pair of shoes,' Ingham said. 'I was sorry about those cuff-links. I loved them.'

'I'm sorry, too.'

'You'd better – Well, it's perhaps safer in the hotel where you are,' Ingham said, 'but if you have anything valuable you might as well put it in one of your suitcases and lock it.'

Jensen listened, expressionless.

'Thanks for the tip,' Ina said. 'I'm pretty lucky, usually. But then I've never been in old Araby before. They're not famous for—' She smiled and looked at Jensen. 'What's the opposite of thievery?' She turned to Ingham. 'You mentioned a canvas jacket you'd lost. I know you're fond of old clothes, darling, but that thing – I remember it.'

'Yes. Oh, that was out of my car, a different matter.' Ingham thought of the old Arab in red pants, and shifted in his chair.

'That was Abdullah,' Jensen put in.

'You even know them by name?' Ina laughed. 'What a place! You must point out Abdullah to me sometime. He sounds like something out of the *Arabian Nights*.'

'We hope Abdullah is no more,' Jensen said.

'Oh, he got his come-uppance?' Ina asked.

'We hope so and we think so,' Jensen said.

'Did somebody knife him?'

Jensen was silent for a moment, and Ingham felt relieved, because it meant Jensen at least knew he should not blurt out the bungalow story. Then he said, 'It seems somebody defended their property for once, and knocked the bastard over the head.'

'How fascinating!' Ina said, as if she were listening to a synopsis for a television play. 'How did you hear?'

'Oh – via the grapevine.' Now Jensen laughed.

'You mean he was killed?'

'He simply isn't around any more.'

Ingham could feel Ina's lively interest in the story. She was about to say something else, when Adams appeared at the end of the terrace and stood looking around for a table. Ingham at once got up. 'Excuse me a minute.'

Ingham asked Adams to join them, and as they walked towards the table Ingham saw that Ina and Jensen were talking again.

'Ina,' Ingham said, 'I'd like you to meet my friend Francis Adams. Ina Pallant.'

'How do you do, Mr Adams.' Ina looked very pretty smiling up at Adams, shaking his hand.

'How do you do, Miss Pallant! How long are you going to be here?' Adams asked.

'I'm not sure. A week, perhaps,' she replied.

That was cautious, Ingham thought. He signalled to one of Melik's sons to come and take Adams's order.

Adams ordered in Arabic.

'You've been here quite a while, Howard told me,' Ina said.

'Yes, more than a year now. I like the climate – as long as one has air-conditioning. Ha-ha!' OWL smiled happily. 'But you've got to tell me all about the States. I haven't been home for a year and a half. All I read is *Time* magazine and the *Reader's Digest* and a paper from Paris or London now and then.'

'What would you like to know? I'm usually holed up in my office, then underground to Brooklyn. I'm not sure I *know* what's going on any more.'

'Oh – the racial thing. And the Vietnam War. And – well – the spirit, the atmosphere. You can't get that out of a newspaper.'

'Um.' Ina smiled a little at Ingham, then looked back at Adams. 'We're having another hot summer, as far as racial riots go. And the Vietnam War – well! I think the opponents are getting better and better organised. But I'm sure you read that, too.'

'And how do you feel, just as an ordinary citizen?'

'As an ordinary citizen, I think it's a waste of time, money and people's lives,' Ina said. 'Not a waste of money to everybody, of course, because war always lines a few pockets.'

Adams was silent for a second or two. His lamb dish was served. Ingham filled his wine glass.

'Are you in favour of the war?' Ina asked Adams.

'Oh, yes,' Adams said with assurance. 'I'm anti-Communist, you see.'

Ingham was pleased that Ina did not bother saying, 'So am I.' She simply looked at Adams with mild curiosity, as if he had said he was a member of the American Legion – which he might well be, Ingham supposed.

Jensen yawned widely, covering it with a large thin hand, and stared off into the blackness beyond the terrace.

'Well, we'll win, of course – even if only technically. How can we lose? But to talk of something more pleasant, what are your travel plans while you're here?'

'I haven't made any yet,' Ina replied. 'What do you suggest?'

OWL was full of ideas. Sousse, Djerba, a camel-ride on the beach, a visit to the ruins of Carthage, a lunch at Sidi Bou Said, a visit to a certain souk, in a town Ingham did not even know of, on its market day.

'I hope I can get around to some of these places by myself,'

Ina said. 'I think Howard wants to work. He doesn't have to entertain me.'

'Oh?' Adams smiled his pouchy squirrel smile at Ingham. 'After all your weeks of solitude, you haven't time to show a pretty girl around the country?'

'I haven't said a thing about wanting to work.' Ingham said.

'I'll be happy to drive you about a bit, if Howard's busy,' Adams told her.

'And I can show you the Spanish fort,' Jensen said. 'My trouble is, I have no car.'

Ingham was pleased that everybody was getting on well. 'But tomorrow is mine,' Ingham said. 'Maybe we'll go down to Sousse or something like that.'

They went to take coffee at the Café de la Plage. Ina loved the Plage. It looked 'real', she said.

When it was time to say good night, Adams insisted that Ingham bring Ina back to his bungalow for a nightcap. Jensen went home. OWL left in his Cadillac.

'Anders is a little sad these days because of his dog,' Ingham said. He told her what had happened.

'Goodness, that's too bad. – I didn't know they were mean like that.'

'Just some of them,' Ingham said.

Ina was enchanted with OWL's bungalow, as Ingham had thought she would be. Adams even showed her his bedroom. The closet was of course, closed, and Ingham knew locked, though the key was not in the door.

'A little home away from home,' Adams said. 'Well, I have no home any more in the States. I still own the Connecticut house.' He pointed to the photograph in the living-room. 'But practically everything's in storage now, so the place is empty. I suppose I'll retire there one day.'

After one drink, Ina said she was exhausted and had to turn in. Adams was instantly sympathetic, and had to figure out exactly what time it would be for her – 7.15 'yesterday'. He almost kissed her hand as they said good night.

'Howard works too hard. Make him get out a little more. Good night, both of you!'

When they were in the car, Ingham asked, 'What do you think of him?'

'Oh, a classic!' She laughed. 'But he looks happy. I suppose they always are. It's the best of all possible worlds and all that.'

'Yes, exactly. But I think he's a little lonely. His wife died five years ago. – I know he'd get a bang out of it if you'd spend a day with him – or part of a day, let him take you out to lunch somewhere.' Ingham meant it completely, but at once he thought of OWL telling her the Abdullah incident, the events of that night, and he felt uneasy. He did not want Ina to hear the details, even the few details Adams thought he knew. What purpose would it serve? It was only depressing and ugly. Ingham drove the car on to the gravelled area before the front doors.

'What's the matter, darling?'

'Nothing. Why?' Could she read his thoughts that well, Ingham wondered, in the dark?

'Maybe you're as tired as I am.'

'Not quite.' He kissed her in the car, then he walked with her into the lobby where she got her key. He promised to call for her tomorrow, but not before ten o'clock.

Jensen was still up when Ingham got home. 'She looks like a good sport,' was Jensen's comment on Ina.

That was probably high praise, from Jensen, Ingham thought, and as such he appreciated it.

CHAPTER NINETEEN

Ingham and Ina went to Sousse the next day, looked at the American battleship at the dock, and drank cold beer (it was frightfully hot) at the café where Ingham had once sat alone. Ina was fascinated by the souk. She wanted to buy some straw mats, but said she couldn't take them on the plane. Ingham said he would post them, so they bought four of varying sizes and design.

'Meanwhile,' Ina said, 'you can use them on your floors. Hang one on a wall. It'll improve the place!' She bought a big glazed earthen ware vase for him and a couple of ash-trays, and for herself a white fez.

The fez was extremely becoming.

'I won't wear it here. I'll wait till New York. Imagine! A good-looking hat for a dollar and ten cents!'

Ina's enthusiasm changed the country for Ingham. Now he enjoyed the toothy grins of the Arab shopkeepers, and the bright eyes of the kids who begged millimes from them. Ingham suddenly wished he were married to Ina. It could be, he realised. It was only for him to ask, he thought. Ina hadn't changed. John Castlewood might as well not have been.

'We could go to Djerba tomorrow,' Ingham said during their lunch. He had taken her to the best restaurant he could find, as she had said she didn't want to eat at a hotel, no matter how good the food might be.

'Your friend Adams is taking me somewhere tomorrow. Tomorrow morning.'

'Oh? He made a date last night?'

'He rang me up this morning just before ten.'

'Oh.' Ingham smiled. 'Okay, I'll work tomorrow then.'

'I wish you had a telephone.'

'I can always ring you. From Melik's or the Plage.'

'Yes – but I like to talk with you at night.'

Ina had rung him a few times late at night from her house in Brooklyn. It had not always been easy, because the telephone was in the living-room in Brooklyn. 'I could be there in person. – Can I, tonight?'

'All night? You don't want to be there for breakfast, do you?'

Ingham said no more. He knew he would go back to her room with her tonight. And not stay for breakfast.

The day went on like a pleasant dream. There was no hurry about anything. They did not have to meet anyone. They went to the Fourati for dinner, and danced a little afterwards. Ina was· a good dancer, but not very fond of dancing. Two Arab men, in neat Western clothes, asked Ina to dance, but she declined them both.

It was quite dark at their table on the open terrace. The only light came from the half-moon. Ingham felt happy and secure. He could sense Ina's question, 'Is it really the same as before? Have you really got no resentments?' and yet Ingham thought it wasn't the right thing for him to make a speech about it.

'What are you thinking?' she asked. 'About your book?'

'I was thinking I love you as much out of bed as in.'

She laughed softly, only a nearly silent breath, or a gasp. 'Let's go home. Well – to the hotel.'

While Ingham was trying to catch the waiter's eyes, she said:

'I must get you some more cuff-links. Do you think they have any good ones here? I'd like to buy Joey some, too.'

When he left Ina that night at a little after one o'clock, Ingham wished that he was sharing her room with her. He wished there might be a second room where he could work in the daytime, of course. Then he thought of his primitive two rooms awaiting him in the Rue El Hout tonight and tomorrow, and he was glad he had those. There was time, he thought. He realised he was a little giddy with fatigue and happiness.

He worked fairly well the next day and produced eight pages. But in his short breaks from the typewriter, he did not go on thinking about his book, but about things like, 'Would Ina stay on the two or three weeks she had, or would she take off for Paris after a week?' and 'Ought he to pack up and go back to the States when she did? If not, why not?' Or 'If he brought up the subject of marriage, just when should he do it?' and 'Shouldn't they have a more serious conversation (matter of fact, they'd had none) about John Castlewood, or was it wiser never to mention Castlewood?' He came to a conclusion only about the last question: he thought it wasn't for him to bring up, but for Ina, and if she didn't he shouldn't.

He rang her hotel from the post office at four-thirty, and she was not in. Ingham left a message that he would call for her at seven-thirty. She should be back by then, he thought.

'You're going out tonight?' Jensen asked when Ingham got back. Jensen was washing in the court.

'Yes. Unless OWL keeps her all evening. Want to join us, Anders? I thought we might go to Tunis for a change.'

Jensen hesitated as usual. 'No, thanks, I—'

'Come on, what's stopping you? Let's find a crazy place in Tunis.'

Jensen was persuaded.

Ingham went off at seven-fifteen to find Ina. He had a funny fan letter to show her which had come that day. A man in Washington State had written him about *The Game of 'If'*, which he said he had borrowed from his local lending library, and he praised the book highly, but offered suggestions as to how the ending could have been improved, and his ideas utterly demolished the theme of the book.

Ina was in. She asked him to come up.

She was dressed, putting on make-up in front of the mirror. He kissed her on the cheek.

'I asked Jensen tonight. I hope you don't mind.'

'No. – He's awfully quiet.' She said it like a criticism.

'Not always. I'll try to make him talk tonight. He's very funny sometimes. – There was a royal wedding somewhere, I think in his own country, and he got fed up with the papers being full of it and said, "Other people's sexual intercourse is always interesting to the public, but it's absolutely fascinating if the sheets have royal monograms." ' Ingham laughed.

Ina laughed slightly, still leaning towards the mirror.

'It's the dry way he says it. I can't do it.'

'He's queer, isn't he?'

'Yes. I told you. – Is it so obvious? I didn't think so.'

'Oh, women can always tell.'

Because homosexuals showed no interest in them, Ingham supposed. 'What'd you do with OWL today?'

'Who?'

'OWL. Our Way of Life Adams.'

'Oh. We went to Carthage. Took a look at Sidi – What is it?'

'Sidi Bou Said.'

'Yes.' She turned from the mirror, smiling. 'He certainly knows a lot. About history and things. And the coffee-house in Sidi is fascinating! The one up the steps.'

'Yes. Where they're all lounging on mats like Greeks. I hope OWL doesn't scoop me on everything there is to show you.'

'Don't be silly. I didn't come here for tourism. I came to see you.' She looked at him, not rushing into his arms, but it was more important to Ingham than if she had kissed him.

She was the woman he was going to marry, Ingham thought, and live with for the rest of his life. Ingham was about to break the spell – which he felt intolerably full of destiny' – by whipping out the fan letter, when she said:

'By the way, is that story about Abdullah true? That he got killed in the hotel grounds here?'

'I don't know. Nobody's got the facts, as far as I know.'

'But you heard him scream, Francis said. He said it was on our terrace.'

Had OWL mentioned the slamming door? Probably. Adams had perhaps told her about the French hearing something fall, too, the clatter. 'Yes, I heard it. But it was two in the morning. Dark.'

'You didn't look out?'

'No.'

She was looking at him questioningly. 'It's interesting, because it seems the Arab disappeared since that night. – Do you think another Arab killed him?'

'Who knows? – Abdullah wasn't liked by the other Arabs. I'm sure they're great at grudge fights.' He thought of telling her about the Arab with the cut throat, but decided against it, because it was a sensational story and nothing more. 'I saw something odd one night by the Café de la Plage. One Arab was a bit drunk. They pushed him out of the door. He stood on the sand a long while, just staring back at the door, with such a look of determination – as if he'd get the guy sometime, whoever it was. I'll never forget the way he looked.'

Ina's silence after a few seconds bothered him. He thought, suppose she finds out the truth, from Jensen, for instance? Then he would be a liar, and a coward also, in her eyes. Ingham had an impulse to tell her the truth before another half-minute went by. Was it so bad?

'You look worried.'

'No,' he said.

'How'd your work go today?'

'All right, thanks. – I love the new mats.'

'No use living like an ascetic. – You know, darling, if tha Arab was hacked to pieces or something, don't be afraid I'l faint. I've heard of atrocities before, mutilations and all that Was that what happened to him?'

'I never saw the guy that night, Ina. And the hotel boy won't say what they did with him. – Maybe Adams know something that I don't.' A vague idea that he was sparin her a nasty story sustained him a little. 'Let's go. I said I' pick Anders up.'

At his and Jensen's street, Ingham jumped out of the ca and ran towards the house. He was some ten minutes late though he knew Jensen wouldn't mind, and probably hadn noticed. Ingham shouted from the court, and Jensen cam down at once.

'Ina thinks you don't talk enough, so try to talk a littl more tonight,' Ingham said.

They went to the Plage, where Scotch was available, too. Jensen had his *boukhah*. Ina had tried it and did not like it. Ingham thought he was stared at more than usual that evening. Or was it because he was with a pretty woman? Jensen did not seem to notice the staring. Only the plump young barman was smiling. By now he knew Ingham.

'You enjoy your visit, madame? . . . Are you here for a long time?' the barman asked Ina in French. 'Not too hot?'

They were standing at the bar.

Ina seemed to appreciate his friendliness.

During dinner at Melik's, Jensen made an effort and asked Ina about her life in New York, and this got Ina on to the subject of her family. She mentioned her two cosy aunts, one widowed, one who had never married, who lived together and came to dinner on Sundays. She told him about her brother Joey, didn't dwell on his illness, but talked mainly about his painting.

'I shall remember his name,' said Jensen.

Ina promised to send Jensen a catalogue from his last exhibition, and Jensen wrote his Copenhagen address for Ina, in case he was no longer in Hammamet when she sent it.

'My parents' address, but I have no flat just now,' said Jensen, 'I'll be in touch with Howard, in case I leave.'

'I hope so,' Ingham said quickly. 'I'll leave before you, no doubt.'

Ingham did not like the idea of parting company with Jensen. Ingham looked at Ina, who was watching them both. Ingham thought she was in a rather strange mood tonight. The single Scotch had not helped her to relax.

'Do you go back to a job in Copenhagen?' Ina asked.

'I paint scenery sometimes for the theatres. I get along. But I'm lucky, my family give me a little every month.' He shrugged indifferently. 'Well, they don't give it, it's mine from an inheritance. No hardship to anybody.' He smiled at Ingham. 'I shall soon see what fresh blood has flowed into our bustling little port.'

Ingham smiled. He realised that with Ina gone, with Jensen gone, and with his book finished except for polishing and retyping, he would be insufferably lonely. Yet he did not want to set a date when he would leave. Unless, of course, he arranged something specific with Ina, made plans to be with her in New York. They might marry, might look for an apartment together. (His wasn't big enough for two.) It wasn't necessary for her to live for ever in the Brooklyn Heights house in order to take care of Joey, Ingham thought. *Something* could be arranged there.

'Would you like to visit the fortress tomorrow morning?' Jensen asked Ina. 'If you would like a walk along the beach it is not far from the hotel, especially if we break the walk with a swim.'

Jensen arranged to call for her at eleven o'clock. He left after coffee.

Ingham thought Jensen had done quite well that evening and waited for Ina to say something favourable, but she did not. 'Want to take a walk along the beach?' he asked. 'What kind of shoes are you wearing?' He looked under the table.

'I'll go barefoot. – Yes, I'd like that.'

Ingham paid the bill. Jensen had left eight hundred millimes.

The sand on the beach was pleasantly warm. Ingham carried Ina's shoes and his own. There was no moon. They held hands, as much to stay together in the darkness as for pleasure, Ingham thought.

'You're a little triste tonight,' Ingham said. 'Does Anders depress you?'

'Well, he's not the soul of mirth, is he? – No, I was thinking about Joey.'

'How is he – really?' It gave Ingham a twinge of pain to ask it, and yet he felt the question sounded heartless.

'He has times when he's so uncomfortable, he can't sleep. don't mean he's any worse.' Ina spoke quickly, then was silent a few seconds. 'I think he should marry. But he won't.'

'I understand. He's thinking of Louise. – Is she really intelligent?'

'Yes. And she knows all about the disease.' Ina's steps grew more plodding in the sand, then she stopped and flexed the toes of one foot. 'The funny thing – the awful thing is, he thinks he loves me.'

Her grip on his hand was light, no grip at all. Ingham pressed her fingers. 'How do you mean?' They were almost whispering.

'Just that. I don't know about sexually. That's ridiculous. But it seems to force anybody else out of his – affections or life or whatever. He should marry Louise. It isn't impossible that he could have children, you know.'

'I'm sure,' said Ingham, though he hadn't been sure.

Ina looked down at her feet. 'It doesn't exactly give me the creeps, but it worries me.'

'Oh, darling!' Ingham put his arm around her. 'What – what does he say to you?'

'He says – oh, that he can't ever feel for another woman what he feels for me. Things like that. He's not always mopey about it. Just the opposite. He's cheerful when he says it. The thing is, I know it's true.'

'You ought to get out of that house, darling. – You know, the house is big enough for you to get someone to live in, if they needs—'

'Oh, Mom could take care of him,' Ina said, interrupting him. 'Anything he needs – and it's really only making his bed. Matter of fact, he's done that several times. He can even get in and out of the tub.' She laughed tensely.

Yes. Joey had his own quarters on the ground floor, Ingham remembered. 'You should still get out, Ina. – Darling, I didn't know what was troubling you tonight, but I knew something was.'

She faced him. 'I'll tell you something funny, Howard. I've started going to church. Just the last two or three months.'

'Well – I don't suppose it's funny,' Ingham said, though he was thoroughly surprised.

'It is, because I don't believe in any of it. But it gives me comfort to see all those – greyheads, mostly, listening and aging away and getting some kind of comfort from it. You know what I mean? And it's just for an hour, every Sunday.' Her voice was uncertain with tears now.

'Oh, *darling*!' Ingham held her close for a minute. A great unspeakable emotion rose in him, and he squeezed his eyes shut. 'I have never,' he said softly, 'felt such a tenderness fo anyone as I do for you – this minute.'

She gave one sob against his shoulder, then pushed hersel back, swept the hair back from her forehead. 'Let's go back.

They began walking towards the town, towards the palel floodlit fortress – monument of some battle plainly lost, a some time, or else the Spaniards would be there.

Ingham said, 'I wish you'd talk to me more about it. Abou everything. Whenever you feel like it. Now or anytime.'

But she was silent now.

She must get out of that house, Ingham thought. It was cheerful-looking house, nothing gloomy or clinging-to-th past about it, but to Ingham it was now a most unhealth house. It was now that he should propose something positiv he thought. But it was not the moment to ask if she woul marry him. He said suddenly, stubbornly, 'I wish *we* live together somewhere in New York.'

Rather to his surprise and disappointment, she made n answer at all.

Only near his car, she said, 'I'm not much good tonigh Can you take me back to the hotel, darling?'

'But of course.'

At the hotel, he kissed her good night, and said he wou find her somewhere after her tour of the fortress wi Jensen. When he got home, Jensen's light was off, a Ingham hesitated in the court, wanting very much to wak him and speak with him. Then Jensen's light came on, Ingham was staring at his window.

'It's me,' Ingham said.

Jensen leaned on the sill. 'I wasn't asleep. What time is i he asked through a yawn.

'About midnight. Can I see you for a minute? I'll co up.'

Jensen merely pushed himself back from the sill, sleepi Ingham ran up the outside stairs.

Jensen was in his levi shorts, which fitted his thin fra loosely. 'Something happen?'

'No. I just wanted to say – or to ask – I hope you won't s anything tomorrow to Ina about Abdullah. You see, I t her the story I told Adams, that I didn't even open my door.'

'No. Well, all right.'

'I think it might shock her,' Ingham said. 'And just now she has problems of her own. Her brother – the one she was talking about who's a cripple. It's depressing for her.'

Jensen lit a cigarette. 'All right. I understand.'

'You didn't tell her anything already, did you?'

'What do you mean?'

It was always so vague to Jensen and so clear to Ingham. 'That I threw the thing that killed him – my typewriter.'

'No, I didn't say that. Not at all.'

'Then don't please.'

'All right. You don't have to worry.'

In spite of Jensen's casualness, Ingham knew he could count on him, because when Jensen had said, 'It just – doesn't – matter,' he meant it. 'The fact is – and I admit it – I'm ashamed of having done it.'

'Ashamed? Nonsense. Catholic nonsense. Rather, Protestant.' Jensen leaned back on his bed and swung his brown legs up on the blanket.

'But I'm not particularly a Protestant. I'm not anything.'

'Ashamed yourself – or of what other people might think of you?'

There was a hint of contempt in 'other people'. 'What other people might think,' Ingham answered. The other people were only Adams and Ina, Ingham was thinking. He expected Jensen to point this out, but Jensen was silent.

'You can count on me. I won't say anything. Don't take it so seriously.' Jensen put his feet on the floor in order to reach an ashtray.

Ingham left Jensen's room with the awful feeling that he had gone down in Jensen's estimation because of his weakness, his cowardice. He'd been truthful with Jensen, beginning with their talk on the desert. But it was funny how guilty he felt, how shaky with Jensen, though he knew he could trust Jensen even with a few drinks in him. Jensen was not weak. Ingham suddenly thought of the scared-looking, but flirtatious and seductive Arab boy who was sometimes loitering in the alley near the house, who always said something in Arabic to Jensen. Twice Ingham had seen Jensen dismiss him with an annoyed wave of the hand. Jensen had used to go to bed with him occasionally, Jensen had said. The boy looked revolting to Ingham, mushy, unreliable, sick. Despite all that, Jensen was not weak.

CHAPTER TWENTY

Ingham could not get to sleep. It was oppressively hot and still. After a bucket shower, he was damp with sweat again in a matter of minutes. Ingham did not mind. He was used to the discomfort by now. And his thoughts entertained him. He was thinking of Ina, and he was filled with tenderness and love for her. It was a large, all-enveloping feeling, taking in all the world, himself, all the people he knew, everyone. Ina was its centre and in a way its source. He thought of her not only as an attractive woman, but in terms of her background and what had made her. She had told him she felt neglected in her childhood, because Joey, being ill from birth, had captured all her parents' affections and attentions. She had tried to do very well in school (this was in Manhattan, where the family had lived then) in order to call attention to herself. She had finally gone to Hunter College and made excellent grades, majoring in English composition. She had been in love with a Jewish boy when she was twenty, a boy more or less approved of by her family (he had been a postgraduate student of physics at Columbia, Ingham remembered), but his family had made Ina feel uncomfortable, because they strongly disapproved, at the same time saying that their son had a right to lead his own life. Nothing had come of the love but a few months of heartache for Ina, and a slightly lower mark when she graduated than she would have got, she had told Ingham, if it had not been for the break-up. Before that, at fifteen, she had had a terrible crush on a girl a little bit older, a girl who was really queer, although doing nothing about it at that time. Ingham smiled a little at that, at the bitter suffering of adolescence, the loneliness, the inability to talk to anyone. Everyone had such experiences and somehow at twenty-five, at thirty, they became forgotten – like rocks in a stream which had to be swum over, causing pain and wounds, yet which the unconscious knew were to be expected, and so like birth pains, perhaps, the agony was not even vividly remembered. And then there was her marriage of a year and a half to that brilliant playwright Edgar something (Ingham was pleased that he had forgotten his last name) who had turned out to be a tyrant, who had drunk erratically, and had struck Ina a few times, and who had been killed in a car accident a couple of years after her divorce.

And now, Ina loved him, and she loved her brother Joey, and she had turned to the church for some moral support and perhaps for some kind of guidance. (How *much* had she turned to the church, he wondered.) But what kind of guidance did the church ever give except to counsel resignation? Stop sinning, of course, but if one were in an awful predicament with husband, family or whatever – or if the problem was poverty, for instance – the church's advice was to resign oneself to it, Ingham felt, and he was reminded of the Arabic religion, uncomfortably.

His thoughts veered away from that and returned to Ina. He was glad he and she were old enough to know the importance of tenderness, to have lost some of the selfishness and self-centredness of youth, he hoped. They were two worlds similar but different, complex yet able to explain themselves to each other, and he felt they had something to give each other. He recalled a few paragraphs he had written in his notebook, in preparation for the book he was writing, about the sense of identity within the individual. (As it turned out he had used none of them in his book, but it was always that way.) He wanted very much to read some of these notes to Ina, to see what she would think of them, what she would say. One note, he remembered, he had copied from a book he had been reading. It concerned under-privileged children in an American primary school. The children had had no joy in life or in learning. All of them lived in crowded homes. Then the school had given each child a small mirror in which he could see himself. From then on, each child

178

began to realise that he or she was an individual, different from everyone else, someone with a face, an identity. The world of each child had changed then.

All at once, Ingham felt acutely the pressure of Joey's tragedy on Ina now, the sadness his disease must cause in her whenever she looked at him – or thought of him – even in the best of moments. And now the mysterious and perhaps insoluble problem of Joey's attachment to her. This onus, this pain, was like something which crept up behind Ingham's back and leapt upon him, sinking its claws. He sprang out of bed.

He had an impulse to go straight to Ina now, to comfort her, to tell her that they would be married – maybe to *ask* her, but that was a technicality – to stay with her the rest of the night talking and making plans until the Tunisian dawn came up. He looked at his wristwatch. Eighteen minutes past three o'clock. Could he even get into the hotel? Of course, if he banged on the door hard enough. Would she be annoyed? Embarrassed? But what he had to say was important enough to cause a disturbance in the night. He hesitated. Wasn't it weak, even fatal somehow, to doubt whether he should go or not? Wouldn't he have gone if he'd been twenty-five, even thirty?

Ingham decided that he shouldn't go at this hour. If Ina had been in a house alone, yes. It was the hotel part.

He cheered himself up by thinking about tomorrow. He would see her at lunch. He'd tell Jensen he wanted very much to see Ina alone at lunch, and Jensen wouldn't mind. And then Ingham would talk about all this, and he would talk also about their marrying. He would fly back with her, or at least very soon after she left, and they would look for an apartment in New York and maybe in less than a month from now, she would be out of that Brooklyn house and living in an apartment in Manhattan with him. That was a very exciting plan. He went back to bed, but it was at least half an hour before he fell asleep.

Ingham awakened at nine-thirty, and found that Jensen had already left the house. Ingham had intended to offer to drive him to the Reine, though he doubted if Jensen would have accepted. Now he would have to keep an eye out for them, if he expected to see them before lunch, Ingham supposed. He worked in the morning, mainly polishing and retyping messy pages in his manuscript, but just before twelve-thirty, he wrote two new pages. Then he put on white dungarees and a shirt, and went to the Café de la Plage.

He was happy to see Ina and Jensen sitting at a table over glasses of vin rosé. 'Knock-knock,' Ingham said, approaching them. 'Can I crash in? Did you have a nice morning?'

They looked as if they had been talking seriously for some minutes before he arrived. Jensen dragged a chair over from another table. Ina's eyes moved all over Ingham – his face, his hands, his body – in a way that pleased him, and she was absently smiling.

'Is the fort interesting?' Ingham asked her. 'I haven't been inside.'

'Yes! Nobody there. We could wander around anywhere,' she said.

'Not even ghosts,' said Jensen.

It was soon evident Jensen was not going to leave. They went to Melik's, and all of them had yoghurt, fruit, cheese and wine, because it was too hot for anything else. Ina might enjoy a siesta, Ingham thought. He might go back with her to the hotel, and they could talk there. Jensen got the bill and asserted his right to pay it, as he had wanted to take Ina to lunch. Then he excused himself.

'I'm going to work for a while – after a nap, that is. Did Fatma turn up?'

'Not this morning,' Ingham said.

'Damn. If she turns up this afternoon, I think I'll send her away. Do you mind?'

'Not a bit,' Ingham said.

Jensen left.

'What's your Fatma like?' Ina asked.

'Oh – about sixteen. Always a big smile. She doesn't know much French. Her favourite activity is turning the tap on the terrace. She just stands there watching the water run and run. Sometimes we give her money to buy food and wine. There's never any change from it. Whatever we give her "exactly enough".' Ingham laughed.

Ina looked as if she were not listening, or was not interested.

'Tired, darling? I'll take you back to your hotel. It's so damned hot – I thought you might like a siesta. Maybe with me.'

'Do you think we'd sleep?'

Ingham smiled. 'I had some things I wanted to talk to you about.' He wished he'd brought his notebook along, but he hadn't, and he wasn't going to the house for it. 'Matter of fact, I almost came storming over to see you last night. At three-thirty. I even jumped out of bed.'

'A bad dream? Why didn't you come over?'

'Not a bad dream. I hadn't been to sleep. I was thinking about you. – You know, darling, you could come back to my place. We could have a nap there.'

'Thanks. I think I'd rather go back to the hotel.'

She'd be of course much more comfortable at the hotel, Ingham realised. But he had the feeling she disliked his place, maybe thought it sordid. He felt a vague defensiveness about his two rooms, even though she had not yet specifically attacked them. They were, after all, the sanctum of his work just now, and as such they were rather hallowed to Ingham. 'All right. Let's go darling.'

He drove her to the Reine de Hammamet. The desk clerk handed her a telegram.

'That's fast communication,' Ingham said, wondering whom it could be from.

'I cabled the office,' Ina said. 'This is from them.'

Ingham waited while she read it, watched her start to frown, and saw her lips move in an inaudible 'Damn'.

'I've got to cable something back,' she said to him. 'I won't be long.'

Ingham nodded, and went to look for a newspaper.

'What was it?' he asked when she was finished.

'It's about a copyright. I told them the story was in the clear, but they were still worried, so they asked me where to look. They want to check it. It's all very tedious.'

Ina took a cool shower, then Ingham asked if he could do the same. The cool, not too cold water felt like heaven. It was a treat also to be able to reach for Ina's scented soap in the niche, to slip it back. There was even a huge unused white towel which he appropriated.

'Ah, delicious,' he said when he came out in the towel, barefoot.

'You know, Howard—' She was lying on the bed, propped up, smoking. 'It'd be nice if you had a bungalow. Why don't we take one – or two?' she added, smiling.

Ingham emphatically did not want to take a bungalow. 'Well, you could – provided they're not full up. Did you ask?'

'Not yet. But your place is so uncomfortable, darling, let's face it. That john! And you're not broke. I don't know why you do it.'

'For a change. I got tired of my bungalow.'

'What's there to get tired of? Good kitchen and bath, everything simple and clean. Francis says you can get an air-conditioner.'

'I wanted to see how the Arabs live, buy stuff in the market and all that.'

'You can see how they live without doing it. It's bloody uncomfortable the way they live. I saw a lot of them this morning, walking with Anders back of the fort.'

'Isn't that a fascinating section?' Ingham smiled. 'The thing is, I'm working so well now where I am. I just think of it as a place to work, you know. I wasn't intending to be there more than a month.'

'Francis thinks you're punishing yourself.'

'Oh? I think he said that to me, too. Sounds strangely Freudian for OWL. Anyway, he's a bit wrong. When did he say this to you, by the way?'

'I ran into him on the beach this morning. Rather he hailed me – from afar. He was out in the water. I went for an early swim. So we sat on the sand and talked for a while.' She laughed. 'He looks so funny with those flippers and that spear, and that waterproof cap with a *visor*. Do you know he swims with it under water?'

'Yes, I know.'

She was silent for a moment, then, 'You know, he says you're not telling the whole story about that night Abdullah was killed. On your terrace, Francis says.'

'Um-hum,' Ingham said, sighing. 'First of all, no one knows if he was killed or not. No one's seen a body. – Adams is acting like an old maid snoop about this. Why doesn't he call the police in, if he's so concerned?'

'Well – don't get worked up about it.'

'Sorry.' Ingham lit a cigarette.

'Is that why you moved?'

'Of course not. – I'm still on good terms with OWL. I moved – because of something I wanted to discuss with you, matter of fact. Or tell you about. It has to do with the book I'm writing. Essentially, it's whether a person makes his own personality and his own standards from within himself, or whether he and the standards are the creation of the society around him. It has a *little* to do with my book. But I found that since being here in Tunisia, I think about these things a lot. What I mean is – the opposite of authoritarianism. And I speak mainly of morals – I suppose. My hero Dennison makes his own, you see. But granted he's cracked.'

Ina was listening in silence, watching him.

'There were moments here in Hammamet, days and weeks, in fact, when I hadn't any letters from you or from anybody, and I felt strange even to myself, as if I didn't know myself. And part of it, perhaps – I know from a moral point of view – was that the Arabs all around me had different standards, different ethics. And they were in the majority, you see. This world is theirs, not mine. You know what I mean?'

'And what did you do about it?'

He laughed. 'One doesn't *do* anything. It's like a state. It's a very troubling state. But in a way, it was quite good for my book, I think. Because it's concerned a little with the same thing.'

'I don't think my moral values would change, living here. I'd really love some plain iced water.'

Ingham went at once to the telephone and ordered it. Then he said, 'Not necessarily change, but you might find them hard to practise if no one around you were practising them, for instance.'

'Give me an example.'

Ingham for some reason balked, though there were any number of examples he might have given. Petty chiselling. Or having a wife and as many mistresses as one could afford, because everyone else was enjoying the same pleasure, and to hell with what one's wife felt about it. 'Well – if one's been robbed five or six times, there might be an impulse to rob back, don't you think? The one who doesn't rob, or cheat a little in business deals, comes out on the short end, if everybody else is cheating.'

'Hm-m,' she said dubiously. At the knock on the door, she waved a hand at him in the direction of the bathroom.

Ingham went into the bathroom. He stared at himself absently in the long mirror beside the tub, and thought he looked rather Roman. His hands were out of sight, clutching the towel from underneath. His feet looked absurd. He was thinking OWL as a bloody meddler. He had alienated Ina, just a little, from him, and for this Ingham detested OWL. If he told Ina about OWL's cock-eyed broadcasts, she would know what a crack-pot he was.

'All clear,' Ina called.

'Western behaviour,' Ingham said contemptuously as he came back. 'Any woman as attractive as you ought to have five men standing around her room in the afternoons.'

Ina smiled. 'But why does OWL think you're not telling the whole truth about that night?' She poured water into a glass.

Ingham went to get another glass from the bathroom. 'You ask him.'

'As a matter of fact, I did.'

'Oh?'

'He thinks you threw something or hit the Arab somehow. Did you?'

'No,' Ingham said firmly, after only a second's hesitation mainly from surprise. 'I know, he's got a door slamming, boys running around, all kinds of details about that night – considering he's a fair distance from my bungalow.'

'But it did happen on your terrace.'

'The yell I heard was near.' Ingham hated the conversation increasingly, yet he knew if he showed this, it would look a bit odd.

'He said the French people behind you heard a door shut, and they were sure it was your door.'

'The French people didn't speak to me about it. Nobody spoke to anybody about Abdullah's disappearance or anything else. Nobody's talking about it except OWL.'

Ina's appraising eyes on him bothered him. It was as if OWL had infected her with his own prurient curiosity, like a disease or a fever.

'That Arab might have got the *coup de grâce* from some other Arab,' Ingham said, sitting down in an armchair. 'OWL thinks the boys dragged him away and buried him somewhere. The hotel boys deny everything. They're hushing it—'

'Oh, no. OWL told me one boy said the Arab hit his head on something. They admitted that much.'

Ingham sighed. 'True. I forgot.'

'You're telling me the whole story. Are you, Howard?'

'Yes.'

'I have the strangest feeling you've told Anders something you haven't told me – or OWL.'

Ingham laughed. 'Why?'

'Oh, you're very close to Anders, face it. You practically live with him. I didn't know you got along so well with queers.'

'I don't get along with them or not get along.' Ina's words seemed stupid. 'I never think any more about his being queer. And by the way, I haven't seen a single boy at his place since I moved in.' Ingham at once regretted that. Was abstinence virtue?

She laughed. 'Maybe he's in love with you.'

'Oh, Ina, come off it. It's not even funny.' But to salvage something, the afternoon maybe, he forced a smile. It was a bad effort.

'He's very close to you – fond of you. You must know that.'

'You're imagining. Honestly, Ina.' How could they have arrived *here* in just a few minutes of conversation? He realized it was impossible to ask her this afternoon to marry him. All because of bloody OWL. 'I do wish OWL would mind his own business. Has he been farting off about Anders, too?'

'No, not at all. Darling, take it easy. It's just what I see for myself.'

'It's not correct. Have you got a bottle of Scotch?' She had given him one bottle.

'Yes, in the closet. Back right.'

Ingham got it. It had been opened, but only the neck of the bottle was gone. 'Like some?' He poured some into Ina's extended glass, then poured for himself. 'Anders and I get along, but there's nothing sexual about it.'

'Then maybe you don't realise it.'

Did she mean on his part, too? Were women *always* thinking about sex, of one kind or another? 'Then it's too damned subtle for me,' he said, 'and if it's that subtle, what does it matter?'

'You don't seem to want to leave him – to take a bungalow.'

'Oh, my God, Ina.' Was it usual for women to take homosexuals so seriously, he wondered. Ingham had always thought they considered queers nothing at all. Zeros. 'I've explained to you, I don't want to move, because I'm working.'

'I think the bungalows have a bad association for you. Is that true?' Her voice was gentle.

'Honey – *darling* – I've never seen you like this. You're as bad as OWL! You know me – but you don't seem to understand me at all any more. – You didn't make a single comment when I was trying to explain how I'd felt in this country, this continent, since getting here. Granted, it isn't of world-shaking importance.' Ingham felt his heart going faster. He was standing with his drink.

'Have you adopted the Arabian moral code, whatever that is?'

'Why do you ask that?'

'OWL said you told him that that Arab's life was of no importance, because he was just a D.O.M.'

That meant Dirty Old Man. 'I said he was a lousy thief

who a lot of people probably wanted out of the way.' Ask Anders, he's eloquent on the subject, Ingham wanted to say.

'Abdullah was the one who stole your jacket out of your car, you said.'

'That's true. I saw him. I just wasn't close enough to catch him.'

'You didn't possibly throw something at him that night like a chair – or your typewriter,' Ina said with a slight laugh.

Her smile was amused, reassuring, though Ingham knew he should not be reassured by it. 'No.' Ingham sighed, as if at the end of an intolerable tension. He wanted to leave. He met her eyes. Ingham felt a distance between them, a sense of separateness. He hated it and looked away.

'Was it Abdullah who took your cuff-links?'

Ingham shook his head. 'That was another night. I wasn't in. I dunno who took the cuff-links. – I think I should go and let you sleep.' He walked into the bathroom to dress.

She did not detain him.

When he was dressed, he sat beside her on the bed and kissed her lips. 'Want a swim later? Around six?'

'I don't know. I don't think so.'

'Shall I pick you up around eight? We could go to La Goulette, the fishing village.'

This idea pleased her, and since it was some distance away, Ingham said he would call for her at seven o'clock.

CHAPTER TWENTY-ONE

Ingham wanted to see Adams. It was four-forty-five, and Adams was probably on the beach. Ingham drove his car the quarter-mile to the sandy lane that led to the bungalows. The bungalows were silent and still in the sunlight, as if everyone were having a prolonged siesta. Adams's black Cadillac was parked in the usual place. Ingham put his car beside it.

He knocked on Adams's door. No answer. Ingham strolled on to the bungalow headquarters' terrace and looked down at the beach. Only three or four figures were visible, and none looked like Adams. Ingham went back to Adams's bungalow, walked to the back where it was shady, and sat down on the kitchen doorstep. Adams's grey-metal garbage pail stood a couple of feet away, empty. After a moment or two, Ingham was glad OWL hadn't been in when he knocked, because he realised he had been a little angry. That wasn't the way. The way was to hint, gently, that OWL shouldn't be so prying, shouldn't be putting ideas into Ina's head, ideas that disturbed her. Ingham was cognizant of the fact *he* was lying, in taking this tack. It seemed to him that that was his business, and that no one else had a right to interfere with it. The police, of course, had a right. But the police were one thing, and Adams was another.

Ingham had been sitting, leaning against the kitchen door, perhaps fifteen minutes, when the click of a lock told him that Adams had arrived. Ingham got up quickly, and walked – slowly now – to the front of the house. Adams would no doubt have noticed his car. The front door was shut, and Ingham knocked.

The door opened. 'Well, hello! Come in! I saw your car.

Nice to see you!' Adams had a shopping net in his hand. He was putting things away in the kitchen. He offered Ingham a drink, or iced coffee, and Ingham asked if he had a Coke. Adams had.

'And how is Ina getting along?' Adams asked. He opened a beer can.

'I think all right.' Ingham had not wanted to plunge in, but he thought, why not, so he said. 'What've you been telling her about the famous night of Abdullah?'

'Why – what I know about it, that's all. She was curious, asked me all kinds of questions.'

'I suppose she did, if you told her you thought I wasn't telling you the whole story. I think you've upset her, Francis.' That was it, Ingham thought, knock the ball into his court for a change.

Adams was choosing his words, but it did not take him long. 'I told her what I think, Howard. I've got a right to do that, even if I may be wrong.' OWL said it dogmatically, as if it were a piece of gospel by which he had always lived.

'Yes. I don't deny that,' Ingham said, dropping into the squeaky leather chair. 'But it's too bad it upset her. Unnecessarily.'

'How do you mean upset her?'

'She began asking me questions. I don't know who the Arab was that night. I never saw his face, and it seems to me only guesswork that it was Abdullah. It's based on Abdullah's apparent disappearance – and to be logical, one should leave open the possibility that he happened to disappear or leave town, and that somebody else hit himself or got hit and yelled – and that nobody at all was killed that night. You see what I mean.'

OWL looked thoughtful, but unchanged. 'Yes, but you know very well that isn't so.'

'How do I know it? You're reasoning on circumstantial evidence and pretty thin evidence.'

'Howard, you must have opened your door, at least. You must've looked out of a shutter. The yell woke you up. Anybody's interested enough to wonder where a yell comes from at two in the morning. And the French people said they were sure the door that shut was yours.'

His bungalow had been quite close to theirs, Ingham realized. Their bungalow had been only twenty-five or thirty feet from his front door, albeit his front door had been on the other side of his bungalow from them. If the French had stayed awake a few minutes, they would have heard the hotel boys coming.

'It's no wonder your girl is a little curious, once she knows these facts. Howard—' OWL seemed to be having difficulty, but Ingham let him struggle. 'She's a nice girl, a wonderful girl. She's somebody important. It's your duty to be on the square with her.'

Ingham had a sick feeling he hadn't experienced since adolescence, when he had looked into some religious books at home, dusty old things that must have belonged to great-grandparents. 'Repent your sins ... bare your soul to Christ ...' The questions and answers had assumed that everyone had sins, apparently even from birth, but what were they? The worst Ingham had been able to think of was masturbation, but since at the same time he had been browsing in psychology books which said it was normal and natural, what was there left? Ingham didn't consider that what he had done that night had been a sin or a crime – if he had killed the Arab at all, which would always be not quite certain, until someone actually found the corpse.

Ingham said, 'I've told you what I know about that night. I don't like it that Ina's bothered by what you told her, Francis. Was it necessary? To spoil part of her pleasure in her vacation like this?'

'Ah, but she knows what I mean,' OWL said quietly. He had not sat down. 'She's a girl with some moral convictions, you know. Oh, I don't like to use the word "religious", but she has some ideas about God, honesty, conscience.'

It was curious to think of OWL as a preacher in a pulpit now, barefoot, barelegged, John the Baptist, swinging a copper-coloured beer can. 'I know what you mean. Yes. Ina's talked to me about going to church of late.' Ingham didn't want to admit how little she had talked, and was annoyed that Ina – because OWL had no doubt encouraged her to speak on the subject – had probably told OWL much more than she had told him. 'She has quite a cross to bear, you might say, with her crippled brother. She's very fond of him.'

'She knows the value of a clear conscience.'

So do I, Ingham wanted to say. He was both irritated and bored.

'You and Ina should marry,' OWL said. 'I know she loves you. But you must make peace with yourself first, Howard. Then with Ina. You think you can sweep it under the carpet, put it out of your sight – because you're in Tunisia, maybe. But you're not like that, Howard.'

Now OWL was just like any one of his tapes. 'Look here,' Ingham said, getting up. 'You seem to be accusing me of having hit that fellow that night. Maybe killed him. So why don't you just say it?'

OWL nodded, with his second variety of smile, gentle, thoughtful, alert. 'All right, I'll say it. I think you hit him with something or threw something – could've been a chair, but it sounded metallic the French said, like a typewriter, for instance – and I think the man died or died later from it. I think you're ashamed to admit it. But you know something?'

Ingham let him pause dramatically, for as long as he wished.

'You're not going to be happy until you make a clean breast of it. Ina's not going to be happy either. No wonder she's troubled! She may be a sophisticated New Yorker, like you, but there's no escaping the laws of God, who rules our being. One doesn't have to be a regular church-goer to know that!'

Ingham was silent. He was a little doped by the words, perhaps.

'And one more thing,' said OWL, drifting towards the closed house door, drifting back. 'The problem is yours. Within you. The police need never be involved. That's what makes this case so different from most such – accidents. The problem is really yours – and Ina's.'

And not yours, Ingham thought. 'It's quite true the problem is my own, if there—'

'Oh, you admit—'

'—if there *were* any problem. So I wish, Francis, for my sake or for Ina's sake, you wouldn't keep on at me like this.' He spoke with careful mildness. 'I'd like to keep our friendship. I can't keep it, if it goes on like this.'

'Well!' OWL opened his hands innocently. 'I don't know why you say that, if I'm trying to do what I can to make you a happier man – a happier man with the girl who loves you, matter of fact! Ha-ha!'

Ingham suppressed his anger. Wasn't it just as silly to get angry with his words now as to get angry with his tapes? Ingham warned himself not to take it all so personally. Yet here was OWL in person, and OWL's words had been addressed to him, specifically. 'I don't think I'd better talk about it any longer,' Ingham said, feeling that he was exerting more control than than most people would have.

'Aha. Well. That's up to you and your conscience,' Adams said, like the voice of wisdom.

It was the last straw for Ingham. The bland, stupid superiority of it was more than he could excuse. He thumped his glass down with the last inch of Coke still in it. 'Yes, I'll be going, Francis. Thank you for the Coke.'

And the way Adams let him out was also revolting. Holding the door, a slight bow, beaming on Ingham as if on a new convert-to-be whom he had just soused with propaganda, who would go home and let it sink in, and be a little more pregnable the next time. Ingham managed to turn around, smile and wave at Adams in the doorway, before he went to his car.

Now Ingham wanted to talk to Jensen. But he thought it was silly to go running from one to the other. So at home, though he heard Jensen upstairs, Ingham kept to himself. He took off his trousers and flopped on his bed, and looked at the ceiling. Adams would never let up, he thought, but he wasn't going to be for ever in Tunisia. He could leave tomorrow, matter of fact, with Ina, if he simply wished to. But alas, it would look like a 'retreat', he supposed, and he didn't want to give OWL even this minor satisfaction. Ingham wiped the sweat from his forehead. Just before the time to see Ina, he would take a bucket shower. He could walk to the beach a couple of hundred yards away, and take a swim, but he didn't want to.

Ingham sat up with a thought. What had Ina asked Jensen this morning about Abdullah? She had seen Jensen just after her talk with OWL on the beach.

'Hey, Anders!' Ingham called.

'Yup?'

'Want to come down for a stone?'

'Two minutes.' He sounded as if he were working.

Ingham got the drinks ready, and when he came back into his larger room, Jensen was standing by the table, looking rather happy. 'Had a good day?'

'Pretty good. I want to work tonight.'

He handed Jensen his drink. 'I just had quite a session with OWL. I feel as if I've been in church.'

'How so?'

Ingham remembered he couldn't tell Jensen about OWL's weekly pro-God-and-America broadcasts. That was a pity, because it would have lent humour, and also force, to his story. 'He's trying to exert moral pressure on me to admit I conked Abdullah on the head. That's doesn't bother me so much as the fact he's filling Ina full of it. He's saying it's got to be me who did it, because it was on my terrace, and only I' – Ingham saw Jensen shaking his head with ennui – 'could have done something, and he says I'd better admit it to Ina and make peace with myself.'

'Oh, merde and crap,' Jensen said. 'Has he nothing better to do with his time? So he gave you a sermon.' Jensen leaned against the table, propped one bare foot on its toes, and laughed.

'He did, invoking God, making my peace with Him and all that. – What did Ina ask you this morning, by the way?'

'Aha.' Jensen looked into space as if trying to remember. 'She had just been speaking with OWL, it seems.'

'I know.'

'Oh, she asked me – yes – if I thought you hit the old bastard with something.' Jensen looked suddenly sleepy. 'I ought to take a nap before I work. This stone will help.'

Ingham wanted to ask Jensen another question, but was ashamed to. He felt he was becoming as small-minded as OWL. 'By the way, OWL and Ina both suggested I might have thrown my typewriter at Abdullah.'

Jensen smiled. 'Really? Where did you see OWL today?'

'I went to his bungalow. After I'd taken Ina to the Reine. I wanted to ask him to stop bothering Ina with all this.'

'You know what you should do, my friend, take her away. I personally would tell Mr Adams to stuff himself, but I think you are too polite.'

'I did tell him to knock it off. What he's really doing is turning her against me. I don't say he means to, but – OWL keeps telling me my conscience bothers me. It doesn't.'

Jensen looked unperturbed. 'Go with Ina somewhere for a week or so. That's easy. – I got a package from home today. Let me show you.' He went up the stairs.

In a moment he was back with a carton. 'Lots of cookies. And this.' He removed the tinfoil from a foot-long ginger-bread man, decorated with hat, jacket and buttons of yellow icing.

Ingham stared at it, fascinated. It was different from American gingerbread men. This one made him think of icy Scandinavian Christmases, the smell of fir trees, and of flaxen-haired children singing. 'That's a work of art. What's the occasion?'

'I had a birthday last week.'

'Why didn't you tell me?' Ingham accepted one of the decorated cookies. Jensen said his mother or sister had made them.

'And these,' Jensen said, fishing at one side of the box. He pulled out a pair of sealskin slippers, the grey fur outside ornamented with blue and red embroidery. 'Not very appropriate for Tunisia, are they?'

Ingham suddenly had such a desire to see Jensen's part of the world, he could not speak for a moment. He held the slippers in his hand and smelled them – a fresh animal smell, of new leather, and the faintest smell of spice from the cookies they had been packed with.

The evening at La Goulette was neither a great success

nor a failure. Ingham had told Ina that he had been to see OWL, because he wanted to tell her before OWL did, but even so – OWL was so quick these days – he was not sure Ina did not already know. She did not.

'I suppose you asked him – not to talk to me any more about the night of Abdullah,' she said.

'Well – yes, I did. OWL knows as little about it as anybody else. Well, not *anybody*. The hotel boys know most.'

'You've talked with them?'

'I thought I told you I tried to find out something from Mokta. He says he doesn't know anything – about the yell and so forth.' It occurred to Ingham that Jensen, speaking his passable Arabic, might learn something from Mokta or the others. The something Ingham was interested in was whether there had been a corpse.

Ina was silent.

'Would you like to go somewhere – like Djerba? I mean, stay at a hotel there? Both of us?'

'But you say you're working—'

'That can wait. You have just a few days here.' That brought up the question of whether he would leave with her, Ingham supposed. Nothing was in its right order any more. He had meant to ask her to marry him, to have that settled by now. That would have made their going on to Paris together, when she left, rather a matter of course. Should he talk to her tonight about getting married? Or was she taking that for granted? Ingham glanced around him: they were at an outdoor table of the restaurant where he had eaten the disastrous *poisson-complet*. Waiters with heavy trays yelled at pedlars and begging children to get out of their way. The light was so dim, they had hardly been able to see the menu.

Ingham did not mention marriage that evening. But he did go back with her to her hotel. They had a nightcap in her room, and they spent a couple of hours together. It was almost as wonderful as the first time after she had arrived. Ingham felt a little more serious. Was that good? And he felt a little sad and depressed when he left.

He kissed her as she lay in bed. 'Tomorrow at nine-thirty,' he said. 'We'll take a drive somewhere.'

CHAPTER TWENTY-TWO

Eight o'clock the next evening found Ingham where he had been the evening before, as far as Ina was concerned. She had enjoyed Sfax, had read about its eleventh-century mosque and the Roman mosaics in his *Guide Bleu*, but he sensed a reserve in her which took away some of his initiative, or enthusiasm. Ingham found a present for Joey, a blue leather case with loops inside to hold pencils or brushes. They had hired a rather heavy rowboat, and Ingham had rowed around a bit with her. They had gone swimming and lain in the sun.

Ingham had wanted to ask her what kind of church she was going to in Brooklyn. It wouldn't be Catholic, he was pretty sure. Her family was vaguely Protestant. But he could not get the question out. In Sfax, he had bought smoked fish, black olives and some good French wine, and he invited Ina to have dinner with him at home.

Jensen had a drink with them, but declined to stay for dinner. By now, Ingham had more dinner plates and three knives and forks. His salt was still the coarse variety, bought in haste one day, and now it was in a saucer, damp. Ingham had two candles stuck in wine bottles on the table.

He laughed. 'Romantic candlelight, and it's so damned hot we have to push them to the very edge of the table!' He pinched one candle out, took a swallow of the good red wine, and said, 'Ina, shall we go to Paris together?'

'When?' she asked, a little surpised.

'Tomorrow. Or the next day, anyway. Spend the last part of your vacation there. – Darling, I want to marry you. I want to be with you. I don't want you to go away from me even for a week.'

Ina smiled. She was pleased, happy, Ingham was sure of that.

'You know, we could be married in Paris. Surprise everyone when we get to New York.'

'Didn't you want to finish your book here?'

'Oh, that! I'm almost finished. I know I keep saying that, but I'm always slow at the end of a book. It's as if I didn't want to end it. But I know the end. Dennison goes to prison for a bit, gets psychiatric treatment, and he'll come out and do the same thing again. – That's no problem.' He got up and put his arm about her shoulder. 'Would you marry me, darling? In Paris?'

'Can I have a few minutes?'

Ingham released her. 'Of course.' He was surprised and vaguely disappointed. He felt he had to fill in the silence. 'You know – I deliberately never talked to you about John. I didn't talk *much*, I hope. Because I didn't think you wanted to. Isn't that true?'

'I suppose that's true. I said it was a mistake, and a mistake it certainly was.'

Ingham's brain seemed to be turning somersaults, turning over facts, choosing none. He felt whatever he might say was of great importance, and he did not want to say the wrong thing. 'Do you still love him – or something?'

'No, of course not.'

Ingham shrugged, embarrassed, but she might not have seen the shrug, because she was looking down at the table.

'Then what is it? – Or do you want to wait until tomorrow to talk?'

'No, I don't have to wait until tomorrow.'

Ingham sat down in his place again.

'I feel that you've changed,' she said.

'How?'

'You're – a little bit tough somehow. Like—' She looked up towards Jensen's rooms. 'He seems to have had such an influence on you, and he's – well, the next thing to a beatnik.' She was not whispering, because they both knew Jensen had gone out.

Ingham felt she was hedging from what she really wanted

to say. 'No, that he isn't. He doesn't come from that kind of family.'

'Does that ever matter?'

'My darling Ina, I haven't known Anders very long, and I probably won't ever see him again – after a few days.'

'Will you tell me exactly what happened the night that Arab – well, what *did* he do, try to come into your house? The bungalow?'

Ingham looked away from her. He wiped his mouth with his napkin, which was a dish-towel. 'I could kick Francis Adams from here to Connecticut,' Ingham said. 'Meddling bastard. Nothing else to do but yak.'

Ina was saying nothing, watching him.

A very inward anger made Ingham silent, too. The stupidity of something like this bothering them, after all the worse things they had weathered, the John Castlewood business, his moping over Lotte which had nearly finished him even after meeting Ina – all that overcome, and now this! And Ingham was now tired of statements, speeches. He said nothing. But he realised that what Ina had said was an ultimatum. It was as if she said, 'Unless you tell me what happened, or that you killed him, if you did, I won't marry you.' Ingham smiled at the bizarreness of it. What did the Arab matter?

He did not go up to her hotel room with her that night. And at home, he couldn't sleep. He didn't mind. In fact he got up and reheated the coffee. Jensen had come in around ten o'clock, said hello and good night to them, and had gone upstairs. His light was now off. It was just after one o'clock.

Ingham lay on his bed. What if he told Ina the truth? She wouldn't necessarily tell OWL. It would annoy Ingham, if she did. But hadn't he decided, days ago, not ever to tell her? But if he didn't tell her – and obviously she suspected already that he had killed the man – he would lose her, and that gave Ingham a feeling of terror. When he imagined himself without Ina, Ingham felt his morale gone, his ambition, even his self-respect somehow.

He sat up, bothered by the fact that if he told her the

truth, he would be in the position of having lied, looking her straight in the eye, for the past several days. He hadn't quite succeeded with his lie, or she wouldn't still be questioning him, but he had succeeded enough to make himself a coward, and dishonest. It was a dilemma. No matter how much Jensen said, 'What does the bastard matter?' the situation had come to matter quite a bit.

Or was it the lateness of the hour? He was tired.

Try to think of it objectively, he told himself. He imagined watching himself in the dark bungalow that night, being scared by the opening of his door (in fact he imagined somebody else, anybody else, being scared), having been annoyed and alarmed by a previous theft from the bungalow. Wouldn't any man have picked something up and thrown it? And then he imagined the Arab alive, flesh and bones, a person known to other people, and morally and legally speaking as important as – President Kennedy. Ingham was ninety per cent sure he had killed the Arab. He had been trying to brush that aside, or minimise it by believing the Arab deserved it, or hadn't been worth anything, but suppose he had killed a Negro or a white man in the same circumstances in the States, a man with a long record of housebreaking, for instance? Something would have happened to him. A short trial or hearing and an acquittal of a charge of manslaughter, perhaps, but not just nothing like here. He couldn't expect to find, in America, a few convenient people to whisk the body away and not mention it.

In spite of the shame of it, Ingham supposed he would have to tell Ina the truth. He would tell her his fear, also his hatred that night. He would not attempt to excuse himself for having lied. He imagined her shocked at first, but finally understanding why it had happened and excusing him, if in fact she would blame him at all. It seemed possible to Ingham that she wouldn't blame him, and that she only wanted to be satisfied that she knew the true story.

Ingham put on the light and lit a cigarette. He turned on his transistor and explored the dial for music or a human voice, and got a baritone American voice saying '... peace towards all'. The tone was soothing. 'America is a land that has *always* extended the hand of friendship and good will to *all* peoples – of whatever colour or creed – the hand of *help* to any peoples who might need it – to ward off oppression – to help them to help *themselves* – win their battles against poverty. . . .' Ingham thought in disgust, All right, then give the land back to the Indians! What a splendid beginning, right at home! Not a piece of lousy desert you don't want, but decent land with some value to it. Like Texas, for instance. (But no, my God, America had already taken Texas from the *Mexicans*!) Ohio, then. After all, the Indians had given the state its name, from the river there. '. . . what every man in the uniform of the American Army, Navy and Air Force *knows* – that with his privilege to *fight* for the United States of America goes a responsibility to uphold the sanctity of human justice, on *whatever* shores he may be. . . .' Ingham turned the thing off so viciously that the knob came off in his hand. He hurled it to the brick floor, where it bounced and disappeared somewhere. It wasn't OWL, that steak-and-martini-filled employee of the Voice of America, or maybe the American Forces Network, but the words could have been OWL's. Did anybody fall for it, Ingham wondered. Of course not. It was just a lot of bland tripe drifting past indifferent ears, which perhaps made some Americans in Europe chuckle a little, something that people endured until the next dance record. Yet the thing must have some influence or they wouldn't keep on with it, therefore some people must be swallowing it. This was a profoundly disturbing thought to Ingham at two-twenty-five. He thought of OWL, just a mile away, dreaming up the same stuff and actually sending it, being paid for it – OWL wouldn't lie about that. And paid by the Russians. Maybe OWL got as little as ten dollars a month for it. Ingham squirmed in his bed, and felt he was in a madhouse world, and that he might not be sane himself.

The memory of his first minute on Tunisian soil returned to him. At the airport. The sudden, shocking warmth of the air. Half a dozen Arab grease monkeys staring at the passengers, at him, under brows that Ingham had felt to be lowering and hostile, though later he had realised that that was how many Arabs' brows looked normally. Ingham had felt conspicuously, disgustingly pale, and for a few unpleasant seconds had thought, 'They must hate us, these darker people. It's *their* continent, and what are we doing here? They know us, and not in a nice way, because the white man has been to Africa before.' For a second or two, he had actually experienced physical fear, almost like terror. Tunisia, that tiny country, on the map not too far below Marseilles (and yet how different!), which Bourguiba had described as a mere postage stamp on the vast package of Africa.

Ingham realised he was in a curiously delicate condition.

Suddenly, he had a thought: speak to Mokta before he spoke to Ina. He couldn't ask Jensen to do it. It might be useless, and yet Mokta might by this time tell him the truth, the fact – if it was a fact – that Abdullah had been killed that night. Why, Ingham thought, should he tell Ina he'd killed him if he hadn't?

CHAPTER TWENTY-THREE

It was Saturday. Ingham had no appointment with Ina. He intended to call at the hotel before noon, possibly see her, or leave a message in regard to meeting her for dinner. Ingham felt she might well want to spend a day without him. But he didn't know if he was correct in assuming this. He felt no longer sure of himself about anything. He blamed part of it on a bad night's sleep, and a couple of disquieting dreams. In one dream, he had been helping to clear the colossal façade of a formerly buried Greek temple. He was with a group that was supposed to remove mud deposits from the Corinthian columns. Ingham had been upside down at the top of a column, clinging only by his knees which were soon to give out and let him drop a vast distance on to stone. He had gone on, ineffectually scraping at the wet mud with a shell-like instrument, and the dream had mercifully ended before he fell, but it lingered in his mind and was very real.

Even as he walked along the narrow alleys towards his car, he felt a clutch of fear, as if the ground might suddenly give way and drop him to a fatal depth.

It was just after 10 a.m. Ingham thought Mokta should be through with his breakfast work. He hoped he would not see Ina. It was more likely he would see OWL, whose bungalow was near.

The terrace of the bungalow headquarters had one occupied table. A man and woman in shorts lingered over the remains of breakfast. Ingham went round to the side door, which was always open. A boy was washing dishes at the sink. Another was fiddling with the big kettle on the stove.

They both looked at him in the doorway and seemed to freeze, as if waiting for their photograph to be taken.

'*Sabahkum bil'kheir*,' Ingham said, meaning 'Good morning,' one of the few phrases he'd memorised. 'Is Mokta here?'

'Ah-h.' The boys looked at each other.

One said, 'He is looking for the plumber. There is a W.C. broken. Lots of water.'

'What bungalow, do you know?'

'That way.' The boy pointed towards the hotel.

Ingham walked past OWL's Cadillac and his own car, keeping an eye out through the citrus trees for Mokta's slim, quick figure. Then Ingham heard Mokta's voice from a bungalow on his left.

Mokta appeared at the bungalow's back door, talking in Arabic to someone in the kitchen. Ingham hailed him.

'Ah, M'sieur Eengham!' Mokta grinned. 'Comment allez-vous?'

Et cetera. Ingham assured him his apartment was still very agreeable. 'You have a moment?'

'But certainly, m'sieur!'

Ingham did not know where they should go. He did not want to take Mokta away in his car, because that would put too much emphasis on the conversation. Almost anywhere else, they would be overheard. 'Let's walk down here for a minute,' Ingham said, pointing to a space between two bungalows.

Beyond, the sand dipped down towards the beach. Ingham wore his white dungarees (already too hot) and his old white sneakers into which the sand trickled unpleasantly.

'I had a question to ask you,' Ingham said.

'Oui, m'sieur,' Mokta said attentively, his expression neutral yet braced.

'It is about that night – the night the Arab was hit on the head. The Arab they think was Abdullah.' The French 'on croît' attached no definite persons to 'they'. '*Was* it Abdullah?'

'M'sieur, I – I don't know anything about it.' Mokta crossed his lean hands on his shirtfront.

'Ah, Mokta! You know one of the boys – Hassim – told M'sieur Adams there was a man that night. The boys took him away. What I would like to know is, was the man dead?'

Mokta's eyes widened a bit more, so that he appeared slightly frightened. 'M'sieur, but if I do not even know who it *was*? I did not see the body, m'sieur.'

'Then there was a body?'

'Ah, non, m'sieur! I do not know if there was a body. Nobody talked to me. The boys told me nothing. Nothing!'

It damned well wasn't true, Ingham thought. He looked impatiently up the sand towards the awning-bedecked bungalow headquarters. 'I am not trying to get anyone into trouble, Mokta,' Ingham said, and realised he would have felt silly saying this if it hadn't been Tunisia, if he hadn't been a tourist. 'Do you know Abdullah?'

'No, m'sieur. – I do not know many around here. I am from Tunis, you know.'

Mokta had told him that before. But Ingham knew the boys had discussed whoever it was, Abdullah or just possibly someone else, whose name they would certainly have found out. 'Mokta, it is important to me. Just me. No one else. I will give you ten dinars if you tell me the truth. If there was a corpse.' He thought ten dinars was a sum Mokta could understand. It was roughly half a month's wages.

Mokta's wide-eyed expression did not change, and Ingham hoped he was debating. But then came the shake of the head. 'M'sieur, I could say something just to gain the money. But I do not know.'

He's a decent boy, Ingham thought. He knew, but he had given some kind of word to his chums, and he was keeping it. 'All right, Mokta. We won't talk any more about it.' The sun was a golden weight on Ingham's head.

As Ingham walked towards the bungalow headquarters, he saw one of the boys pause in his clearing of a terrace table and stare at the two of them.

Mokta must think that it was quite important for him to have offered ten dinars, Ingham thought. He supposed Mokta would tell that to his friends, maybe increase it to twenty. It would, Ingham realised, lay him open for blackmail, because why should he have offered money? It did not bother Ingham. Was that because he intended to leave so soon, or because he didn't believe any of the boys would be clever enough to effect blackmailing? It didn't seem to be worth it to ponder this.

'You still work very hard, m'sieur?' Mokta asked as they reached level sand near the bungalow headquarters' terrace.

Ingham did not answer, because at that moment, he saw Ina coming from the direction of OWL's bungalow, Ina in a short belted robe and sandals. She looked at his car, then looked around and saw him. Ingham waved.

'Your American friend!' said Mokta. 'Au revoir, m'sieur!' He darted for the kitchen door.

Ingham walked towards Ina. 'Visiting Francis?'

'He asked me to breakfast,' Ina said, smiling. 'Were you taking a walk?'

'No. Came to see if there was any mail they hadn't sent on. Then I was going to call on you – or leave you a note.' He stood near her now, near enough to see on her cheeks a few freckles that had come out since she had been here. But he sensed the distance between them that he had last evening. Her expression looked politely pleasant, as if she were gazing at a stranger. Ingham felt wretched.

'That's your Arab friend – that boy, isn't he?' she asked. 'The one who helped me with my luggage at first?'

'Yes, Mokta. He's the one I know best. I'd very much like to talk to you. Could we possibly go to your room?'

'What's the matter, darling? You look pink around the eyes.' She moved towards his car.

'I was reading late.'

In the car, they said nothing. It was a very short way to the main building.

'How's Francis?' Ingham asked as he stopped the car. 'His old cheery self?' Ingham wondered suddenly if OWL had shown Ina his suitcase with the tapes and made her swear to tell no one, not even him, about them. That would be funny.

'Filled to the brim with OWL-ish glee, yes,' Ina said, smiling. 'I wish I knew his secret.'

Fantasy, Ingham thought. Illusions. He followed Ina into the hotel. She had a letter.

'From Joey,' she said.

In her room, she said, 'Excuse me while I get out of this

suit,' and went into the bathroom, taking shorts and a shirt.

Ingham stood by the closed terrace shutters, wondering how he should begin. But he never got anywhere planning the beginnings of things he had to say.

Ina came back, wearing the pale blue shirt outside her shorts. She took a cigarette. 'You wanted to talk to me?'

'It's about that night. I wasn't telling you the whole story. I saw someone coming in the door, and I threw my typewriter and hit him in the head. It was very dark. I'm not sure it was Abdullah – but I think so.'

'Oh. And then?'

'Then – I shut the door and locked it. The door hadn't been locked because I forgot that night. I waited to find out if there was anyone else with him. But all I heard was – some of the hotel boys coming to drag whoever it was off the terrace.' Ingham went into the bathroom and drank some water from the cold tap. He was suddenly dry in the mouth.

'You mean he was dead,' Ina said.

'That's what I don't know. The boys here won't tell me anything, believe it or not. I was just asking Mokta, offered him ten dinars to tell me if the man was dead. Mokta says he didn't see anything and the boys didn't tell him anything.'

'That's very strange.'

'It isn't. Mokta knows. He wants to deny there was *anyone* around that night.' Ingham sighed, baffled and tired of the subject. 'They want to hush up anything about thieving. In Tunisia, I mean. And that old Arab, let's face it, nobody's going to make a stink about *his* life – if he was killed. You see, I don't know, Ina. I know it was a hard blow. It bent the typewriter.'

She said nothing. Her face looked a little paler.

'The police didn't come into it. – There's one thing I'd like to ask, darling.' He came closer to where she was standing. 'Don't tell OWL this, would you? It's not his business, and he'd only gloat because he suspects something like this happened. He'd keep telling me it's on my conscience, I ought to tell the police or something, when as a matter of fact it's not on my conscience.'

'Are you sure? You seem to be taking it pretty seriously.'

Ingham put his hands in the pockets of his dungarees. 'I may take it a bit seriously – *if* I killed him. It's not the same thing as its being on my conscience. The guy was coming into my bungalow, maybe not for the first time. I've got a right to throw something at somebody who's coming into my place at night in a stealthy manner, intending no good. It wasn't a hotel guest who'd made a mistake and walked into the wrong bungalow!'

'You could see it was an Arab?'

'I think he had a turban. He was like a black silhouette in the doorway, sort of stooped. God, I'm sick of it,' Ingham said.

'I think you could do with a Scotch.' Ina went to her closet. She fixed his drink in the bathroom, with a splash of water.

'Don't you want to read your letter from Joey?'

'I can tell by his handwriting he's all right. – You told Anders about this?'

'Yes. Only because he knows more about Tunisia than I do. I asked him what I should do, what I should expect. He told me not to do anything.'

'And that the Arab's life was worthless. – It's a funny country.'

'It isn't funny. They just have their ways about things.'

'I can understand another Arab throwing something, but it seems a little violent from you. A typewriter!'

The Scotch was a comfort. 'Maybe. I was scared. – You know, a couple of months ago, I was walking back from Anders's place in the dark, and I stumbled over a man lying in the street. I struck a match – and I saw that his throat had been cut. He was dead. An Arab.'

'How awful!' She sat down on the edge of her bed.

'I wasn't going to mention it. It's just a horrible story. I suppose these things happen more often here than they do in the States. Though maybe that's debatable!' Ingham laughed.

'So what did you do?'

'That night? Nothing, I'm afraid. The street was dark, nobody around. If I'd seen a policeman, I'd have told him, but I didn't see a policeman. And – yes. That was the night

Abdullah was hovering around my car, or rather he'd just fished my canvas jacket out of the back window which was open a little. Anyway, I yelled at him and he scuttled away. He could scuttle like a crab!'

'You seem to think he's dead.'

'I think it more than likely. – But if I can't get it out of Mokta for money, even promising him I won't tell the police, do you think the police are going to get anything out of anybody?'

'Or out of you?'

'The police haven't asked me anything.'

She hesitated. 'I think, Howard dear, you'd go to the police in the States just by way of protecting your property. I think you don't want to here because you probably killed the man. It's no doubt awkward here if—'

'Less awkward, probably.'

'Wouldn't you talk to the police in the States if you thought you'd killed someone?'

'Yes. I think so. But – you'd have to imagine chums of the thief – or maybe chums of mine – dragging the body away. I suppose it could happen in the States. But in the States it's a little hard to get rid of a body. The real point is, why should I go and announce that I've killed someone when it's not necessarily true? The point is—'

'But you said you think he's dead.'

'The point is, my house was broken into. Or entered. That's worth reporting in the States, yes. But here, why bother? It happens all the time.' Ingham saw that his argument irritated her. 'And any corpses are just buried in the sand somewhere.'

'The point is,' she said, 'as a member of society, you should report it. In either place. It'll bother you if you don't.'

'It doesn't bother me. You sound like OWL.'

'I'm sorry you didn't tell me all this from the start.'

Ingham sighed and put down his empty glass. 'It was an unpleasant, vague story.'

'Even when the boys dragged something off your terrace?'

'Suppose Abdullah was simply knocked out? Suppose he went to another town – considering his unpopularity here?'

'I think I will have a Scotch after all.' When she had made it, she said, 'What about the hotel people? The management. Don't they know?'

He sat down near the foot of the bed. She had leaned back against a pillow.

'I doubt it. The boys wouldn't report it, because they're supposed to keep prowlers off the grounds.' He shrugged. 'If the management knew, I don't think they'd tell the police. They don't want the rumour spreading that the Reine has burglars.'

'Mm-m,' she said on a dubious note. 'Curious reasoning. But you're an American. It's customary to report things like that. I mean attempted robbery. Maybe the police wouldn't do anything to you, if he's found dead. He was invading your house. All right. But they must have a census or registration of some kind, and presumably Abdullah's missing.'

Ingham smiled, amused. 'I can't imagine a very accurate census here, I really can't.'

'You – just didn't consider reporting it,' she went on.

'I considered it, and gave the idea up.' After talking with Anders, he thought, but he didn't want to mention Anders again.

It hadn't helped, his telling her. He could see that she would always disagree with him. Ingham felt adamant about not reporting it – especially at this late date it seemed silly – but he wondered if that would be the next ultimatum, the next hurdle he had to take to please her?

'In view of the atrocities going on in some parts of Africa,' Ingham said, 'Arabs massacring blacks south of Cairo, murders as casual as fly-swatting, I dunno why we make so much over this. I didn't murder the fellow.' He took her hand. 'Darling, let's not let this throw a gloom over everything. Please don't worry, Ina.'

'It's not really for me, it's for you – to worry.' She said it with a shrug, looking towards the window.

The shrug hurt him. 'Darling, I want to marry you. I don't like – secrets between us. You wanted me to tell you the truth, so I did.'

'You compare it to a lot of Africans or whatever killing

each other. But you're not an African. I just find it surprisingly callous of you, I suppose. When you see a man fall – I presume – knowing you'd hit him, wouldn't you turn on the light and see what had happened to him, at least?'

'And get hit over the head myself by his pals who might be on the terrace? Imagine yourself. You'd throw the heaviest thing you could, then shut the door!'

'Yes, a woman might.'

'Then I'm not very noble. Or manly.' Ingham got up. 'Think about it for a bit. Till tonight. I thought you might like to be alone for a while today.'

'I think I would. I've got a couple of letters to write. I'll just sit in the sun and be lazy.'

A minute later, he was gone, walking down the carpeted corridor towards the wide staircase. He felt worse than ever, worse than when he had been lying to her. He stopped before he reached the bottom of the stairs, and looked up, wondering if he should go back, *now*, and talk with her. But he could not think of anything he could say that he had not already said.

He drove quickly back home, thinking only of talking with Jensen.

Jensen was home. The smell of turpentine was powerful in the warm air. Jensen was reheating a pan of boiled coffee. Ingham told him about his talk with Ina.

'I don't know why you told her,' Jensen said. 'You can't expect her to understand. She doesn't understand this part of the world. Anyway, women are different.' He poured the coffee through a strainer into two cups. 'A man may not like causing a death, but it can happen. Mountain-climbing. A mistake with the rope, a slip and *fwit* – your partner, maybe a good friend, is dead. An accident. You could say what you did was an accident.'

Ingham remembered his arm with the typewriter drawn back, his effort to get a perfect aim. But he knew how Jensen meant 'accident'. 'I told you why I told her. Last night I asked her to marry me. She practically said she wouldn't or couldn't until I told her the truth about that night. She knew I wasn't telling the truth, you see.'

'Um-m. Now Adams is going to hear about it. It wouldn't surprise me if he told the police. Not that you should worry.'

'I asked Ina not to tell him.' But Ingham couldn't remember that Ina had given him a promise that she wouldn't. 'Yes—' Ingham stretched back on Jensen's sloppy bed, and pushed off his tennis shoes. 'Is it social responsibility or bloody meddling?'

'Bloody meddling,' said Jensen, staring with nearly closed eyes at his canvas in progress. The picture was of two enormous soles of sandals with the tips of brown toes showing. A reclining Arab's face was tiny between the sandals.

'I'm going downstairs to sleep,' Ingham said, 'despite your good coffee. I had a bad night last night.'

'Don't let her upset you! Good God, I see she's upsetting you!' Jensen was suddenly rigid and spluttering with anger.

Ingham laughed. 'I want her, you see. I love her.'

'Um-m,' said Jensen.

At his sink, Ingham washed his face, then put on pyjama pants. It was ten to twelve. He didn't care what time it was. He lay down on his bed and pulled the sheet over him, and after a minute threw it off, as usual. One last cigarette. He made himself think for a few minutes about his book. Dennison was having his semi-realised crisis. His appropriations had been discovered. Dennison was stunned, though not completely puzzled, by the public's attitude. What was worse for him was that a few of his friends were shocked that he was a 'crook', and had dropped him, though even these, later, were going to repay the money he had given them. Ina had had an idea the other night: have the money repaid with interest, over a long period if need be, so that Dennison's bank could not say he had cost them the money his stolen money would have earned. It was going to amount to a fantastic lot of money. Ingham put out his cigarette.

He turned on his side and shut his eyes, and suddenly he thought of Lotte. It gave him as usual a pleasant-painful jolt. He thought of getting into bed with her at night, every night, always a delicious pleasure to him, whether or not they made love. He had never tired of Lotte physically, in those two years, and he remembered thinking that he saw no

211

reason why he should ever tire of her, despite what some people said about boredom always setting in. He had never quarrelled with Lotte. It was funny. Maybe that was because they'd never talked anything at all complex, such as what he'd just been talking to Ina about – and he'd always been quite content to let Lotte have her own way. He supposed Lotte was happier now, with the extrovert idiot she had married. Maybe she had even decided to have a child.

Ingham heard the front door being opened, a wooden squeak against the threshold. Fatma, he thought, damn her.

A knock on his door. 'Howard? Anybody home?' It was OWL.

'Just a minute.' Ingham pulled on his pyjama jacket. He hated being seen in pyjamas. He started to put on his sneakers and gave it up. He opened the door.

'Aha! Sleeping late. Sorry if I disturbed you.'

'No, I went back to bed. I had a lousy night.'

Adams wore neat Bermuda shorts, a striped shirt, and one of his little canvas caps. 'How so?'

'The heat, I suppose. Gets worse and worse.'

'Ah, that's August! Have you got a few minutes, Howard? It's reasonably important, I think,' he said briskly.

'Of course. Sit down. Would you like a drink or a beer?'

OWL accepted a beer. Ingham got two cans from the bucket of water on the floor. The foam spewed up. They were not very cool, but Ingham didn't apologise.

'I had breakfast with your girl,' OWL said with a chuckle. 'If that sounds funny, I met her on the beach this morning. I invited her for scrambled eggs.'

'Oh.' OWL hadn't noticed his car, Ingham gathered. Ingham sat down on his bed.

OWL had taken the chair by his table. 'A bright young woman. An exceptional girl. She goes to church, she told me.'

'Yes, so did I tell you. I think just recently.'

'Protestant. Called St Ann's, she said. She told me about her brother, too.'

What was he leading up to?

'She's a little worried about you. – She said she'd tried to

212

talk you out of living here and get you to take a bungalow. Just for your own comfort.'

'I'm not uncomfortable. I can understand that a woman wouldn't like it.'

'She tells me you've got a very nice apartment in Manhattan.'

Ingham resented the remark, as if it were somehow an intrusion on his privacy. And what would OWL think if he knew John Castlewood had killed himself there, and if he knew why?

'Ina'll be leaving in another week or so, she told me. You're staying on, Howard?'

'I'm not sure. If my book is finished – the first draft – I suppose I'll go back to New York.'

'I thought maybe you'd be going back with her.' Adams smiled pleasantly, and put his hands on his bare knees. 'Anyway, I'd hang on to her, if I were you.'

Ingham sipped his beer. 'Is she so keen to hang on to me?'

'I would think so,' OWL said with a sly wink. 'Would she have come to Tunisia, if she weren't pretty sold on you? But I hope you'll be honest with her, Howard. Honest in everything.'

Ingham thought suddenly, Ina hadn't told *him* much about her feelings for Castlewood, speaking of honesty. She might have given a fuller accounting. 'Perhaps adults, people as old as we are, always have some secrets. I don't know that I want her to tell me everything about her past. I don't know why some things can't remain private.'

'Maybe. But one's heart must be open to the one we love, to the one who loves us. Open and bare.'

As always, listening to OWL, Ingham saw the actual thing, the heart, cut open, full of limp valves, bloodclots, as he had seen hearts in butchers' shops. 'I'm not sure I agree. I think actions in the present count more than those in the past. Especially if the other person wasn't even in that past.'

'Oh, it doesn't have to be so long past. Just an honest attitude, that's all I mean.'

Ingham smouldered gently. He drained the last drops of his beer and set the can down a little hard on the crate that he used for a night-table. He wiped his mouth on the back of his hand. 'I hope I'm honest enough to satisfy Ina.'

'We'll see,' said OWL, with his happy, paunchy smile. 'If she leaves before you or if you both leave together, we've got to have a big send-off. I'll miss you both. – Would you like to have some lunch at Melik's, Howard?'

'Thanks, Francis. I think I'd like some sleep more than anything.'

When OWL was gone, Ingham drank a big glass of water, and tried the bed again. He felt as if he seethed inside, deeper than even a sleeping pill could touch, if he had had one. It was a sensation like repressed anger, and Ingham detested it. He heard Jensen's soft tread on the outside steps, and was delighted when Jensen tapped on his door.

'Wasn't that our mutual friend OWL?' Jensen asked.

'Correct. Have a stone, my friend.'

'How did you guess?' Jensen went to the kitchen. 'And you?'

'I don't mind if I do.'

Jensen sat down. They drank.

'OWL is urging me to confess, and he doesn't know I've already done it,' Ingham said. 'Imagine confessing something that you might not have done?'

'OWL should go back to New England, or wherever it is.'

'And of course he's urging me to hang on to Ina.' Ingham flopped back on his bed. 'As if his advice would influence me in something like that!'

'He's a funny little fellow. "What a funny little man you are," as Bosie said to the Marquis.' Jensen laughed with sudden mirth.

And Ingham smiled, too. 'I'll go by the Reine around seven and see how Ina's doing.'

'I have never seen such meddling people – maybe not Ina, but I can see you depend on what she thinks. Do you know what I would do to the man who stole Hasso? I won't put into words what I would do, and I would do it slowly, and I wouldn't give a damn what anybody thought of me for doing it.'

Ingham drew comfort from Jensen. 'It's not entirely Ina

214

and OWL. I think I live through the same kind of crisis in my book. That happens.' Ingham had told Jensen about Dennison.

'Oh, yes, that happens. You don't mind if I have another stone? Or a pebble?'

CHAPTER TWENTY-FOUR

Ingham went to find Ina at seven o'clock. He had slept a couple of hours, had gone for a swim, and had written three pages in an effort to make it seem a day like any other. But he felt odd, and had come to no conclusion as to what he should do if Ina's attitude was this or that. The church business bothered him in an amorphous way. How *much* was she involved with the church? And it was not so much the situation now that he thought about, but future ones, in which she might take an attitude with which he couldn't cope, in which she might go off on tangents that would make him feel like someone from another world – which would be in fact true.

He rang Ina's room, and she sounded in a good mood and said she would be down in ten minutes. Ingham sat down on a lobby sofa and looked at a newspaper.

Ina came down in a pale pink dress. She had a white chiffon scarf in her hand.

'You look marvellous,' Ingham said.

'The scarf is in case we go for a walk. The breeze.'

'You're counting on a breeze?' Her perfume, as usual, pleased him. It was so much more interesting than jasmine. 'Would you like to go somewhere in particular, or should I think of something?'

'Francis rang up and asked us for a drink. Do you mind?'

'No,' Ingham said. They got into Ingham's car. 'What's Joey's news?'

'Nothing much. He's painting. Louise comes over nearly every day.'

'She lives near by? I forgot.'

The car rolled on to the nearly silent sandy lane that

curved towards Adams's bungalow. Adams's terrace light was on, and he greeted them at the door before they had time to knock.

'Welcome! I'd suggest the terrace but it's much cooler inside. Ha-ha! Come in and see!'

Adams's terrace faced the gulf and had a glider, table and chairs. There were canapes of cheese and black olives on the mosaic table in the living-room.

Ingham hoped Adams wouldn't want to join them for dinner. Then he thought it might be better if he did join them. Why was Ina so cheerful? Ingham wasn't sure how to interpret it. Had she given him up? Had she 'understood' and decided to tell him so? Whatever she said tonight, Ingham thought, he would ask her just one more question about John Castlewood: had she liked or loved him merely because he had loved her? Castlewood's declaration of passion had been a surprise to Ina, she had written. It often seemed to Ingham that women fell in love with men who were already in love with them, men whom they wouldn't otherwise have noticed.

Adams entertained Ina with bits of Arabic lore, of which he had so much. Such as that the Mohammedans expected their messiah to be born a second time, and via a man, hence the baggy pants that they wore in expectancy. And there was talk of the Arab refugees west of the Jordan River. It was astounding how much wreckage had resulted from a war lasting only six days.

'I hope you've extended your leave from your office, Ina,' Adams said, refilling Ina's glass from his silver shaker. He had offered them daiquiris ('Jack Kennedy's favourite cocktail') which he had made before they arrived and stored in his refrigerator.

'Yes, I cabled today. I'm sure I can have another week, because I promised to come back if something urgent turned up.'

OWL's smile took in Ingham. He beamed goodwill on both of them. 'You said something about going to Paris, didn't you, Howard?'

Had he? 'That was if I finished my book.'

'I think I said I'd thought of it,' Ina said.

'With Howard? Good. I think he's getting restless,' said OWL.

Ingham wondered what had given him that idea. OWL, as the talk drifted on, glanced from one to the other of them, as if trying to perceive what they had 'decided', how much in love they were, how happy or maybe not so happy. And Ingham more and more sensed a detachment in Ina. Here in OWL's living-room, where he had so often sat having friendly, ordinary conversations with OWL, Ingham tried to brace himself to turn loose of Ina – in an emotional sense – because he felt that was what she was going to suggest. How much would it hurt? And would it be his ego or his heart that would be hurt? Ina looked at him, smiling with a slight amusement, and Ingham knew she was a little bored, like himself.

'I think I'm within two days of finishing,' Ingham said in answer to Adams's question about his book.

'Then you should have a real holiday with a change of scene. Yes, Paris. Why not?' OWL bounced on his heels, as if he were seeing a vision of a classic honeymoon, blissful, in Paris.

They left after two drinks. OWL had showed no sign of wanting to come with them.

'He's sort of an angel, isn't he?' Ina said. 'Very fond of you. – You're awfully quiet tonight.'

'Sorry. I think it's the heat. I thought we might try the Hotel du Golfe tonight.'

The restaurant of the Hotel du Golfe – where Ingham had looked so often for letters that never came, letters from John and Ina – was nearly full, but they were able to get a well placed table for two.

'Well, darling,' Ingham said, 'did you think any more about what we were talking about today?'

'Of course I thought about it. Yes. I understand things are different here. I suppose I was making too much of it. – I really didn't mean to be telling you what to do.'

And yet in a way, that was what Ingham wanted.

'If it doesn't bother you, it doesn't bother you,' she added.

Did she mean it ought to? Ingham gave a laugh. 'Then let's not talk about it any more.'

'Do you want to go to Paris? Next week?'

Ingham knew what that meant. She had taken him back, accepted him. Go and maybe come back to Hammamet? But he knew she didn't mean it that way. 'You mean, go on to New York from there?'

'Yes.' She was calm, quite sure of herself. She smiled suddenly. 'I don't think you're bubbling with enthusiasm.'

'I was thinking I'd like to finish my book before going anywhere.'

'Isn't it as good as finished?'

It was, and he was the one who had said so, but he did very much want to finish his book here, in that crazy room where he was now, with Jensen's paintings and Jensen upstairs. Not going to Paris wouldn't necessarily mean losing Ina. 'If you could stay here – if you could bear it, the heat, I mean, I could be finished in less than a week.'

She laughed again, but her eyes were gentle. 'I don't think you'll finish in a week. But you may not want to go to Paris.'

'And you want to go to Paris instead of staying here. I understand.'

'Just how long do you want to stay here, darling?'

The waiter was showing them a skillet with two raw white fish in it. Without knowing a thing about the fish, Ingham nodded his approval. Ina might not have seen the thing. She was watching him.

'I'd like to stay till I finish. I really would.'

'All right, then, you stay.'

An awkward silence.

'I'll see you next in New York then,' Ingham said. 'That won't be terribly long.'

'No.'

Ingham knew he might have said, knew she was expecting him to say, something more affectionate. He was suddenly unsure about the way he felt. And he knew this stuck out all over him. He could make it up later, he told himself. It was just a sticky moment. His uncertain feelings gave way to a sense of guilt, of a vague embarrassment. He thought of the day in the bungalow at the Reine, when he'd suddenly had a hunger for Henry James, felt that he couldn't live through the rest of the day and the evening, if he could not read some prose by him, and he had driven to Tunis and bought the only thing he could find, a Modern Library edition of *The Turn of the Screw* and *The Lesson of the Master*. He wanted to tell Ina about that, but what had it to do with tonight, with now?

They had a brandy after the meal. The evening, externally, improved. There were no more difficult moments. But Ingham continued to feel unhappy within himself. Phrases of OWL's tripe drifted through his mind maddeningly. That and the happiest recollections of being in bed with Ina. He thought of being married to Ina, living in a comfortable apartment in New York, being able to afford a maid to make life for both of them easier, entertaining interesting people (he and Ina tended to like the same people), and of maybe having a child, maybe even two. He was sure Ina would want a child. He imagined his work developing, burgeoning, in that atmosphere. So why didn't he jump at it?

He simply couldn't jump that night.

But he did go back to Ina's room with her. Ina asked him, and he accepted.

It was 3 a.m. when he got home. He had wanted to do some thinking, but he fell fast asleep almost at once. They had had, as usual, quite a nice and exhausting time in bed.

Ingham awoke in the dark, a little suddenly. He thought he had heard something at the street door, but when he listened, he heard nothing. He struck a match and looked at the time – four-seventeen. He lay back on his bed, tense, alert. How much did Ina love him? And wouldn't he be guilty of rather bad behaviour if he pulled out now? And yet there *had* been John Castlewood, who'd entered the picture after Ingham, and presumably Ina had taken it for granted they'd be married. Ingham had asked Ina about John tonight, in her room. He had asked her how much she had loved him. But the only thing he had got out of her was that she had felt, or she had believed, they might make a go of it. John Castlewood had loved her very much, and so forth, and maybe that was true. But Ina's answer seemed a little vague to Ingham now, or there was no definite phrase that stood out in it, anyway. His mind shied away from the problem, and he thought of the crazy situation he was in, here, and wondered how it had all come about. Castlewood's assignment, of course. Then OWL with his unbelievably corny broadcasts, and being *paid* for them! Ingham had, on one occasion in OWL's bungalow, seen an envelope with a Swiss stamp on it in the wastebasket. OWL had said he was paid via Switzerland. The return address of a bank had given no clue as to the payer, of course. Could it be possible, Ingham wondered, that OWL was having a fantasy about all of this, about having met the Russian who would pay him for such broadcasts? Was he pretending to himself that some of his own dividends, which might be coming from Switzerland, were payments for his talks? What was possible and what wasn't? Ingham's months in Tunisia had made this borderline fuzzy. The fuzziness, or inversion of things, now involved Ina. He felt it was not quite right they should marry, which was the same as saying that he didn't love her enough, and maybe she did not love him enough either, and that she was not 'quite right', whatever that was, and maybe something quite right did not exist for him. But was this feeling due to some strange power of Tunisia to distort everything, like a wavy mirror or a lens that inverted the image, or was the feeling valid?

Ingham lit a cigarette.

And Jensen. Jensen had a character, a background, a history, which Ingham did not know, which he could never know any more than partially. He knew Jensen only enough to like him quite a bit. (And Ingham recalled one night when he'd gone along to the coffee-house called Les Arcades, and had come near to taking home a young Arab. The Arab had sat at the table with him, and Ingham had stood him a couple of beers. Ingham had been both sexually excited and lonely that evening, and the only thing that had deterred him, he thought, was that he hadn't been sure what to do in bed with a boy, and he hadn't wanted to feel silly. Hardly a moral reason for chastity.) He was surrounded by a sea of Arabs who were still mysteries to him, with the possible exceptions of Mokta, and the cheerful Melik, a kindly fellow who certainly wasn't a cheat, either.

Ingham realized he must come to a decision about Ina and tell her, preferably before she left for Paris, which she wanted to do in about five days or less. If he turned loose of Ina, would it be stupid? He could see her marrying someone else very quickly, if he did. Then he might be sorry. Or was this a bastardly way to be thinking? He had the awful feeling that in the months he had been here, his own character or principles had collapsed, or disappeared. What was he? Presumably someone with a set of attitudes on which his conduct was based. They formed a character. But Ingham now felt he couldn't think, if his life depended on it, of one principle by which he lived. Wasn't sleeping with Ina a form of deception now? And he didn't even feel uncomfortable about it. Was his whole past life then a history of phoneyness? Or was all this now the falseness? He was suddenly sweating, and lacked the initiative to get up and pour a bucket of water over himself on the terrace.

He heard a scratching noise, a whimper, down at the door on the street. Jensen must have put out his garbage. Usually it attracted cats. The scratching kept on. Anger got Ingham out of bed now. He turned on his light and took his flashlight. He went down the four steps, tense, prepared to yell at the cat who was probably trying to dislodge a sardine can from under the door.

The dog looked at him and growled low.

'Hasso? – Hasso, it *isn't*!'

It was. The dog looked awful, but it was Hasso, and Hasso remembered him – just enough not to attack him, Ingham could see.

'*Anders!*' Ingham yelled, his voice cracking wildly, 'Anders, *Hasso's* here!'

The dog crawled up the steps towards Jensen's rooms, its legs limp.

'What?' Jensen leaned out his window.

Hysterical laughter started in Ingham's throat. Jensen knelt on his top step and embraced the dog. Ingham, for n reason, turned on all the lights he had, and also the terrace lights. He poured a bowl of tinned milk and added a dash of water lest the milk be too rich. He took it upstairs to Jensen.

Jensen was kneeling on his floor, looking the dog over. '*Vand!*'

'What?'

'Water!'

Ingham went to Jensen's tap to get it. 'I've got sardines. Also some frankfurters.'

'Look at him! But he'll live. No bones broken!' That was the last thing Jensen said for several minutes that Ingham could understand. The rest was in Danish.

The dog drank water, ate ravenously of a few sardines, then abruptly abandoned the dish. He was too starving to take on much at once. An old brown collar was around his neck, trailing a length of metal chain. Ingham wondered how he had broken or chewed the chain, but the last links were worn so thin and flat, they gave no clue. The dog must have walked miles.

'He really has no wounds,' Ingham said. 'Isn't that a miracle?'

'Yes. Except this scar.' There was a tiny bald patch in front of one of Hasso's ears. Jensen thought they had had to knock the dog out to catch him or to put the collar on him. Jensen was looking at Hasso's teeth, at his feet which were scabby and bloody. Some bad-looking patches in his hair were only mud or grease.

Ingham went down to get his Scotch. He brought the rest of the tinned milk. Jensen had heated some water and was washing the dog's feet.

They sat up talking a long while. The dawn came. The dog lay down on a blanket Jensen had put down for him, and fell asleep.

'He was even too tired to smile, did you notice?' Ingham said.

And so the time passed with remarks like that, remarks of no consequence, but both Ingham and Jensen were very happy. Jensen speculated as to what had happened. Someone must have taken him miles away and attempted to keep him tied up. They must have had to toss food at him, because he wouldn't have allowed anyone to come near. But how had they captured the dog in the first place? Clubbed him? Used chloroform? Not likely. And Ingham was thinking that it was all cock-eyed, except this, except Hasso's return, which was the most unlikely thing he could have imagined would ever happen. And he knew he would speak to Ina tomorrow, rather today, and tell her that he could not marry her. That was correct, the correct thing to do. And in three more days, he would finish his book, he was positive. He made this announcement to Jensen, about his book, but he doubted if Jensen took it in.

The whisky put them both, towards 7 a.m., in a relaxed, happy mood. Jensen was positively drunk. They both went to sleep in their respective beds.

CHAPTER TWENTY-FIVE

At eleven-twenty that morning, Ingham was walking along the beach, carrying his sneakers, towards the Reine de Hammamet. The sun poured down, turning the sand white. The sand, if he walked quickly, was bearable between his toes. The sky was a cloudless deep bright blue, like the shutters and doors of Tunisia. He had bought a chicken and a form of leg of beef for Hasso this morning. Jensen's hangover, if any, was totally lost in his concern for Hasso's welfare. The dog, this morning had been well enough to smile, and he had smiled at Ingham, too.

Now Ingham was thinking, with as usual no success in preparation, of what he was going to say to Ina. The hour to him did not matter. It might as well have been 4 a.m. Ah, destiny! He was convinced that his decision to sever himself from Ina was of a little more importance to him than to her. He imagined her meeting another John Castlewood, or some substitute for himself, in a matter of weeks. He was sure she could more easily find a man she liked than he could find a woman. For this reason, he felt that he was not going to hurt her very much.

He also might not find her in. Ingham was prepared to be told that Miss Pallant had taken an all-day bus-ride somewhere.

Miss Pallant was not in but she was on the beach.

Ingham went back to the beach, and walked on in the direction from Hammamet, because he was sure he had not passed her.

He recognised her chair by her beach robe and a script bound in a blue cover. With his eyes nearly shut against the glare, he faced the sea and examined the surface of the water.

It couldn't be, but it was true: OWL's spear broke the surface with its black arrow, just a hundred yards out and a bit to the left. Ina's white-capped head emerged beside it, her face gasping and laughing, and finally OWL's ruddy visage came up behind the spear. Naturally, the spear was empty. Had OWL ever caught anything?

They saw him, and waved. Ingham stood waiting, dry and hot, the skin on his face and forearms gently toasting, while they came out of the sea.

A burst of greetings from OWL. Why hadn't he brought his swimming trunks?

'Why aren't you working?' Ina wiped her face with a towel.

'Hasso came home last night. Anders's dog,' Ingham said.

'My goodness! The one who was lost?' OWL was agoggle with surprise. 'Yes, Ina! Did I tell you? Anders's dog disappeared – How long ago was it?'

'Six weeks, anyway,' Ingham said.

Ina was also incredulous and glad about the good news.

Adams asked them to his bungalow for a beer, to cool off, but Ingham said:

'Thanks, Francis, can I take a raincheck?'

Adams understood. He understood, anyway, that Ingham wanted to talk to Ina.

Ingham and Ina walked towards the hotel. Ina paused to shower under the bare, outdoor tap where Ingham had seen the Americans who he had thought were Germans. In silence, they went directly to her room. Ina again removed her bathing suit in the bathroom, and came out in a terry-cloth robe like his own, but white.

'I know what you're going to say, so you don't have to say it,' Ina said.

Ingham had sat down in the one big chair. Ina leaned across him, one hand braced on the arm of the chair, and she kissed his cheek, then briefly his lips.

I can't get married, Ingham thought. What should he say? Thank you?

'Would you like a Scotch, darling?'

'No, thanks. – It was a strange night last night,' he said stuttering slightly. 'I was awake, and I heard Anders's dog

226

scratching at the door. Only I didn't know it was the dog. So I went down – and it was unbelievable, to see this dog after so many weeks. Skinny, of course. He looks awful, but he'll live. It's a miracle, isn't it?'

'Yes. Six weeks, did you say?' She was sitting on her bed, facing him, with a deadly air of politeness.

'Six weeks maybe, I haven't counted them.'

Their eyes met briefly.

Ingham had a mad impulse to push her back on the bed and make love to her. Or if he did, would he find himself incapable? 'I'm sorry I dragged you here.'

'You didn't!'

He could predict the next exchanges. It was awful. They came, and at last he was saying, as he had hoped not to, 'Why should I put you in a trap? I suppose I don't love anyone. I suppose I can't.'

And she obliged with, 'Oh, you have your work. Writers think about so many sides of things, they never choose any one thing. I'm not blaming you. I understand.'

How many times had Ingham heard that in the years before Lotte? Little did the girls know. But one thing was true, they were jealous of his work. 'It isn't that,' Ingham said, feeling stupid.

'What do you mean, it isn't that?'

She was supposed to cut through all this underbrush with a clear rapier brain, Ingham thought. He didn't know what to say. She *did* blame him, and it might have been a lot better if she were angry. 'It isn't enough to get married on,' he said.

'Oh, that's obvious.' Her hand moved in a limp, hopeless gesture.

Ingham looked away from her hand. 'You'll meet someone else easily enough, I think. Maybe even before you leave Tunisia.'

She laughed. 'OWL?' Then she got up and made Scotches. 'How're you going to finish that book if you don't get any sleep?'

'I'll finish.'

She was leaving for Paris in two days, or possibly

tomorrow, and Ingham thought it would be tomorrow. She had had a cable from her office saying she could have another week. And of course the heat here was a bit much. The Scotch nearly knocked Ingham out, but he didn't mind, in fact was grateful.

'Shall we all have dinner tonight? You and I and Anders? Maybe OWL?'

'I simply can't. If you don't mind.' There were tears in her eyes.

Ingham knew he had said the wrong thing, that he couldn't improve things by proposing that they have dinner together alone. He stood up. The only thing he could do to please her was to leave. 'Darling, I'll ring you tomorrow to find out when you're leaving.'

'I didn't say I was leaving tomorrow.'

She was standing barefoot in the white robe. He wanted to embrace her, but was afraid she would reject him. 'I'll call you anyway.' He went to the door. 'Bye-bye, darling.'

He pulled the door to, and thought of nothing until he was down on the beach again, where he removed his sneakers. Now the hotter sand made him run fast to the water. He splashed in, wetting his dungaree cuffs, rolled them up, and plunged on towards Hammamet, ankle-deep, splashing. He had no doubt that Ina would see OWL tonight. OWL would express regret and disapproval.

In his room, Ingham felt calmer. He made coffee, and drank it in sips as he tidied up. Jensen was quiet upstairs. Maybe both he and the dog were sleeping. With a second cup of coffee, he sat down to work. But before he could collect his thoughts about his chapter in progress, he thought of Lotte. The throb of loss, or maybe of lust or maybe love, went deeper this time. He had an impulse to write to her now (the only address he knew was their old one, but the letter might be forwarded), and to ask her how she was, ask her if she might like to see him sometime in New York, for a drink or for dinner, if she ever came to New York. Was she happy or unhappy? Might she possibly like to see him? They'd have very few mutual friends. There was no one Ingham could ask in New York about her. She'd been in California for over

228

a year. He realised he wanted her back, just as she was. She had that incredible quality – not a virtue, not an achievement – which let her do no wrong. That was to say, no wrong in his eyes. She had made mistakes, she had behaved selfishly sometimes, but Ingham had somehow never blamed her, never resented, never found fault. Was that love, he wondered, or simply madness? He decided that he must not write to her, though it was a brinkish decision.

Another five minutes walking around his room, another cigarette, then he sat down and worked. Dennison was out of prison. The period had been seven years, which Ingham had compressed into five pages of intense prose of which he was rather proud. His wife, faithful always, had remained faithful. Dennison was forty-five now. Prison had not changed him. His head was unbowed, not at all bloodied, just a trifle dazed by the ways of the world that was not his world. Dennison was going to find a job in another company, an insurance company, and start the same financial manoeuvrings all over again. Other people's hardships were intolerable to Dennison, if merely a little money could abolish them. Ingham, sweating, shirtless, in sticky white dungarees, produced five pages by four-thirty, got up from his chair and dropped on his bed. The air in the room, though everything was open, was motionless and saturated with heat. He was asleep within seconds.

He awakened with the now familiar logginess of brain that always took fifteen seconds to clear. Where was he? What was up or down? What time of day was it? What day of the week? Was there anything he had to do? Hasso was back. He had talked with Ina. He had got through the awful speech to her, or she had made it for him. One more day's work, maybe a day and a half's work, would finish *Dennison's Lights*.

Ingham took off his clothes and poured a bucket of water over himself on the terrace. He put on shorts, and soaked his sweaty dungarees in the bucket which he filled at the sink. Then he went up to see Jensen.

He found Jensen painting, his blond hair dark with sweat. Jensen wore nothing but cotton underpants. The dog slept on the floor. 'Can I invite you for dinner *chez moi?*' Ingham asked.

'Avec plaisir, m'sieur! J'accepte!' Jensen looked bleary with fatigue, but happy. He was working on his picture of the Arab with the two huge sandals in the foreground. A jar of vaseline was on the floor near Hasso.

'Did you write your family about—' Ingham pointed to Hasso.

'I cabled them. I said I'd be home in a week.'

'Really? – Well, that's news.' As the dog breathed, Ingham could see his ribs rise and fall under the black and buff hair.

'I don't want anything else to happen to him. The Choudis were very nice this morning. I think they were as glad as I was!'

The Choudis were the Arab family next door.

Jensen's face glowed with a simple and rather angelic happiness.

'You're going to collapse in this heat,' Ingham whispered. 'Shouldn't you take a nap?'

All around them, the town seemed to be sleeping. There was not a sound beyond the windows, only thick, silent sunlight.

'Maybe I will. Shall I bring some wine and some ice?'

'Don't bring anything.' Ingham left.

He went out for the shopping, thinking he might be too early for the butcher's to be open, but he wanted to buy a lot, and he might have to make two trips, anyway. The ten-year-old daughter of the Choudis was sitting in her open doorway, arranging round stones on the doorstep. She grinned at him with bright eyes, and said something Ingham could not understand.

Ingham replied in French, with a smile also. He thought she had said 'Hasso', but even this word was different when she said it. Her little face was warm and friendly. Ingham walked on. He felt suddenly different towards the family next door, felt they were friends of his and Jensen's, instead of just a family who lived there. He realised he had vaguely suspected them of having had something to do with Hasso' disappearance.

The dinner that night was the best Ingham could provide, given the town's resources. He had gone to the Reine's little grocery. There was salami, sliced hard-boiled eggs, lambs' tongues, cold ham and roast beef, potato salad, cheese and fresh figs. Jensen had brought *boukhah*, and of course there was Scotch and cold white wine. Hasso was there, too, and ate bits of meat which they handed him from the table.

'I don't usually do this, but tonight's a special occasion,' said Jensen.

'Is he keeping everything down?'

Hasso was, said Jensen. Jensen still looked very happy, too happy even to sleep, perhaps. 'And Ina? How is she?'

'All right. I think she's with OWL tonight.'

'She might stay another week, you said.'

'No, I think she'll go on to Paris. Maybe day after tomorrow.'

'And you, too?'

'No.' Ingham said a little awkwardly, 'I told her I didn't think we should marry. – It's not the end of her life, I'm sure.'

Jensen looked puzzled, or maybe he had nothing to say. 'Nothing to do with that dead Arab, I trust.'

'No,' Ingham laughed a little. He wanted to mention Lotte, to say he was still in love with her, but first he was not sure that was true. He was not at all sure Lotte had been the main reason why he had decided not to marry Ina. The Castlewood affair had shaken Ingham more than he had realised when he first heard about it. 'Did you ever have someone in your life,' Ingham said, 'who's like the one great love? The rest just can't ever be as good.'

'Ah, yes,' said Jensen, leaning back in his chair, looking at the ceiling.

A boy, of course, but Ingham felt that Jensen knew exactly what he meant. 'It's a funny thing – the feeling that such people can't do any wrong, no matter what they do. A feeling that you'll never have a complaint against them.'

Jensen laughed. 'Maybe that is easy if you don't live with them. I never lived with mine. I never even slept with him. I just loved him for two years. – Well, for ever, but for two years I didn't go to bed with anybody.'

But Ingham meant, even if you did live with someone, as he had with Lotte. Ingham let it go. He realised he would miss Jensen painfully when he left.

CHAPTER TWENTY-SIX

Ingham saw Ina off at the airport the next day. She left on the 2.30 p.m. flight to Paris. OWL went with them in Ingham's car. Ingham had rung her just before eleven o'clock from Melik's, and Ina had told him her arrangements.

'I was just about to send a messenger to you – or something,' she said, blithely enough.

Ingham wasn't sure whether to believe her, but he knew she had his address. 'I'll take you in the car. We can have some lunch at the airport.'

'Francis wants to take me.'

'Then ask him to come along in my car,' Ingham said, a bit irked by the ever-present OWL. 'I'll be there in about half an hour.'

Then he went home and changed, and started out almost at once. Ina hadn't wanted to stay one more day. Ingham knew that 2.30 p.m. flight. It left every day.

Ina was settling her bill in the lobby. Then through the glass doors Ingham saw Adams's black Cadillac pull up outside the hotel. Adams had a small bouquet of flowers.

'So – you're missing a Paris holiday in delightful company,' OWL said with his squirrel smile, but Ingham could see that Ina had told him they were not going to marry.

Ingham insisted, over OWL's protest, on taking his car, and they got in. There were the usual remarks on the seascape by OWL.

Ina said to Ingham, 'I'll check on your apartment as soon as I get home.' She was in the front seat beside Ingham.

'Don't hurry. – Anyway, I might be home in ten days myself.'

She laughed a little. 'How long have you been saying that?'

They lunched in the slightly mad restaurant of the airport. Service was sporadic, but they had plenty of time. Again the departure and arrival announcements were inaudible beneath the radio's claptrap. Ina made an effort (so did Ingham), but he could see a certain sadness, a disappointment in her face that pained him. He really was so fond of her! He hoped she was not going to cry on the plane, as soon as she was out of his sight.

'Is there anyone you know in Paris now?' OWL asked.

'No. But one usually runs into someone. – Oh, it doesn't matter. I like walking around the city.'

Two-ten. It was bound to be time to start boarding. Ingham paid. A kiss at the gate, OWL got a smack on the cheek, too, a second quick, passionless kiss for Ingham, then she turned and walked away.

Ingham and Adams walked in silence back to Ingham's car. Ingham felt sad, depressed, slightly impatient, as if he had made a mistake, though he knew he had not.

'Well, I gather things didn't work out,' OWL said.

Ingham set his teeth for an instant, then said, 'We just decided not to marry. It doesn't mean we had a quarrel.'

'Oh, no.'

At least that shut Adams up for a while.

Finally Ingham said, 'I know she enjoyed meeting you. You were very nice to her.'

OWL nodded, staring through the windscreen. 'You're a funny fellow, Howard, letting a wonderful girl like that go by.'

'Maybe.'

'There's not someone else in your life, is there? I don't mean to be prying.'

'No, there isn't.'

Ingham was back home by four o'clock. He wanted to work, but it was an hour before he could settle down. He was thinking of Ina.

He produced only two pages that day. One more day's work would certainly see the book finished, Ingham thought. As usual at the end of books, he felt tired and somehow depressed, and wondered if it was something akin to post-natal depression, or was it some doubt that the book wasn't as good as he thought it was? But he had had the same depression after books he knew were quite good, like *The Game of 'If'*.

The following day it took him three dragging hours to produce the four pages that ended the book. After a few minutes, he went upstairs to tell Jensen he had finished.

'Hurray!' Jensen said. 'But you look gloomy!' Jensen laughed. He was cleaning brushes with a messy rag.

'I'm always like this. Pay no attention. Let's go to Melik's.'

Ingham picked up after some drinks with Jensen before dinner. Jensen had gone to a hotel that afternoon and arranged his flight to Copenhagen for next Friday, just four days off. Ingham felt absurdly forlorn at the news.

'You'd – better make sure your canvases are dry, shouldn't you?'

'Yes. I won't paint any more. Just draw a little.' His smiling face was in great contrast to Ingham's gloom.

Ingham replenished Jensen's Scotch and water.

'Come with me, Howard!' Jensen said suddenly. 'Why not? I'll tell my family I'm bringing a friend. I already told them about you. Stay a week or so. Longer! We've got a big house.' Jensen was leaning towards Ingham. 'Why not, Howard?'

It was exactly what Ingham wanted to do, to take off when Jensen did, to see the North, to plunge into a world completely different from this one. 'You mean it?'

But there was no doubt Jensen did.

'I'll show you Copenhagen! My family's house is in Helle-rup. Off the Ryvangs Alle. Hellerup's sort of a suburb, but not really. You'll meet my sister Ingrid – maybe even my aunt Mathilde.' Jensen laughed. 'But we'll bum around the city mostly. Lots of good snack bars, friends to look up – and it's cool, even now.'

Ingham wanted to go, desperately, but he felt that it would be a postponement of what he had to do, which was get back to New York and start his life there again.

Copenhagen would be like a five-day Christmas celebration. He really did not want that.

'What's the matter?' Jensen asked.

'I'd like to very much, but I shouldn't. I can't. Not just now. Thank you, Anders.'

'You're just melancholic tonight. Give me one good reason why you can't come.'

'I suppose I'm a little disturbed. It would be self-indulgent. It's hard to explain. I'd better get back on my own tracks again. But can I – maybe visit you sometime, if you're there?'

Jensen looked disappointed, but Ingham thought he understood. 'Sure. Make it soon. I may go away again in January.'

'I'll make it soon.'

CHAPTER TWENTY-SEVEN

Four days later, Ingham drove Jensen to the airport. They stood in the terminus bar and drank *boukhahs*. Hasso had already been loaded in his box on to the plane. Ingham made a fierce effort to be cheerful, even jolly. It actually worked a little, he thought. Jensen was obviously so pleased to be going home, that Ingham felt ashamed of his own depression. They embraced at the gate like Frenchmen, and Ingham stood watching Jensen's tall, lank figure, lugging portfolios, until he reached the turning point at the end of the corridor. Jensen looked back and waved.

Ingham went straight to the ticket office of the terminus and bought a ticket for New York for Tuesday, four days off.

Jensen's empty rooms upstairs made Ingham think, perversely, of a tomb that had been robbed. He tried to put the floor above out of his mind, pretend it wasn't there, and he certainly had no intention of going up to look at the rooms, even to see if Jensen might have forgotten something. The only happy thought was that Jensen was very much alive, and that he would see him again somewhere, in a matter of months if he wished.

The other happy thought was of course his finished book. It would be pleasant to do some more polishing in the days he had left here, work that required no emotional effort. He was pleased with the book, and only hoped his publishers would not think it dull after *The Game of 'If'*. Dennison had a less primitive attitude than most people about money, and he hoped he had made that point. Money to him had become impersonal, essentially unimportant, like an umbrella that can be borrowed to hold over someone's head, an umbrella that could be returned like the umbrellas in the racks at some railway stations that Ingham had heard about, somewhere. Banks did the same thing, even extracting interest, and hoped that there wouldn't be a run on them.

He began slowly to prepare for leaving, though there was absurdly little he had to do. He had no bills in town. He wrote to his agent. He sent off Ina's mats, and spoke to the post office, giving them a date at which to start forwarding to his New York address, and he gave the man a tip. He called on OWL to inform him of the news, and they made a date for dinner the night before his departure. Seeing him off was unnecessary and awkward, Ingham said, because he had to return his rented car in Tunis.

'But how're you going to get to the airport then?' OWL said. 'I'll come with you in my car to the rental place.'

There was no dissuading OWL.

Now when there was no need of routine, because he wasn't writing, Ingham particularly stuck to one. A swim in the morning, a little work, a swim again, a short walk before lunch, work again. He was taking his last looks at the town at the Café de la Plage, all male always, even down to the three-year-old tot seated at a table of wine-drinkers. Strange things crossed Ingham's mind, some that made him laugh such as, how easy it would have been to hire an Arab for a few days to pose as the missing Abdullah, to satisfy Ina that Abdullah was not dead. But that would not have made any essential difference in his and Ina's relationship, Ingham knew.

The morning before he left, he had two pieces of mail, one a postcard from Jensen. It read:

Dear Howard,
    Will write later, but meanwhile have this. I will torture you by saying I sleep under a blanket here. Please visit soon. Write me. Love, Anders

The picture on the card was of a greenish-roofed building surrounded by a moat or canal.

The second item was a letter, much forwarded, and Ingham caught his breath when he saw the handwriting i the centre of the envelope. It was from Lotte. The original postmark was California. Ingham opened it.

July 20, 19—

Dear Howard,

I am not sure this will reach you, as I only know our old address. How are you? I hope well and happy and working well. Maybe you are married by now (I heard something along this line via the grapevine) but if not, knowing you, I feel sure you are involved, as they say.

I am coming to New York next month and thought we might meet for a drink for old times' sake. I've had a rough last year, so don't expect me to look the picture of happiness. My husband was a charmer to quite a few others too, and we at last decided to call the whole thing off. No children, thank God, though I had every intention of having some. (You won't believe that, but I have changed.) I hope to stay in New York for a while. Even sunshine can become boring, and I found California so full of weirdies I finally felt as square as the Smith Brothers in comparison. There was a rumour here that you had gone to the Near East to write a play or something. True? Write me c.o. Ditson, 121 Bleecker Street, N.Y.C. Won't be staying there, but they will forward letters to wherever I am. In New York by August 12 about.

Love,
Lotte

When he had read it, Ingham breathed again. Ah, fate! It was as if she had read his thoughts. But it was more than that. So much more had had to happen to her than to him to make the letter possible. So she was free now. Ingham began to smile in a dazed way. His first impulse was to write her that he would like very much to see her, then he realised he would be in New York tomorrow night. He could give her a ring from his own apartment – rather the Ditsons, and ask where she was. He didn't know the Ditsons.

At Melik's that night, OWL commented on his good mood. Ingham felt very merry, and talked a great deal. He realised OWL thought he was happy merely because he was leaving. Ingham could have told him about Lotte, but he did not want to. And despite his apparent good humour, he was feeling very compassionate towards Adams and a little sad about him. Adams seemed so lonely under his own cheer, and his cheer seemed as bogus as the phrases he dictated to his tape machine. How long could such pretence sustain anyone? Ingham had a terrifying feeling that one day OWL would pop like a balloon, and collapse and die, possibly of heartbreak. How many more people would turn up in the months ahead to keep OWL company? OWL had said he had met three or four people he had liked since being here, but of course they always went away after a while. OWL plainly saw himself as a lonely guardian of the American Way of Life, in a desolate outpost, keeping the lighthouse aglow.

The next morning at the airport, OWL gripped Ingham's hand hard. 'Write me. I don't have to tell you my address. Ha-ha!'

'Good-bye, Francis. You know – I think you saved my life here.' It may have sounded a bit gushy, but Ingham meant it.

'Nonsense, nonsense.' OWL wasn't thinking about what Ingham had said. He poked a finger at Ingham. 'The ways of Araby are strange as her perfumes. Yes! But you are a son of the West. May your conscience let you rest! Ha-ha! That rhymes. Unintentional. Bye-bye, Howard, and God bless you!'

Ingham walked down the corridor that Jensen had. He felt as if he were being borne slowly up into the air, higher and higher. Even the typewriter in his hand weighed nothing at all now. There is nothing, he thought, nothing so blissful in the world as falling back into the arms of a woman who is – possibly bad for you. He laughed inside himself. Who had said that? Proust? Had anyone said it?

At the end of the corridor, he turned. OWL was still standing there, and OWL waved frantically. Carrying things, Ingham couldn't wave, but he shouted a 'Good-bye Francis!' unheard in the shuffle of sandals, the din of transistors, the blare of the unintelligible flight announcements.